Emyr Humphreys

Old People Are A Problem

seren

Seren is the book imprint of
Poetry Wales Press Ltd
Nolton Street, Bridgend, Wales
www.seren-books.com

© Emyr Humphreys 2003
First published 2003
Reprinted 2004

The right of Emyr Humphreys to be identified as the
Author of this Work has been asserted in accordance with
the Copyright, Designs and Patents Act, 1988

ISBN 1-85411-331-3

A CIP record for this title is available from
the British Library

*The publisher works with the financial assistance of the
Welsh Books Council*

Cover photograph: *Dilys* (detail) by Cassandra Jones

Printed in Plantin by Bell and Bain, Glasgow

Contents

Old People are a Problem

I

Old people are a problem. What other conclusion could he come to? It seemed as though nothing on earth would persuade Mary Keturah Parry to move out of the chilly squalor of Soar chapel cottage into a comfortable room, or even a suite of rooms, in Cartref Residential Home. Alderman Parry-Paylin felt responsible for her. She was ninety-three and his mother's only surviving sister. And there was the question of how much time he could afford to spend on such a fruitless enterprise. He wasn't feeling too young himself. That very morning he had exhausted his strength trying to break in and then stable one of his mountain ponies. He was pushing sixty and made to realise how much stronger the pony was than himself. There was the depressing possibility, on such a bright summer morning, that he might have to give up this hobby. Then as if to demonstrate further the strength and intractability of youth, no sooner had he succeeded in stabling the wild animal than his only daughter turned up, breathless with triumph, from demonstrating and protesting in Genoa. And in tow, like campaign trophies, she brought a wispy unmarried mother and her snivelling offspring.

'Thought we could put them up for a while,' Iola said. 'A bit of rest and recuperation.'

It becomes clear that the young are a problem too. When your daughter corners you, it is hard to decide whether this world is too big or too small.

'Where has she been this time?'

His aunt was glaring at him as she crouched over a small fire, cooking peppermint-cake in a dirty little saucepan. At the heart of the glare lay the congealed reproach of a lifetime. He had gone over to the enemy and she would never allow him to forget that that was still the way she looked at it. All he had done in effect was

9

marry the daughter of Penllwyn Hall, in her view the pretentious home of a family of turncoats. At some stage well within Keturah Parry's copious memory, his late wife's grandfather, a mean and grasping quarry owner, had deserted Methodism for the established church. These fragments of local history did not concern him much, except to remind him, on occasions such as this, of the appalling narrowness of his aunt's views. They were no more relevant to modern living than her working wig that rested low over her forehead like an inverted bird's nest. He could never venture to laugh at her. She knew too much. He had a perfect right after his marriage to abandon primary school teaching, and to go into business in a limited way as a property developer, but she had a way of referring to the transformation as something vaguely discreditable. As far back as he could remember there was always accusation in her glance. When he was small in chapel, if he became restless during the service, she would never fail to transfix him with a glare across an expanse of sparsely populated pews.

'Genoa,' Mihangel Parry-Paylin said.

He pronounced the name clearly for the benefit of her hearing. She took quiet pleasure in getting it wrong.

'Geneva,' she said. '*From Bala to Geneva*. Nice little book. Things were so much more civilised in those days.'

She had acquired the perverse habit of appropriating the life experience of her parents' generation as her own. The world had taken a definite wrong turning in 1914. The Alderman said that may well have been the case: but since Keturah was only seven at the time, there would have been very little she could have done about it.

'Genoa,' he said. 'Where those terrible riots took place. A young lad was shot dead there.'

'I haven't got a television,' she said. 'You know that.'

She had a wireless that was fifty years old but she only heard what she wanted to hear. She liked to complain about Radio Cymru. Too much noise and not enough sermons.

'I've been telling you for years, Mihangel Paylin,' she said. 'You spoil that girl.'

He could only agree with her. On the other hand, what else could he have done? She was still in school when she lost her mother and he lost a wonderful wife. Easy enough for an old witch to talk. What had she ever lived for except the chapel and the good name of her family: and both these were no more, he suspected, than extended aspects of her own absorption in herself. All these things he thought and could never really tell anyone since Laura died. His closest friend Morus had moved to live in the Dordogne. His daughter Iola had driven off Charlotte Sinclair, who with a great deal of persuading, might have become his second wife, on the grounds that she was too English and should never be allowed to defile her mother's bed or Penllwyn, which was in fact her mother's inheritance.

'You want to bring her to heel,' Auntie Keturah said. 'I've told you before. Her mother was weak enough with her. Spare the rod and spoil the child.'

Mihangel Paylin sat in the uncomfortable wooden chair despairing of his situation. No movement seemed possible on any front. His only daughter was impervious to argument. This old woman would never budge. She loved squatting in her squalor, so what could he do about it? He looked up at the shelf above the open fireplace and stared at a tin with Mr. Gladstone's stern features painted on it, staring back at him. That was where she kept her pennies for the Foreign Mission. They were still there long after pennies had ceased to be legal tender. That's the kind of woman she was. Wedded to the past. Like one of those clothed and crowned skeletons that hang in the crypts of Sicilian churches. A bride of silence. If the chapel was to be sold somehow or other she had to be moved out. As things stood she would only leave feet-first in a box.

And how are things at home he asked himself. Will somebody tell me exactly what is happening?

II

The first thing he noticed in the dining room was the absence of his framed photograph on the Welsh dresser. It was taken when he was the youngest mayor ever to be elected by the County Council. He wore the splendid mayoral robes. The chain itself was worth several thousand pounds. A colour photograph, tastefully lit, demanded a substantial frame. There was no good reason why a man should not be allowed to take a certain pride in his appearance and achievements. People had been known to remark he was a fine figure of a man.

'Where's my picture?'

Iola was fussing about helping the unmarried mother to feed her little son who seemed to be rejecting unfamiliar food.

'In the drawer, with your albums. Standing behind the Queen opening the new by-pass. Church parade in full regalia. It's all there. Safe and sound.'

'What did you want to do that for?'

'Well it's a bit out of date, isn't it? And you wouldn't want people to think you were self-important, would you?'

Who were 'people'? This wretched girl and her wretched boy. Iola said her name was Maristella and the boy she called Nino. What were they to him that his daughter should remove his mayoral portrait from its place of honour on the dresser? The furnishing at Penllwyn was unchanged since his wife died. And she in her day had cherished her family antiques with a religious care. They still stood as memorials of her quiet devotion – in such contrast to his daughter's iconoclastic inclinations. Did the girl do anything these days except protest, and when she could spare the time, call the whole purpose of his way of life into question? It was his habit to be genial and generous. They were essential qualities for public life. Smiles all round. You needed to work the familiar streets, dispensing cheerful greetings and armed with pockets full of goodwill. Did that mean he had to be genial and generous to this unlikely pair? He had a legal right to turn them out. Flotsam and jetsam didn't have a vote. There were facts to be established. He addressed his daughter in a tongue the new arrivals could not understand.

'Where did you find this one?' he said.

He made a stiff effort to be judicious and impartial.

'On the ground,' Iola said. 'A policeman was kicking her. And hitting her with a truncheon.'

He knew these things happened. Outside the limits of his council's administration there existed a dangerous world. There was his regular evening television viewing to demonstrate this ferocious fact. But why should his only daughter want to plunge into the heart of it? Such a perfect quiet child. She was twelve when she lost her mother and a light went out of his life. She grieved so quietly. So intense. So determined. It was only worrying about her, and the increasing demands of public life – he would tell sympathetic colleagues when they were inclined to listen – that kept him sane. She showed every sign of academic brilliance. And then just before her sixteenth birthday a police car brought her home from some large-scale language protest. Her forehead was bleeding and he had never seen her look happier. That had to be the take-off of a great career of protest. For years it was something to tolerate. From prison or from foreign parts she would come limping home to recuperate. He could not but welcome her. She was his only daughter. Remonstration proved ineffective. Iola was an excellent cook and it became her practice to prepare a celebration supper as soon as she felt she had recovered. This, however was a new departure and it made him nervous. This was his home; his citadel. He needed the privacy, the space; the relaxation that belongs to a proprietor at the heart of his estate. Did she propose to turn it into a refugee centre?

'We won't be in your way, Mici Paylin.'

She had a way of creating a variety of versions of his name and using them, in the first instance, as badges of affection. As time went on and he felt her character toughen, it would all depend on her tone of voice: it could vary from habitual affection to thinly veiled contempt. With both these women, as it were at both ends of his life's candle, he was obliged to be so circum-spect. They had never much taken to each other. His theory used to be, because they were too alike: stubborn and intractable. Even when Iola was small her great-aunt was displeased with her prolonged stubborn silences. 'I don't understand this girl at all,' she would say: as if her inability to fathom Iola's hidden depths were entirely the little girl's fault. And now when Keturah Parry was clinging so stubbornly to her unhygienic and desperately independent life, he had noticed how little interest and sympathy his daughter had with the old woman's predicament. 'Go and visit your aunt,' he would say. 'She doesn't want to see me,' she would answer. 'We don't have anything to say to each other. We live in two different worlds. It's your problem, Alderman Paylin,' she would say. As if it were only one more of his civic responsi-bilities instead of a family problem that reached in fact, right back to his childhood and even to his birth. With all her capacity for indignation, Iola could be quite heartless.

'I need help in the house and in the garden. There's an awful lot to be done. You'll be free to attend even more committees, Mici P. Think how much more good you'll be able to do.'

Was that snide or was it sincere? These were the questions that beset him latterly; almost whenever his daughter spoke. How much good in fact did he do? Public Health, Education, Ways and Means, Planning. Why should there always be a question mark over Planning? There was a crying need for better housing and it had been no more than coincidental that the three barren fields below the closed quarry were part of the Penllwyn estate. It was a social necessity, and the purchase price came at a crucial time.

'I think you ought to know, Alderman Paylin. Maristella and your darling daughter have been through the fire together.'

He inquired more closely. It transpired that Maristella had been tear-gassed at the E.U. summit in Nice. This had aroused her ire and stiffened her sinews. Protesters of the world unite! You have nothing to lose except your unemployment benefit. The world was disintegrating and there were fragments flying in all directions and what good was that supposed to do? There was a string of sarcastic remarks he could make that remained still-born in his brain. He managed to mutter a question in Welsh about the identity of the little boy's father.

'She was raped.'

Iola snapped her answer out rather than saying it. For a moment she seemed to be the voice of women through the ages. It was up to him to accept the universal guilt of his sex.

'By a Corsican.'

And that was that. The subject was closed. He could not inquire whether there were black Corsicans. Any further enquiry would have been unpardonably indelicate. He had his own thoughts to cultivate. What was this girl any more than one of those decorative drifters who hung about Riviera resorts? She knew how to be still and unobtrusive like a piece of furniture. It was possible to discern that, in her own fragile way, she had once been decorative. And here they were, old comrades in arms, who couldn't have known each other more than three weeks or possibly a month: and Iola using a blowlamp flame of enthusiasm to create twin souls. Strangers were settling under his roof protected and patronised by his only daughter and there was so little he could do about it. At what point would he be able to inquire more closely into her motives and purposes?

'I thought I'd make a bread and butter pudding, Tada. Would you like that?'

The least he could do was show he was melted for the time being by the warmth of her smile.

III

In the damp vestry of Soar chapel Mihangel Paylin marvelled at the transformation in his aunt's appearance. And in her manner. She was no longer an ancient witch, crouching over a bunch of hot cinders, stirring a brew in a battered saucepan. In some way she was more alarming. A lighter wig was mostly concealed by a black hat of ancient vintage trimmed with a skimpy veil. The black costume she wore had a green tinge and a square shouldered war-time cut. He saw her as an emaciated simulacrum of the stern deacon and Sunday School teacher who had tyrannised his childhood. The washing facilities in Soar cottage across the road were limited. In any case it was possible that in old age Keturah had got out of the habit. The creases on her neck and the wrinkles on her face seemed lined with venerable grime. She had unlocked a safe and was laying out documents on the green baize of the deacon's table.

'You will be fascinated by this, Dr. Derwyn. A membership paper. Or ticket should I say? Dated April 15th 1819. "Let it be known that Jane Amelia Parry who bears this paper is a full member of the Christian Society gathered in Soar chapel, Llandawel." Isn't it wonderful?'

Dr. Derwyn Dexter had no choice but to agree. He was a tall thin man with a prominent nose and a small mouth set in a propitiating smile. Since he had been placed in charge of the university archive he had cultivated a manner of inoffensive shrewdness.

'Well yes indeed,' he said. 'Yes indeed.'

He clasped his hands behind his back and bent to scrutinise the faded paper more closely.

'My great great great grandmother,' Keturah said. 'She thought nothing of walking thirty miles to a preaching meeting.'

Her voice was loud with triumph. Dr. Dexter half turned to indicate that by the same token Jane Amelia would have been related to Alderman Paylin too, since his late mother was Keturah's sister. To Keturah in her present elevated mood this could be no more than a peripheral detail.

'1822 this sanctuary was built on the foundation of the original chapel which had been a barn. "A delightful wayside temple," Dr. Peate called it. I was standing just there when he said it. "If I had the funds," he said, "I would love to transport this chapel stone by stone all the way to the Folk Museum at St. Fagans." "No indeed," old William Cae Clai said. "Indeed not, Dr. Peate. This is a place of worship and it shall remain so as long as I live." "Well of course William Jones" Dr. Peate said. "Quite right too". Poor William did not live so long after that.'

Dr. Derwyn saw a chance for a pleasant diversion.

'Ah, Dr. Peate,' he said. 'He put me in the second class for the Crown Poem in '74 was it? He was dead against *vers libre*. "If this competitor is under twenty-one, there is still hope for him." I was twenty-seven at the time so I gave up competing. No crown for me. He knew his stuff though. About architecture. And about poetry if it comes to that. I was never meant to be a poet.'

Keturah Parry paid little attention to the archivist's anecdote. She had the pressing anxiety of a peasant woman who has arrived late at the market to display her wares. From a drawer in the deacon's table she extracted a rusty key that opened the stiff door of a wall cupboard. Inside there were stacks of notebooks.

'Now this is something,' she said. 'Really something. The sermons of five generations of ministers. And all of them notable preachers. Just look at them.'

Mihangel Parry-Paylin shuffled to one side and left the responsibility of looking to the archivist. Keturah took down a notebook as if to display a sample. She opened it and held it at a distance to read the handwriting.

'"*Beloved, now are we the sons of God, and it doth not appear what we shall be*"... John Jones's last sermon. My grandmother remembered it you know. The chapel was full to overflowing and they sang, she said, full of joy and thanksgiving for the blessing of holy eloquence. It all happened here. Those were the days, Dr. Derwyn. Those were the days. They had something to sing about.'

Keturah stared at each of the men in turn defying them to disagree with her assessment.

'A better world inside these walls,' she said. 'Simple people wrapped in love and righteousness.'

Dr. Derwyn felt obliged to make a judicious comment.

'A simpler world certainly,' he said. 'Less complex. Less loaded with distractions.'

'It will come again,' the old woman said. 'It will come again. Only if we keep the flame alight. John Jones had a wonderful sermon you know on the parable of the ten virgins. The church is One you see. The living and the dead keep the lamp burning. We need money Dr. Derwyn. There's the roof you see and other repairs. Now then. If you take this wonderful collection of documents into your care, the question is how far could you help us?'

Dr Derwyn's small mouth opened and shut as he pondered a sufficiently tactful reply. Keturah made a visible effort to contain her impatience.

'Men like to talk business,' she said. 'Mihangel here is a Trustee. We have to save this place one way or another. I'll go and make a cup of tea.'

Leaning on her stick she moved carefully to the small kitchen and scullery attached to the vestry. She opened the rear door to empty the teapot of a previous infusion. An early section of the graveyard stretched between this rear door and the lean-to toilets that needed painting. The headstones were mostly in slate and dated from the nineteenth century.

Alderman Parry-Paylin took hold of Dr. Derwyn's arm and led him into the body of the chapel. They were in solemn mood, both very conscious of their responsibilities. They sat close to each other in the shadow of the mahogany pulpit, so that they could exchange views without being overheard by the old woman. Because of the reverberation in the chapel their voices barely rose above a whisper.

'Don't think I am unsympathetic,' the Alderman said. 'But you can see my difficulty, can't you?'

'Difficulty?'

Dr. Derwyn repeated the word slowly as if he were trying to give himself more time to think. He found himself in a situation far more awkward than he had anticipated. His best defence was an air of unworldly detachment. Mihangel's whisper grew more vehement. It seemed to whistle through his clenched teeth.

'What are we reduced to?' he said. 'This place has more trustees than members. Could this be described as a building of distinction? I hardly think so. I expect Dr. Peate was just being nice to the old people. He could see how much Soar meant to them. In any case, it was a long time ago. I was never all that happy here myself. She was a bit of a tyrant you know in her day. A fierce spinster. She disapproved of my father. He was a sailor and he had no business to go and get himself torpedoed. She doesn't really approve of me either. Just because I married into a family of better off Methodists. Talk about sectarianism. Makes you think, doesn't it?'

Dr. Derwyn had come to a decision.

'We could take those papers and all the written records,' he said. 'And care for them properly. But we couldn't pay for them. A courtesy *ex gratia* maybe, but nothing more than that. As you well know these things are regulated by market forces. I don't suppose there is an overwhelming demand for handwritten sermons in our dear old language.'

The acoustic was too sensitive to allow them to chuckle at his mild academic joke. Alderman Mihangel Parry-Paylin clenched his fist under his moustache to demonstrate the intensity of his sincerity.

'I try to be understanding,' he said. 'And tolerant. It's no use being in public life without being tolerant on a wide range of issues. The truth is she lives in the past.'

He made a sweeping gesture to implicate the rows of empty pews in front of them.

'She still sees this place filled with God-fearing peasants. A whole world away. And what kept them in good order? Fear. The fear of death. Weren't they dropping like flies under things like typhoid and tuberculosis? The N.H.S. with all its faults has done away with that, for God's sake. So what is she on about? I used to sit over there you know and sit as still as a graven image while some old preacher went droning on, just in case she should catch me fidgeting or sucking a sweet. She could glare like a basilisk. She still can when she feels like it. You can see what she's like can't you?'

This was a whispered appeal for sympathetic understanding. Dr. Derwyn was minded to be put in possession of more of the facts before he could unreservedly extend it. He knew the Alderman was Chairman of the County Council Planning committee as well as a Trustee of the chapel.

'Forgive me for asking but am I right in thinking this chapel is scheduled for demolition?'

Mihangel Parry-Paylin could only lean forward to bury his face in both hands. Dr. Derwyn was moved by the strength of his reaction.

'I'm sorry,' he said. 'I didn't wish to be inquisitive. It is widely rumoured. And these things are happening. I read something in the Chronicle that said they were still coming down throughout the Principality at the rate of one a fortnight.'

He submitted this as a melancholy statistic from which the Alderman might derive some comfort. The moving finger of history had written and in its own roughshod manner was moving on.

'It isn't that,' Parry-Paylin said.

He stared into the middle distance as if it were inhabited by a seething multitude of problems.

'It wouldn't worry me all that much to see the place come down. It's the vested interests involved. You are lucky, Doctor Derwyn. You don't have to deal with vested interests.'

'Oh I wouldn't say that...' The archivist was unwilling to have the difficulties of his profession diminished.

'People can be very sentimental,' Parry-Paylin said. 'You can't ignore that. And yet in public life the guiding principle must be the greater good of the greatest number. The road needs widening. There can be no question about that. On the grounds of public safety. On grounds of commercial and industrial necessity. There are jobs involved. And progress. There's always progress isn't there with a capital 'P'. Politicians can't survive without visible Progress. She's ninety-three. She can't live for ever. The roof is leaking. Who is going to pay? Should we let the weather and neglect finish the job. You see my difficulty?'

His jaw froze as he heard his Aunt's measured approach. She appeared in the open door to practice a gesture of old fashioned hospitality.

'Now come along, gentlemen. What about a nice cup of tea?'

IV

The sun shone and the verandah's sharp shadow spread across the drive as far as the first herbaceous border. The Alderman paced back and forth somewhat in the manner of a captain on the bridge of his ship. In the bright light of morning the problems that beset him had to be more amenable to solution. There had to be a residue of authority in the very place where he stood. His late wife's great-grandfather had been far sighted enough to build his mansion on the brow of a hill that commanded a view of a magnificent mountain range, as well as the slate quarry he needed to keep an eye on. The quarry had long been closed and the bitter criticisms Mary Keturah made about the old minister's hypocrisy and bogus religiosity were no longer in any way relevant: nevertheless the owner of Penllwyn, (the 'Hall' had been dropped on the insistence of his dear wife who found it insufferably pretentious) was in an ideal position to lift up his eyes to the hills from which help and inspiration were bound to come to a man of good will such as himself, devoted to public service.

He stretched himself and blinked in the sunlight. There were interesting smells wafting through the open kitchen window where his daughter Iola was busying herself with baking cakes. From the walled garden he could hear the little boy Nino laughing as he dodged about the raspberry canes while his mother picked the fruit. Iola had persisted in drawing his attention to how phenomenally well behaved the little boy was; not to mention his mother who seemed to tremble gently in her anxiety to please.

Iola insisted that a great movement of peoples was taking place: not unlike the great waves of emigration that gave the nineteenth century its special character. He smiled as he took in her youthful exaggerations. At the same time he acknowledged it was wise for a man in public life to lend an ear to what the young were saying. There were great unseen forces at work as difficult to fathom and control as the world's weather. And since his house had nine bedrooms he had to admit he was in a privileged position. He had to accept that it was her benevolent intention to lead him gently into the new paths and patterns of positive existence. "You are never too old to learn, Mici?" she said. Her innovations, surprising as they were, he had to believe would in no way detract from his civic responsibilities; it was up to him to make sure that, if anything, they would enhance them. It was not impossible at any rate while the sun shone, that he would come to be proud of his daughter's colourful eccentricities.

The little boy's laugh provided the amenities of Penllwyn with a new and pleasant dimension. It was Parry-Paylin's habit before committee meetings to take a walk in the wooded area above the house in order to rehearse arguments and sometimes test oratorical phrases aloud. Primroses grew among the trees in the spring and crocuses in the autumn. He was always ready to enthuse about the views he could enjoy throughout the changing seasons. Yesterday he had looked down at a wild corner of the gardens and saw the little boy chasing butterflies among the overgrown buddleia bushes. He was raising his little arms and trying to fly himself. The alderman was so pleased with what he saw he wanted to race down the slope and chase the butterflies himself.

Bicycle wheels crunched across the drive and a young man braked and skidded with a flourish, to pull up in front of where the alderman was standing with his hands behind his back enjoying the undisturbed beauty of the morning.

'Lovely day, isn't it?'

The alderman had little choice but to agree. The young man's hair was dyed yellow and sprouted around in indiscriminate directions. It wasn't a spectacle that he could contemplate with pleasure and he was obliged to look up at the sky as though a sudden thought had occurred to him he needed to hold on to.

'Iola back then? Hell of a girl, isn't she?'

This wasn't a statement he could disagree with either. This was Moi Twm, Iola's friend and devoted admirer. Not a suitor he had long been given to understand by his only daughter. This only brought limited relief. They were, Iola said, "partners in crime". What could that mean except, an unappetising procession of raucous protests? Moi Twm kept a book shop in an unfrequented corner of the market town. The books in the window were fading in spite of the cellophane he wrapped around them. He lived behind the shop among heaps of magazines and papers and flags and slogans of protests gone by. It was his way of life he said. Living on a pittance was the best guarantee of eternal youth. This light-heartedness might fill his daughter with admiration; all it brought him was suspicion and foreboding. He had an Uncle Ted who wrote a muckraking column in the local weekly. Uncle Ted followed the proceedings of the Council with relentless diligence. The more so because he had failed to get on the Council himself. There was always the possibility Moi Twm could wheedle secrets out of Iola; which meant he had to take extra care when talking to his own daughter: and that in itself was an unnatural curtailment on the resources of family life. If he couldn't talk to his own daughter, who else could he confide in? It all made the business of local government more irksome than it needed to be. And this thin and hungry looking young man with his silly hair a less than welcome visitor.

'I wanted to see you too, Alderman, Sir. If you can spare a moment.'

Moi Twm had a trick of cackling merrily as though the simplest statements he came out with were potentially a huge joke. Iola had said she couldn't be sure whether this was evidence of a depth of insecurity, a need for affection or just a nervous tick; whenever he heard it the Alderman closed his eyes and racked his brain for an avenue of escape.

'About Soar chapel, Alderman Paylin. I've got just the answer. A rescue operation.'

The alderman restrained himself from saying Soar chapel was none of his business. His long experience of public life had taught him the value of a judicious silence.

'It could make a lovely book shop of course,' Moi Twm said. 'But Miss Parry would never allow that would she? She's a hell of a girl, I have to say, but we have to respect her wishes.'

Parry-Paylin winced in anticipation of another cheerful cackle.

'You must know this,' Moi Twm said. 'Being one of the children of Soar yourself. But I have to say it came as a complete surprise to me. R.J. Cethin was the minister at Soar for ten months in 1889.'

The alderman did not know this and saw no reason why he should have known. The name of R.J. Cethin meant little to him. Moi Twm was an amateur antiquarian as well as a bookseller and he had an irritating habit of displaying his arcane knowledge at inopportune moments. It often came with a brief cackle.

'A deep dark secret,' he said. 'At Soar I mean. You wouldn't have heard Miss Keturah mention it, I expect?'

'I wouldn't be sure,' the alderman said.

He resented being cross-examined. A shuffle of his feet on the verandah floor suggested he had more important matters calling for his attention.

'I dug into it,' Moi Twm said. 'Nothing I enjoy more than a bit of research. There was just a paragraph in the old *North Wales Gazette* for February 1890. But it was enough to give the game away. The fact is he got the organist's daughter pregnant. They fled and started a new life in the United Sates. He became pastor of a Unitarian Church in Toledo, Ohio. And began to write pamphlets in English about workers' rights and female emancipation and all that sort of thing. Author of *Christ the Socialist, The Church against Poverty,* and *The Land for the Poor and the Poor for the Land.* He's very well known over there now. As a pioneer. Not much honour for a prophet in his own country though. The old story Alderman Paylin.'

There was a powerful cackle.

'Anyway, I don't want to keep you. Now this is my idea. Why not turn Soar into a nice little museum? A tourist attraction you could call it on the lowest level, so to speak. But in the true interest of culture and local history it could really be made into something. With your personal associations, it could be a jewel in your crown. So to speak. Don't take any notice of my frivolous manner, Mr. Paylin. It's a silly habit I can't get out of. I'm making a serious suggestion. And who would have thought of it. The great R.J. Cethin the minister of Soar chapel Llandawel. Ten months or ten years. What does it matter? And the organist's daughter into the bargain. I haven't investigated her background yet. But it's bound to have interesting local connections. As you said in the council last month. We needed to diversify. In the face of the decline of agriculture and the quarries closed and being too remote to attract new industry. Tourism is our best chance. Our best resource if handled properly. With taste and discretion of course. How else?'

The alderman gave so deep a sigh, the young man grew apologetic. For the first time his enthusiasm subsided sufficiently for him to become aware of another person's reactions. For the alderman, he had taken the bloom off the morning.

'It's only an idea,' Moi Twm said. 'I just thought I'd mention it. A contribution. People ought to know about these things.'

The alderman's silence implied he was wondering whether in fact they should. He was startled by a yelp of delight as his daughter rushed out of the house. Down on the drive below him, Moi Twm and Iola became locked in a fierce embrace. They were like two footballers who had managed to pierce the defence and score the winning goal. He had to look away. He was always embarrassed by too much explicit emotion. And it was hardly right that these young things should be so close. People were talking freely about 'partners' these days. In that case could someone tell him what was to become of the family? It was as if he had to live with a veiled threat of being thrust out of his own nest.

'You little devil,' Moi Twm was saying. 'You just shot off without telling me. Without a word. I'm furious with you. You know that, don't you?'

'Listen you old bookworm. I've got a surprise for you. A lovely surprise.'

'Chocolates? Pearls? Green bananas?'

She took his hand and dragged him towards the walled garden.

'Something you've been looking for, for ages. The nicest girl you could ever wish to meet.'

V

In a matter of days Iola established a routine at Penllwyn that her father found moderately reassuring. Price the gardener who came three half days a week remarked, not for the first time, how much she reminded him of her dear mother and how Iola had always been a young lady who had a way with her. This was the kind of music the alderman liked to hear and he heard it again from Mrs. Twigg the diminutive cleaner who was ever faithful but had a chronic inability to detect dust anywhere higher than her eye level. Maristella and the boy Nino were proving satisfyingly low-pitched and even docile. It amused him to detect that when they passed his study they moved on tip-toe. The flow of chatter through the house did not disturb him unduly. When he stopped to listen it was invariably Iola that was doing most of the talking. The guidelines of dispensation had been laid down skilfully enough to avoid disrupting in any way his own focused way of life.

It was summer and the new arrivals had contrived to make themselves pleasing figures in the landscape. Maristella had a knowledge of plants and was very willing to go on her knees and do some weeding, even without gloves. In the orchard, Price the gardener put up a primitive swing for the little boy and Iola drew her father's attention to the child's remarkable capacity for amusing himself for hours on end. "It's the Garden of Eden for the child," she said in a subdued tone that was loaded with darker implications. It suggested too that her father could derive satisfaction from the knowledge that he had helped to rescue a child from an unmentionable fate. The Corsican father was a gendarme in Marseilles notorious for his brutality. The Alderman would have liked to learn more. He had to be content with the knowledge that Maristella, in spite of her courageous nature was extraordinarily naive. Her father must have noticed, Iola said with a passing sigh, how often it happened that nice girls were taken in by the most awful shits. It was in the end a phenomenon that could only be attributed to some obscure force that surfaced from a primaeval past in the animal kingdom.

Supper time became a pleasing occasion. The strangers were transformed into guests and out of courtesy the Alderman spoke more English. Maristella for her part clenched her small fist and declared her firm intention to *dysgu Cymraeg*. This caused much pleasant laughter. The Alderman was especially pleased when Iola prepared a lamb stew with mixed herbs in exactly the way her mother used to do. It was in the middle of this meal, he could only assume for want of a fresh crusade, that she returned to the attack.

'I hear there are plans afoot to bury toxic waste at the bottom of Cloddfa Quarry.'

Alderman Paylin looked longingly at his plate. There was a lot of delicious stew left and he would have liked to enjoy it in peace.

'In a democracy I suppose we have to put up with incredibly stupid and vulgar politicians. At least until the population arrives at a higher level of education: and that seems a long way off. But you are in a position of authority, Tada. You can make decisions. Or see to it that decisions are made. Whose idea was it?'

Public life could never be that easy. The blonde bookseller, and his daughter's bosom friend, had this horrid uncle who wrote a column in the local paper and haunted council meetings in search of scandal and the raw material of muckraking.

'Planning.'

He answered briefly, in the vain hope of heading off further discussion.

'Well, that's your committee, isn't it? Your special baby!'

'We are running out of landfill sites,' he said. 'In a high consumption society, this is becoming a problem.'

'Everything is a problem with you Alderman Paylin. It's not problems we need. It's solutions. What about this cyanide business?'

'Cyanide? Who said anything about cyanide?'

He was provoked and his stew had gone cold.

'Moi Twm's Uncle Ted. And when Ted's your Uncle you can smell monkey business a mile off. Who is the Treasurer of the golf club these days?'

'Ennis Taft. And has been for years. As you well know.'

'Taft Bronco Products. With cyanide drums to dispose of before they can sell their redundant premises for redevelopment.'

The Alderman raised his hand to his brow and Maristella looked at him anxiously. Plainly her genial benefactor had been struck by a sudden headache. The Alderman rubbed his forehead and wondered why the resemblance between his dear wife and only daughter should be so superficial. Laura was a romantic and an idealist in her own way. She had none of this unwholesome passion for smelling rats and conspiracies all over the place. It had to be a generational change of consciousness. This was just the kind of philosophic thing his friend Morus loved discussing. Perhaps it was time to take a holiday in the Dordogne. Summer should be a time to relax and reflect and recuperate. Perhaps he was getting too old and shouldering too many responsibilities.

'It's up to you to put a stop to it, Tada. They're our quarries after all.'

Did 'our' mean she was anticipating her inheritance? Why should she make these hints and threats when all he had done, all his life, was cherish her. At the first opportunity he excused himself and made for an early bed. Whichever way he laid his pillows, sleep eluded him. This was an annoyance in itself. He was a man who depended on and cherished eight hours solid sleep. His window was open and as the sun went down there was a noisy commotion among the crows' nests in the tallest trees above the house.

It seemed as if he could cope with anything except what was left of his own family. Long ago the family had been a source of strength and encouragement. He had his mother's resolve and courage to emulate. When his father was lost at sea, she went out to work as a daily domestic in order that her Mihangel should enjoy a proper education. They had lived in a small terrace house with his grandmother and both women had seen to it he was well fed and given peace and quiet to study before the open fire in the little parlour. The initial objections to his marriage to the heiress of Penllwyn Hall were overcome and the family background and family backing were enlarged and immensely strengthened. His father-in-law became his mentor and patron. Now it was all gone. All that remained was a cantankerous maiden aunt and a headstrong daughter.

The sad fact was that he enjoyed more encouragement and companionship in the golf club than in his own home. After a prolonged tussle in the Ways and Means committee where else could he turn to for a drink and a joke and a measure of inno- cent relaxation? Old Ennis Taft would be waiting there at the bar, ready to slap him on the back or on the shoulder and say things like, 'Now then San Fihangel, what are you going to have?' Ennis was on all the committees raising funds for all the charities God sends. It helped to soothe his conscience. He said so himself. 'Not that I've got all that much. It's drinks and laughter and fair play and decency. And a bit of a singsong. Those are things that mark the man of goodwill, San Fihangel. Now then, how about another?'

It was possibly Ennis's whisky-soaked lips that let those wretched drums of cyanide out of the bag. He was too fond of boasting about his wealth and influence. Uncle Ted had his spies in the golf club. What harm could a few drums of cyanide do buried deep in the bottom of the quarry? Poison the water supply once the drums had rusted away. Always ready with an answer, Iola. How could a man sleep in peace in his own bed in his own house?

In the end he fell into a trouble-haunted sleep only to be awakened by a piercing scream and then the wail and whimper of a child crying. He sat up in bed seething with indignation. There was a full moon and in the wardrobe mirror he could see a white ghost that was nothing more than his own dishevelled image. A man devoted to public service deserved a decent night's sleep. There were more committees tomorrow and he would need all his wits about him to steer through a minefield of amendments. There were enemies on all sides ready to oppose the creation of positive compromise. He was in the chair precisely because of his ability to steer though the waves of controversy to the calm water of any other business. Was there singing going on as well as wailing? He could never get back to sleep. He was the victim of his own benevolence.

There was a piercing scream, he swore, sufficient to shatter the universe. He had to get up and register stern disapproval. This was the kind of disturbance that should not be allowed to continue. It may be a city was going up in flames and his mother lying unconscious in the street and the tentacles of anarchy were tightening around his little throat so he had to scream; but it had to stop. Down a moonlit corridor he saw Maristella sitting on the floor outside the door of the little boy's bedroom. She was in a skimpy nightdress, nursing a large white bath towel. She said she was waiting there in case little Nino woke up again.

'They come sometimes,' she said. 'These nightmares. Soaking in sweat. I think it is my fault.'

He could only respond with a sympathetic stance.

'I'm afraid he will disturb Iola,' Maristella said. 'Iola can't function without her eight hours sleep.'

The phrase was so obviously his daughter's. Repeated in this soft exotic accent it sounded like a confession of faith. He was abruptly reminded of his own long-suffering mother and his own childhood.

'I had nightmares,' he said. 'When I was small. I used to think I was drowning. Sinking to the very bottom of the sea.'

This was another mother trying to bring up a fatherless son. An emblem of anxiety, patience, and suffering.

'If it is my fault,' she said. 'He may grow up to hate me.'

The alderman smiled to reassure her.

'I don't think so,' he said. 'I don't think so at all.'

She raised a hand to let it rest on his arm. The scent of tender feminine concern was a comfort he had forgotten.

'You are so good to us,' Maristella said. 'So good. We thank you.'

When he returned to his bedroom it seemed emptier than when he left it. There were forms of consolation, beyond language, that could still exist.

VI

A series of meetings of local government specialists called the alderman first to Cardiff and then to London. He fussed over the preparation but it was a relief to get away. At meal times when he was inclined to make polite inquiries into the kind of life that his guests had emerged from, it seemed incredible that such a docile creature as Maristella had been turned out of a prosperous home in Bordighera. Iola would commandeer the conversation with more probing questions about the Council's planning policies and particularly about the extension of the landfill in Cloddfa Quarry. When Iola spoke Maristella lapsed into respectful silence. It was difficult too for him to establish any reaction on her part to Iola's sporadic and rather crude efforts to push the unmarried mother in Moi Twm's direction. Could both the creatures be so much under his daughter's thumb that they would go to any length to please her? It was none of his business and yet he had a right to know what was going on under his own roof. He found Moi Twm's increasingly frequent visits distinctly nerve-racking. He claimed now to have established contact with a J.R. Cethin Society, in Toledo, Ohio, through the internet. He also claimed that Dr. Derwyn the college archivist was showing a keen interest in his discoveries. He even had the temerity to suggest he interviewed Miss Keturah Parry. He was certain the old woman would have more information about the affair with the organist's daughter. In such a closed society, he argued, knowledge of such a scandal would be vigorously suppressed but not forgotten. There could even be papers still kept under lock and key.

The meetings in Cardiff and London were pleasant occasions. His expenses were paid and comfortable accommodation provided. There was the mild excitement of brief conversations with celebrated politicians. Old acquaintances were renewed and new friendships made warm with promises of being useful in the future. An old farmer who used to accompany him earlier in his civic career called the process 'setting out mole traps.' A more recent phrase he learnt was 'networking.' The meetings resembled social occasions enlivened with a measure of pomp and conviviality. Consensus or a genial agreement to postpone were both easy to arrive at. This led him to observe to jovial colleagues that government on the larger scale was infinitely more tractable than squabbles on the home patch.

However diverting the excursion, he was always glad to catch the first glimpse of Penllwyn in the taxi from the station. The old minister had set that stark strong square house on the brow of the hill and it still exuded its own endowment of mid-Victorian confidence. He had designed the place himself, and in a sense it would have been true to say he was monarch of all he surveyed: the theocratic ruler of pulpit and workplace, composing sermons and hymn tunes, and opening quarries and investing in ships that seemed to have gone down in storms with monotonous regularity. There was something about the old man's arrogance that made the Alderman shudder slightly and he had been relieved when his late wife removed the full length portrait in oil from the drawing room to the attic. The past was to muse upon at leisure, the present was alive with problems that cried out to be solved. There were clouds scudding along high in the blue sky above the hill and he was glad to be home.

The house was empty and it was the sound of the little boy's laughter that led him to the orchard. There his mother was rocking him to and fro in the swing Price the gardener had put up for him. She pushed the swing with one hand and with the other held on to a floppy hat that threatened to fly away in the breeze. She wore a thin pink and white frock, and mother and son together made an attractive picture. He took his time before making his presence known.

'Where is everyone?'

It was something to say. He didn't really want to know. It was agreeable to have the place to themselves.

'They have gone to the Rally in Caernarfon,' she said. 'In support of the coffee workers of Nicaragua. Iola leaves me to look after your house. And my son of course.'

'You mean Iola and her partners in crime.'

Maristella took time to interpret the phrase and decide whether or not the alderman was joking. She offered to make tea and he was pleased to accept. She was a good listener whether or not she understood everything he was saying. For too long the house had lacked the attentions of a woman prepared to listen to a man of some consequence who returns from a conference primed with tell-tale fragments of the gossip of high politics. Ministers spoke more freely in a convivial social context. Would Maristella be interested to know that the minister had pulled a grim face and said something needed to be done about the Teachers Union? Her response would be more satisfying than his daughter's. All he would have got from Iola would be yet another disparaging remark.

'Alderman...'

She had something to ask. Was it too soon to suggest she used a less formal mode of address? Was there too wide a gap between his title and his first name? Would she have been able to pronounce Mihangel? Iola's frivolous modes of address could well have confused her, which was a great pity. Youth was so obviously the antidote to all the uncomfortable premonitions of old age.

'I have seen the piano in the drawing room,' Maristella said. 'Would you allow me to give my Nino music lessons? He is not too young to learn.'

'But of course.'

It was such a pleasure to be generous and gracious. This would be an opportunity to inquire more closely into her background. It was an operation that needed to be conducted with a degree of delicacy and expertise. He had a reputation for success in interviewing candidates for all sorts of posts. These enquiries of course would be far more friendly and intimate. Maristella had gone to the kitchen to make tea and left the Alderman and the little boy gazing at each other in a state of benevolent neutrality. There was the sound of tyres on the gravel outside. Parry-Paylin saw Dr. Derwyn emerge in some haste from his economical little car. He became aware instantly of trouble afoot. Derwyn was not his usual restrained and urbane self. Something serious had ruffled the slippery smoothness of his feathers.

'I'm so glad you are back,' Dr. Derwyn said. 'Something of a crisis I fear. Keturah Parry has locked herself in the chapel.'

Derwyn's small mouth was twitching. Under different circumstances, at a distance perhaps, the disclosure could have been amusing. A nonagenerian had caught up with the methods of the age of protest.

'I have to admit, to some extent, the fault was mine. That notion of Moi Twm Thomas's about a museum for R.J. Cethin. Professor Dwight Edelberg of Toledo was quite enthusiastic about it. On the e-mail. Americans when they're enthusiastic are always in a hurry, aren't they? They like to get things done. He was all for a joint operation by his department and mine. I told Moi Twm Thomas to wait until you got back. But your daughter was all for striking while the iron was hot. And they made matters worse, you see. I told them the approach was too crude. Turn Soar into an R.J. Cethin Museum or see it demolished for the new road scheme. This is her response. She's locked herself in the chapel.'

Maristella appeared from the kitchen with the tea tray.

'Shall I get another cup?' she said.

The alderman was too angry to answer. He stalked out of the house. Dr. Derwyn hurried after him.

'I'm sorry to be the bearer of bad news,' he said. 'She's taken her paraffin stove into the chapel. A lamp on the communion table. And blankets. And a chamber pot. She's ready for a long siege.'

'That woman is the bane of my life.'

Dr. Derwyn stepped back in the face of such a blaze of indignation.

'And that young devil... mischief makers have made matters worse.'

'I did stress that it would be wiser to wait until you got back. I did stress that.'

Alderman Paylin raised both arms and let them fall again.

This academic had no idea how to handle people. He was just the type to rush in where any sensible experienced angel would fear to tread.

'She's mad,' the Alderman said. 'And she's been mad for years. Do you realise we had an electric stove installed in that cottage thirty years ago? She had it taken out. She sold it and gave the miserable price she got for it to the L.M.S. She lives in a nineteenth-century time-warp. You've seen it for yourself. She's completely out of touch with reality.'

He waved a hand to specify the unique solidity of their surroundings, the house and the gardens and the woodland above them: the view of the noble mountain range: the honourable scars of the quarries: the sea on the western horizon. This was reality.

'Did you speak to her yourself? What did she have to say? As if I couldn't guess.'

'She said R.J. Cethin was a heretic and a scoundrel and the sooner his name was forgotten the better. She said I should be ashamed of myself not giving the sermons of five glorious ministers a place of honour. She said I had joined the worshippers of the Golden Calf. Both of them she said. The English Calf and the Money Calf. It was quite upsetting.'

The Alderman allowed himself a grim smile.

'She said something else too. The organist's daughter was one of your family. On her mother's side. It was a terrible secret!'

'One of her hobbies. Making family trees. I used to tell her if we went back far enough we'd find we were all related.'

'Will you speak to her Alderman Parry-Paylin? She's in quite a state.'

The Alderman shook his head. At least he could give the archivist a brief lesson in the exercise of authority and the management of people.

'Let her stew in her own juice,' he said. 'She'll soon get fed up in there. Chamber pot and all.'

VII

Iola was the first to point out that in the kind of community in which they lived people would soon start talking. Since when may he ask had she and her ilk worried about what people were saying? He slumped in his chair at the head of the table as though he were sitting for a portrait of a brooding monarch. He could see that his bad mood was disturbing Maristella and her little son; whereas Iola was just treating the whole affair as a joke. The only way he could wipe the grin off her face would be to threaten to turn the strangers out of the house. That would be worse than a futile gesture. It would deprive him of the few crumbs of comfort available. In the worst possible case if he tried to turn his only daughter out she would go around the place screaming that he had deprived her of her mother's heritage. And that would cause more talk than the scandal of the old woman locking herself up in Soar chapel. The only measure of discipline he had been able to impose was to insist that Moi Twm be kept out of his sight. However this did nothing to diminish the frequent mutterings and chatterings that took place at the back of the house or down by the road gate.

Within twenty-four hours he was perched precariously on top of a tombstone trying to communicate with his aunt through a chapel side window above the level of green opaque glass. To maintain his balance and make himself heard he was obliged to lean forward and place his hands on a stone sill that was covered with green slime. The grass grew high between the gravestones. He was made to realise that the volunteer caretakers had become too old to cut the grass. A cloudy drizzle was looming to put a damper on everything. Soon the place would be overrun by creeping brambles and briers and what on earth was he to do about it?

'You are breaking the Law!'

Against his better judgement he had to shout. It was the only way he could make himself heard. The old woman seemed to treat his warning as a joke. From the end of the pew where she sat she was raising her hands to warm them above the paraffin stove in the aisle.

'The moral law, Mihangel Paylin,' she said. 'That's something you don't know too much about.'

'I offered you rooms in Penllwyn years and years ago. You know that as well as I do.'

In his uncomfortable position he made a strenuous effort not to sound cross.

'Your poor grandfather would turn in his grave if he knew you were living in the enemy's citadel. That's what he called your precious Penllwyn. The enemy's citadel.'

The old woman was enjoying the reverberations of her own voice in the empty chapel. The sound was an incentive to preaching. She stood up and placed a hand on the back of the pew in front to support herself. She was ready to address an invisible congregation.

'That was your grandfather, auntie. I said your grandfather. It was a very long time ago!'

He struggled to maintain his balance as he raised his voice. His aunt persisted with her litany.

'Persecuted he was. Gruffydd Owen Parry. Driven out of his smallholding by a vicious landlord for voting against him. Driven to work in the quarry and driven out of Cloddfa by that old monster of Penllwyn. Driven to work as a farm labourer and walking ten miles a day there and back for fourpence a day. But he never soured in spirit. He was the leader of song in this chapel for forty years.'

She started to sing in a quavering voice, '*Driven out of Eden and its blessings I came to kneel before the Cross...*'

The effort was too much for her. She sat back in the pew to mumble the words of the hymn to herself. For his part Mihangel could no longer hold his precarious position. A drizzle was beginning to fall.

'I'll be back.'

He shouted as he waded through the long grass.

'I'll be back. We've got to be sensible about this. It's got to be settled.'

In reality he had little idea how. The weather wouldn't allow him to pace to and fro among the trees above the house and Penllwyn itself was being given a thorough cleaning by Iola assisted by Maristella and Mrs. Twigg. There would be no peace there. In any case they had no idea of the depth of his problem.

He repaired to the golf club. Ennis Taft was already there enjoying, he said, his first Dubonnet before a light lunch. He insisted Saint Mihangel should join him. Didn't they have a whole agenda to discuss? Over fish, he said, which was good for the old ticker and a bottle of white wine, in no time at all they could set the world to rights. He was full of a new scheme to deal with industrial waste products and make a healthy profit. There was also an amusing crisis at the Comprehensive school where the kitchen staff were threatening to go on strike. It took Ennis Taft some time to apprehend that Parry-Paylin was weighed down with a critical trouble of his own. After an initial burst of amusement, which included an embarrassing rendition of a vulgar ditty about two old ladies locked in the lavatory, Ennis Taft became serious and intensely resourceful.

'The poor old biddy,' he said. 'She must be suffering from senile dementia. There's only one thing to do, San Fihangel. Section her. Or whatever it is they call it. All they need to do is ask her a few questions. What's the name of the Prime Minister of New Zealand? What day is it the day after tomorrow? That sort of thing.'

He grew excited with the sharpness of his own intelligence and the fumes of the white wine. Parry-Paylin had to beg him to keep his voice down. This was a family matter and he found it intensely embarrassing. His friend and colleague was not to be put off his brilliant line of thinking. He continued in a fierce whisper that was hardly less audible than his raucous laughter.

'A doctor and a policeman,' he said. 'That's all you need. And a court order maybe. That should be easy. You're a serving magistrate. I don't want to be callous but you've got to look ahead. Have her put away and you could have the chapel demolished in the twinkling of an eye. And the road widened and the lorries rolling by and everything in the garden will be lovely.'

There was no comfort anywhere. Certainly not in the voice of Ennis Taft. The Alderman sat at the wheel of his car in the spacious golf club car park, stricken with paralysis and the sense of no longer being in charge of anything. This ludicrous crisis called the whole romance of his career into question. In his heart of hearts it had always been a romance: the sacrifices his mother and his grandmother made to ensure his higher education. He was never all that academically bright and he would be the first to admit it, but he had worked hard and overcoming obstacles that in this more comfortable age would have been counted daunting. His greatest triumph had been his marriage. It couldn't be seen as less than a triumph. The daughter of the big house giving him the courage to confront her formidable father to ask for her hand in the most charming old-fashioned manner: with nothing to offer in return except a decent measure of good looks, a winning smile and a manner that, again in this day and age, would be counted a touch too ingratiating. But it was good for politics and his father-in-law set him on the right road. Laura said that was what fathers-in-law were for.

If only Laura were with him now. Their life together was a wonder and a marvel. Laura had presided over a golden age. She knew how to handle everybody. In the case of Mary Keturah she plied her with delicious home-made cakes and jam and praised her grubby mintcake as though it were manna from heaven. She did more than that. Chauffeuring the surly spinster from one eisteddfod or singing festival or preaching meeting to another. The centre of gravity of his existence had been lost since the day Laura died and in some baffling way both his daughter and this impossible aunt seemed determined to hold him responsible for a loss that he felt far more keenly than either of them were ever capable of doing. There seemed to be very little left for him to do except feel acutely sorry for himself.

VIII

It did not take long for the substance of Ennis Taft's advice to her father to reach Iola's ears. While the Alderman brooded in his study, she bustled about the place increasingly excited by the notion of nurturing a plan of her own. She tried to explain the background of the situation and the opportunities it offered to Maristella, and became impatient with her when she was slow to understand.

'Taft Bronco is hardly the World Trade Organisation,' she said. 'But the principle is the same. A chance to wake up the community. Get the people to reassess their sense of values. If we plan this carefully and get Moi Twm's Uncle Ted to write it all up in his column we could start a home-grown revolution.'

'What are you going to do?'

Maristella would at least understand action and showed that she was as ready as ever to take part in it. She had every confidence in Iola's leadership. This was a woman who knew how to act and bring about satisfactory change. She owed her a great debt and was ever ready to pay it.

'We'll join her,' Iola said. 'We'll have a sit-in strike in Soar. The only thing is we have to keep Moi Twm well away from the place.'

Maristella frowned hard as she struggled to follow Iola's line of reasoning.

'They rubbed her up all the wrong way. All that half-baked nonsense about a museum to the memory of R.J. Cethin. It was a daft idea.'

'But you encouraged, I think...'

'Well it didn't work did it. And things have moved on. The essence of revolutionary practice is to seize the moment. I'll get Mrs. Twigg to look after Nino and we'll go and talk to her. Right away. There isn't a moment to lose.'

Maristella felt obliged to listen intently while Iola communicated with Moi Twm on her mobile phone in a language she didn't understand. Somehow or other troops of protesters, mostly from the student body of the colleges within a reasonable radius, were to be put on standby. When Iola gave the signal, the ancient bus that Moi Twm used to collect support for rallies would rumble into action and collect enough bodies to lie in the road when the local authority and the police attempted to take possession of Soar chapel. Iola switched off and waved the mobile phone under Maristella's nose.

'Democracy is a fine thing,' she said. 'We've just got to learn how to manage it.'

She became so excited with the potential of her gift for management that she could no longer keep still. They would go now and she would make immediate contact with her great-aunt herself.

In the car she turned to make Maristella appreciate that a dialogue with Mary Keturah would not be all that easy. There were historical difficulties that had to be overcome. Sectarian difficulties in fact. Did Maristella have any idea of what sectarian difficulties could be like? Her best hope she supposed was that blood in the end would be thicker than the bitter waters of contention. That much Maristella could understand. They stared at the unpretentious façade of the chapel. The west wall was slated from roof to the overgrown path.

'Soar,' Maristella said. 'Like soar up to heaven, yes?'

Iola was so amused she embraced her friend and shook with the effort of controlling her laughter.

'Is it Welsh then?'

Iola breathed deeply to stop laughing.

'Hebrew, you ignorant Papist. Did you never read your Bible? Soar was saved from the destruction of Sodom and Gomorrah.'

Iola embraced her again.

'Don't look so worried. Now then. Here we go.'

Iola grasped the iron ring on the main door.

'My ancestors built this,' she said. 'Some of them did anyway. Quite a lot of them are buried over on the left there. Those gravestones buried in the long grass.'

She began to bang the door determinedly.

'Auntie! Auntie Ket! It's Iola. Let me in, won't you? Let me in!'

She realised she spoke with too much authority as if she had automatic right of entry. With an effort she injected a note of pleading into her voice.

'Auntie. It's Iola. Please Auntie. I want to speak to you.'

Mary Keturah's voice was harsh but noticeably feeble when at last she spoke with her face close to the closed door.

'Who's there with you? Not that Moi Twm Thomas? You keep him well away from this place.'

'Are you alright Auntie Ket. I've brought you some milk and fresh bread.'

'Men do not live by bread alone,' Mary Keturah said. 'She was your great-grandfather's cousin.'

'Who was?'

Iola beckoned Maristella to bring her ear closer to the door. Maristella shrugged and shook her head to show she couldn't understand a word either were saying.

'That girl who ran away with that false prophet R.J. Cethin. So you be careful.'

'I don't care about R.J. Cethin, Auntie. I only care about you. And Soar of course.'

'If you marry that stupid Moi Twm Thomas you'll be making the biggest mistake of your life.'

'I wouldn't dream of marrying him, Auntie. People aren't getting married any more.'

Iola pulled herself up and tried to turn the dangerous observation into a joke.

'It's gone out of fashion. So there you are. You were well ahead of your time, Auntie Keturah.'

There was no response to her attempt at humour. For an old woman who attached so much importance to family how could the demise of marriage be something to laugh at? What would become of the family tree that hung in her bedroom and stretched back generations? And what about the first chapter of the gospel according to St. Mathew?

'There's got to be a succession,' the old woman said. 'Things can't carry on without a succession. If you were as old as I am, you would know that. Where's your father?'

'We want to come in, Auntie Keturah. We want to join you. We want to support you.'

'Do you indeed.'

'Really we do. We want to save Soar.'

'I've never seen you darken these doors before. Dashing about the world getting into trouble. That's what I hear. You run off now, child, and get your father. He is a Trustee. It's his responsibility. He's let the whole fabric of this building run down. It's his job to repair it. And the sooner he starts the better. You go and tell him that. Him and his precious County Council. And tell him I'm not budging out of this chapel until they start repairing it. You tell him that.'

'Won't you let me in? Please.'

'No, I won't. Go and get your father.'

IX

Iola was too furious to speak. The old woman had left her to glower at a closed door. Maristella was standing behind her, a model of patience, waiting for some form of explanation. She was no more than a refugee in a foreign country, without the language or any acquaintance with local custom. All she could gather was that her champion and benefactor and friend was hugely displeased. On the way home Iola kept repeating the same imprecations under her breath.

'The old witch. She's impossible. She always was impossible. Who wants families anyway? They should be done away with.'

A cloud of gloom and despondency descended on Penllwyn. There was a sharp and unforgiving exchange between the Alderman and his only daughter that Maristella could not follow and from then on they stopped speaking to each other. Meal times were particularly uncomfortable. Nino was quick to sense an atmosphere of discord and clung more closely to his mother. His large eyes scanned the faces of father and daughter at either end of the table. The Alderman, when he thought Iola wasn't looking, extended an open hand in Maristella's direction as though looking for sympathy and then closed it abruptly. He was cut off from his habitual source of consolation and comfort at the golf club by a compelling desire to avoid Ennis Taft's poking and probing. Iola, for her part was reluctant to contact Moi Twm. She would have to admit her scheme was a total failure and she had put him to great trouble for nothing. It seemed as if they could not agree what to do about Mary Keturah, they would never be able to agree about anything.

After lunch, Maristella led Nino to the drawing room to give him a music lesson. It was something he had already begun to enjoy. He had two or three notes he could strike in the treble clef so that his mother could tell him they were playing a duet. He hammered away delighted with his own efforts and his mother was pleased too. The volume of sound increased. Iola marched into the room.

'For God's sake, won't you stop that row?'

When she saw how much she had startled them she clapped a hand to her brow.

'I'm afraid I've got a horrible headache,' she said. 'It's not at all my day. I tell you what. Why don't you go and visit Moi Twm in his precious shop. Tell him the sorry tale. You can stick Nino in front of the telly. I'll keep an eye on him.'

Maristella was reluctant to accept the suggestion.

'I don't know what to tell him,' she said. 'I find it difficult to talk to him. He speaks so quickly. I don't really understand what he say. Most of the time.'

'Not good enough for you, is he?'

'Good. He is good of course. Very good.'

'You prefer to be knocked about a bit. Bit of a masochist aren't you, on the quiet?'

Maristella was slow to understand that Iola in her frustrated mood was looking for a fight. She grew pale and took what comfort she could from the little boy clinging to her side.

'Just you remember, if you don't like it here, you can leave tomorrow. I can turn you out the minute you feel like that.'

Her display of nasty temper seemed to bring her some temporary relief. When she saw that both the mother and child were crying, she left the room. It seemed large and empty when she had gone. In the corner of a sofa Maristella nursed and comforted her little boy. They were only here on sufferance. They were isolated in a cold unfriendly world. Within less than half an hour Iola was back again, contrite and full of apologies.

'I'm so sorry my dear. I'm such a nasty spoilt bitch. I know I am. I try to control it. I'm one of those miserable creatures trapped in their own nature.'

She came around the back of the sofa and laid her cheek on the top of Maristella's head. The little boy shrank closer inside his mother's arms. Iola whispered more urgently.

'It comes bursting out sometimes. You do forgive me don't you? Say you forgive me.'

When Maristella nodded she stroked her cheek tenderly.

'We've been through so much together. You are so good for me, Maristella, my guiding star. You help me escape from myself. I mean that. Doing good is more than a back-stairs method of getting your own way. You taught me that.'

She moved around the sofa to sit on the floor at Maristella's feet. She took hold of her hand to squeeze it. The little boy gazed at her with his mouth open, wondering what she would do next.

'The Dominican Republic,' she said. 'There's enormous work to be done there. Shelter are very keen on starting a housing project. It's something to think about Maristella, isn't it? You can speak Spanish?'

'Only very badly.'

Maristella sighed deeply. She was anxious to please Iola, but there were simple facts that had to be faced.

'It's an idea anyway. Something to think about. I have to get away from this place. There's so little I can do about it. You can see that for yourself. It's my home of course. I have a deep deep attachment. But what good can I do? It's sunk so deep in a morass of complacency. There's nothing I can do about it.'

Her father and her great-aunt only seemed to exist to make

her uncomfortable. She shifted up to the sofa from the floor and sat so close to Maristella that Nino was crushed between them. He gave a little squeak of protest and this amused her.

'Go and bang at the piano,' she said. 'Bang it as hard as you like.'

Once he had more space, the little boy was reluctant to leave his mother's side.

'You do what you like,' Iola said. 'Don't ever let people bully you especially me. We've got to think about what to do next, haven't we, Maristella? Whatever happens we've got to be in the same boat.'

X

At four o'clock in the morning Alderman Parry-Paylin was woken up by a loud cry. He studied his wristwatch on the bedside table trying to decide whether it was part of a dream, or the little boy having another nightmare: considering the oppressive atmosphere in the house the previous day, it would not have been surprising. He had seriously considered the possibility of asking the little boy's mother to act as some sort of go-between or mediator, between his difficult daughter and himself; only to conclude that such a move would have been too ridiculous. Since when had a foreign girl been able to intercede between a widowed father and his only daughter, who in any case had no excuse to be harbouring imagined wrongs. As so often happened in these matters, it was a case of sitting it out: just waiting until all the parties concerned came to their senses. In all his dealings throughout his life, he had relied on common sense to prevail.

He was slow to become aware of a blue light outside revolving in the grey mist of early morning. He saw the police car in the drive. In a state of agitation he stumbled around the bedroom aware of an impending emergency but uncertain how to prepare for it. Half dressed and carrying a rain-coat he walked down the stairs to be met by Inspector Owen Evans a police officer with whom he had good relations. In their dressing gowns Iola and Maristella stood in silence on either side of the bottom of the staircase. Iola reached out to take her father's hand. He had to assume she was prepared to offer him comfort. In any event, it looked right. The Inspector was a large avuncular figure who liked to say that he was a farmer's son from Meirionydd, who had to make a choice between the ministry and the police force, and had settled the matter in his own mind by making his professional manner a mixture of both.

'Sad news, Alderman. And bad news. I've already informed these young ladies. A fire at Soar. I'm very sorry to tell you Alderman Parry-Paylin your dear old aunt has passed away.'

'A fire?'

The Alderman gripped the curved balustrade to steady himself.

'Yes. Well now then, I thought it was the least I could do to come and tell you myself.'

Iola reached out to take his hand.

'Daddy. I'm so sorry. I really am.'

Her sympathy was a form of reconciliation and he smiled at her. The Inspector placed his large hand on the Alderman's shoulder, and Mihangel Parry-Paylin lowered his head in gratitude for so much thoughtfulness and consideration. The Inspector looked at Iola and she bestirred herself to make some tea. The Inspector and the Alderman made their way at a solemn pace to take tea in the study.

'A nasty accident,' the Inspector said. 'It's too soon to jump to conclusions but I suspect it was that paraffin stove. It is a great sadness of course, but in my job, alas, we have to deal with these tragedies every day. At least here, my friend, there was a touch of heroism in the story and good deeds are bright lights in a wicked violent world. Nick Jenkin the postman was on his way to work and saw the smoke billowing out of one of the windows and from under the door. He didn't hesitate. He soaked his jacket in the river, put it over his head, smashed the door open with the jack from his van and dragged the old woman out. Too late of course, but a fine gallant action. She was dead of course, overcome with the fumes.'

They shook their heads and contemplated the postman's courageous action as they sipped their hot tea.

'They put the fire out,' the Inspector said. 'But the dear little chapel is little more than a smouldering ruin. There was a lamp you know on the communion table. Was it the lamp or the paraffin stove? Did she knock it over? Was she desperate to escape? She was very old of course. But old people are still people, aren't they? I know how upsetting it must be for you. I know you thought the world of Soar. All those family associations. When you have recovered sufficiently I want you to come with me and look at the damage. Not much we can save I'm afraid. Plenty of scorched papers fluttering around. You, more than anyone else will have to decide what is to be done. And of course, when you feel up to it, we shall need to identify the body.'

XI

In the portico of Moriah, one of the largest chapels in the county town, Uncle Ted drew on the fag end of his cigarette while Moi Twm stood alongside him anxious to find a seat inside. The chapel was filling up rapidly.

'There'll be room in the gallery,' Uncle Ted said. 'Above the clock. That's where I like to sit. Keep an eye on things.'

Moi Twm was embarrassed by the note of cynicism in his Uncle Ted's rasping voice. There was a limit to the extent you could suspect everyone and everything. The death of the old woman and the destruction of the chapel had touched him deeply. He had washed the colour out of his hair and had his head shaved like a Buddhist monk. He hoped people would take his transformation seriously. It was not such a big step, he said, from protest to pilgrimage. Uncle Ted's comment he found thoughtless to the point of being hurtful. He said it made him look like an overpaid professional footballer.

'Here they come.'

Uncle Ted's small eyes ferreted about.

'Two by two the animals enter the ecumenical ark.'

He threw his fag end away and pushed Moi Twm forward to climb the gallery steps on the left side of the vestibule. The weather had taken a turn for the worst. Umbrellas and raincoats abounded and a steamy atmosphere gave the impression that the chapel was packed. In the gallery there was more room, and from his chosen vantage point above the clock, Uncle Ted and Moi Twm could take a close view of the proceedings. The coffin, mounted on a wheeled chromium-plated bier, was parked under the elaborately carved pulpit, where the communion table usually stood. It was adorned with one large wreath of white lilies and red roses. The pulpit itself was overshadowed by the shining mountain of pipes of the powered organ. The curved deacon's-pew was occupied by ministers of all the denominations, including the Anglican Archdeacon and the Roman Catholic priest.

'I wonder what the old girl would have had to say about that...'

Uncle Ted fidgeted about the pew so that he could get closer to Moi Twm's ear. There was ceaseless comment he wanted to make for his nephew's edification.

'Quite a bing-bang you know at the Ecumenical Council. How best to take advantage of the occasion. The Bishop was there you know. Agreed to Moriah, provided the Archdeacon made an address all designed to prove the old girl died to prove the church was One and indivisible.'

Moi Twm made an effort to shift further away from the buzz of his Uncle's excited whispers. The organ had begun to play low sonorous music. He wanted to be left alone with his own solemn thoughts. Uncle Ted had too much to say for himself. This wasn't the place to be dishing dirt.

'The Press is here you know. We are on the verge of a mini-media event. Jones Llandudno Junction has been trying to get the tabloids interested. Working himself up no end concocting tasty headlines – *Nonconformist spinster sets fire to herself.*

He began to shake as a sequence of witty elaborations occurred to him. In the end he had to clap his hand over his loose dentures to stop them slipping out. He seemed incapable of sitting still. He leaned over the edge of the gallery in case persons of importance might be sitting at the back of the chapel. Moi Twm tugged fiercely at the tail of the black coat his uncle wore to attend funerals.

The two front pews according to custom had been left vacant for the immediate family. Mihangel Parry-Paylin and his daughter Iola occupied the first.

'Not much of a family.'

Uncle Ted felt obliged to comment. He was surprised almost to the point of outrage when Maristella and her little boy took their place in the second pew. Before she sat down Maristella genuflected in the direction of the coffin and crossed herself.

'Good Lord! Did you see that Moi Twm? Did you see that?'

It was a neat and unobtrusive gesture, but surprising in a nonconformist chapel.

'What do you expect her to do?'

Moi Twm was fed up with his uncle's prattle. The man was tied to his bad habits like a wayside goat on a tether.

'She's a Latin, isn't she? It's a mark of respect. We could do with a little more of it around here.'

In a brief address, the Archdeacon said that he was speaking on behalf of the county branch of the Ecumenical Movement. This was a special occasion. By her sacrifice this lonely old lady had brought the whole community closer together and made it aware of all the present dangers that threatened its Christian roots. The fate of our little nation, he said, was inextricably interwoven with the faith that gave it birth in the first place. There was such a thing as an apostolic succession on the humblest level and by her untimely death, Mary Keturah Parry had made a whole community more aware of this vital fact. Uncle Ted made notes in his own peculiar form of shorthand and grunted full approval of the Archdeacon's eloquence.

Mary Keturah Parry was buried in the new cemetery plot opposite the ruin of Soar chapel. For this service the mourners were far fewer in number. When the interment was over, Alderman Parry-Paylin stretched out a hand to hold back Maristella.

'I wonder if I could have a word,' he said.

They stood still on the wet grass as the straggle of mourners went past them. There was some curiosity to take a closer look at the ruins of the chapel. Someone said the pews were still smouldering.

'Something I've been wanting to say.'

The Alderman breathed more deeply to gain courage to speak.

'If you and your little boy wanted to make Penllwyn your home, I would be very glad for you to stay.'

Maristella looked down as if she were measuring the degree of tenderness in the proposal.

'You are very kind,' she said. 'You have been very kind to us both.'

'Will you stay?'

There was a level of pleading in his voice. He had his own problem, being obliged to grow old alone. This gentle unmarried mother could be the answer. He had to make the offer.

'I don't know,' she said. 'I shall have to ask Iola.'

'Ah well, Maristella. I am sure you will find life more comfortable in Penllwyn than wandering the wildernesses of this world. Much easier you know.'

'I don't think my life was ever meant to be easy,' Maristella said.

In her deep black, Iola was approaching to ask them what they had stopped to talk about.

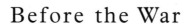

Before the War

I

'Sheltered accommodation!'

Elsie Probert drew the attention of her great niece to the nervous capers of a wren above the thick hedge behind the garden trellis.

'Out there and in here. Are you interested in birds, Non?'

Her great-niece made a gesture that could have meant anything: a pout of her young red lips and a slight shrug of the shoulders. There was a microphone on the chair between them.

'Your grandfather used to collect birds' eggs. I wasn't allowed to touch them.'

Non raised her eyebrows and tilted her head making just a shade too much effort to show interest. Elsie returned her attention to the behaviour of the bird.

'There's a pair in there,' she said. 'They're monogamous. And they have a problem keeping warm because they build too many nests and have too many to choose from.'

'Really,' Non said. 'I didn't know that.'

In spite of herself she touched the microphone and it became clear she wanted to start asking questions and recording. Her great-aunt was a bird-like creature herself; too small for the large armchair and her little white head was inclined to dart about. Her bones were delicate but not brittle. At eighty-six she was a spinster who some people would judge as pretty as she had ever been. And she had a pert precise manner that went well with her decoratively neat appearance.

'How is your young man?'

It wasn't the kind of question Miss Probert would normally ask. Whether or not she smiled when she said it, it did sound inquisitive, if not vulgar even. However she had agreed to speak freely and in these matters there should be a degree of give and take. Non's young man was called Gilbert and he worked for an American publisher in London. He was twenty-six years old and very ambitious. The problem was Non wouldn't move up to London and Gilbert would not move down to Wales.

'He can be a bit difficult at times,' Non said.

'Men are, aren't they?'

Elsie smiled understandingly. After all they were both women as well as being related. Non was already blushing and it made her look prettier than ever. She was determined never to trade on her good looks. She might not have taken all that much interest in her great-aunt before, but now she was all set to make her the temporary centre of her little academic universe. And when the thesis was well and truly finished and she had her Ph.D. she could tread with Master Gilbert on a more or less equal footing. He should know she too had her career to think about.

'What I thought you could tell me, Auntie Elsie, if you would, just what it was like in Llannerch before the war.'

Non leaned forward to press the button on the tape-recorder with studied care.

'Which war, my dear?'

Non was disconcerted. She looked at her note pad and at the tape-recorder as if uncertain whether or not to switch it off and start again.

'I'm only teasing. When I was a child 'before the war' always meant before 1914. Or the year before I was born. There's always a 'before' isn't there? In those days it meant when everybody went to chapel and a handful went to church, and the poor had parish relief and the twin-set, bless it, hadn't been invented. And the threshing machine came rumbling up the lane drawn by a great team of horses. In our time it was a steam engine. We used to love steam-rollers. And the smell of tar. Especially when they came passing our house. Your grandfather said that when he grew up he was going to drive a steam-roller. I was convinced he would. You're not recording this rubbish are you? You know how old women go rambling on.'

'It's fine, Auntie. Really I want you to say whatever you like.'

'Goodness knows what I'll say. Rambling on.'

'That's fine. We've got all the time in the world.'

Non's anxiety to please amused her great aunt.

'Have I? That's nice to know.'

'You know what I mean.'

'Yes I suppose so.'

Elsie looked lovingly at the garden. She called it her amphitheatre, furnished with plants and flowers. The birds and the small animals came and went as if they were doing their best to entertain her.

'It's very nice here,' she said. 'I'm really pleased with the place. All day to sit around and nothing to worry about. I used to be an awful worrier.'

She began to carol a hymn in a thin quavering soprano.

'The strife is o'er, the battle done

Now is the victor's triumph won...'

She clapped her hand over her mouth and pointed at the microphone.

'Oh dear,' she said. 'Am I being naughty?'

Non shook her head vehemently.

'Good heavens no, Auntie. You can say whatever you like. Absolutely!'

'That would be fun wouldn't it? I used to think we'd be singing that in church because we'd won the war. Or at least my father had. There was the Rector, up in the pulpit, shutting his eyes tight and throwing his head back and croaking out in that constricted voice of his, 'Alleluia!' That was the Reverend Justin Jones, M.A. The Oxford man. And there was Miss Prydwen Parry, my adored teacher, bouncing away in front of the narrow pipe organ because the bellows had broken and there was no one to mend the thing. And the Rector's wife, drooping over her hymn book. We thought she had sleeping sickness. It was the drink of course. And my father, your great grandfather, my dear, sitting alone at the back of the church, which was almost empty anyhow, because of his artificial leg you see. He never took communion either. I never found out why. It couldn't have been just his leg. I used to sing with all my might because I thought my father was the victor. Everybody said it had been a terrible war and that's why the church was so dead quiet when we stopped singing. Such a silence. We were embalmed in peace thanks to my father, I thought. Did you know your great grandfather was a war hero? Major David Owen Probert M.C. Did you know that?'

'Well I suppose I did. Vaguely.'

'So long ago. Have you made your family tree? No family ties without a family tree, you know. No funeral complete without them. We all need one. Especially in a place like this. A better class of old people's home. You need the information to hand when you haven't got the time or the energy to go in search of it.'

'So you went to church, Auntie.'

'Oh, we *were* church. "All aboard" my Dad used to say. "Get a seat in our little Anglican lifeboat or you'll drown in a nonconformist sea." He liked to make pronouncements. That is, when he felt like talking. There were days when he didn't talk at all. We thought it was because of his leg. He'd gone to war you know when he didn't really need to. He had two children. Your grandfather and me. I don't think my mother was pleased. In a way I think she never forgave him'.

She studied the garden more closely and pondered the mystery of her parent's relationship. What had they seen in each other in the first place? Such secrets were buried forever in the past and yet had so much to do with why a woman of eighty-six and another of twenty-three were making this taped recording. If they were related could she speak her mind as if she were talking to herself? Hardly. She had a lifetime to understand the difference between what you were saying and what you were thinking. It was a game to be played, and a game was better than fear and distrust and edgy loneliness. She could tell her great niece whatever she chose to tell her and she could think what ever she chose to think.

'I never saw him do any work,' she said.

'Who was that Auntie?'

Non was intent on making notes to qualify whatever was on the tape.

'Your great grandfather. My father. That's going back a bit, isn't it? Before the war. Before the flood. He always behaved like a gentleman of leisure. If we made too much noise we got on his nerves. Gelli Wen stood in its own grounds and we had a gardener believe it or not. Elfed his name was. We thought he was the oldest man in the world. And we had a maid. Girlie my father called her because she came from Caegwrle. Priscilla her real name was but she preferred being called 'Girlie'. All on his war pensions I suppose and my mother's annuity. They were the props that kept our little world in place although I hadn't any notion about things like that then. I thought Gelli Wen was the centre of the universe. Trees on the slopes around the back and the big garden between us and the country road that led to the outside world. Shabby genteel would be the phrase to describe us. We went to the local church school so there were no fees to pay. Nothing more than twopence a week anyway. I never knew what the twopence was for. A penny for your grandfather and a penny for me. Tada said it was to keep Mrs. Jones the Rectory in gin. When you're a child of course you take your world for granted. Even the gloom and doom. And our house was full of gloom and doom. And then along came the wonderful Miss Prydwen Parry. You've never seen such a beautiful head of yellow hair; all bangs and curls. And a sweet smile with dimples. And long legs for running and jumping. We'd never seen anything like her. She was a nonconformist but the Rector got round her to play the organ in church. The congregation didn't grow any bigger. In those days people didn't change their denomination for the sake of a head of yellow hair. It was all fixed you know. Loyalty the major virtue. Like the Law of the Medes and Persians.'

Non's eyes were bright with enthusiasm.

'It sounds wonderful, Auntie. And everybody speaking Welsh. It must have been like the earthly paradise.'

Miss Elsie Probert nodded.

'Yes it was,' she said.

And she immediately thought otherwise.

II

I adored your grandfather, young lady, but I'm afraid he didn't adore me. Not a very good beginning when you come to think of it, and these days I come to think of it more than ever. You must have more of his genes than mine. They go on a lot about things like that these days. In olden times, before we started counting wars they used to believe in bad blood, inherited guilt and wayward inclinations, family weaknesses. I suppose the language and the treatment may differ but the disease remains incurably the same. That is not a cheerful thought but I can live with it as I clutch my hymn book. In the same sense, history always happens when you're not looking. You read about it afterwards and you let it fall into place like a collection of old calendars in the attic.

I can see Tom's face this minute as he scowls at me and puts a finger to his lips. Tada is in the garden leaning on his stick and his back is turned. Tom is about to make his escape through a well-concealed hole in the hedge. Should I raise my voice, give a shout, or remain silent? I could do either. It was a fleeting but exhilarating taste of power. I could exercise authority over my brother who was nearly four years my senior and never ceased to remind me of that vital fact. If only there had been time to bargain; like me more or I'll shout! It was fear that kept me silent. Fear of retribution. The threat like thunder in his face. And no hope of reward. Ever. It was more than that special form of patronising contempt that elder brothers can exercise over a younger sister. Or used to anyway. All the boy's magazine stories he read had heroes with annoying younger sisters. That could have been a pattern set by the manners of age. Then of course he could have been reproducing the condescending attitude my father had towards my mother. Perhaps he assumed that this was standard practice by any self-respecting male to any female. As for me, I positioned myself at his beck and call in the hope of some muttered word of approval, however brief.

Another of life's mysteries to be mulled over but never resolved: why my mother and father were so desperately unsuited to each other. The married state remains an ideal I've no doubt but most of the examples I dwell now on seem to suggest otherwise and allow me to accept my spinsterhood as something of an uncovenanted blessing. It is true that my father went off to war either against her wishes or without telling her; and came back minus a leg. And that could be sufficient reason for those prolonged silences. He had disappointed her, condemned her to a shabby genteel existence and she took it out on him by finding sexual intercourse distasteful. They slept in separate rooms. He had an old army chum he called Mog Rees who would turn up in a variety of large motor cars to transport them to unknown destinations: regimental reunions, and maybe assignations? When he got back, a week or more would pass before my parents spoke to each other. Essential messages would be conveyed by Girlie or by Tom or by myself. I would knock on the door of his study before opening it and he would peer at me through a cloud of pipe tobacco smoke as if I were some strange and unfamiliar apparition. I may well have been. I was thin and nervous and had a habit of rubbing my ankles together which he plainly disliked. He was an avid reader of history books and hated to be disturbed. I knew how he felt even then. I was an avid reader myself and never liked being called away from my book. My father made notes in a common-place book, and he said once he was arming himself against the coming darkness. As far as I was concerned the darkness had come already. Hardly a day passed without one member or another of our household finding me an impediment or a nuisance. There was nobody there to take pleasure in my company. My mother wore a perpetual frown as she concentrated on treading the high wire of keeping up appearances. My father amused himself by a close observa-tion of the absurdities and pretensions of local life and much to my mother's annoyance he would garner local gossip from Elfed the gardener, finding out, she said, miserable little facts it would be better for our standing in society not to know. Worse still, he encouraged Elfed to lean on his spade and grind out gossip when there was so much work to be done.

The garden was intended to be an outward and visible sign of my mother's gentility; a decorative bulwark to prevent the outside world and the overly inquisitive from detecting the gloom that governed the interior behind an undistinguished façade. When I saw the place again, several years ago, it was not without charm and it could have provided a small girl with a pleasant playground. It seems sad that it didn't.

III

From the beginning there was a fairy tale quality about Miss Prydwen Parry. She touched me with a magic wand and my life took a new turn. Her little Austin Seven drew up outside the pretentious gates of Gelli Wen that were rusting under their coat of cheap brown paint, and to my astonishment both my father and my mother were pleased to see her. My mouth and my eyes were wide open as I recognised for the first time the power of charm in operation. Would they allow Elsie to join the girls weekend camp at Castell Cawr? Open air and all that: three bell tents, ground sheets and mattresses stuffed with straw. Farmer Roberts was very obliging. The tithe barn if the weather broke. Games of course. Some new ones. Singing certainly. A dip in the river if parents allowed it. Of course they would. My father was all for it. 'That chap Hitler has some good ideas. Very go ahead, the Jerries. Strength through Joy. We could do with a bit of that sort of stuff in this country' Once he had warmed to a theme he expected the world to listen. The year before it had been Lloyd George and 'I can conquer unemployment,' and copies of that yellow pamphlet stacked in the cloakroom.

'The trouble with this village,' he liked to say, 'they've got no idea what's going on in the world. Not the faintest!'

He said it more than once to Miss Parry. I could see he much preferred talking to her than to my mother. The marvel was my mother didn't mind. Could she, too, be taken with Prydwen Parry's spirited beauty; that brilliant, understanding smile? In return her mouth was set in one of her own impassive Mona Lisa smirks. If only Miss Prydwen Parry could take up residence in Gelli Wen my whole world would be transformed. She was a star you could wait around for, just in order to trip along in her trail of glory.

We were a group of girls all longing to please her and hoping to be like her. This was a new way of life. She made us all believe we were born to be happy. When I stumbled out of the tent at dawn and trod in a cowpat or a bed of nettles I didn't mind a bit. I was seeing the world as I had never seen it before. There was a new sun burning away the morning mist. Down by the river I saw trout jumping and I jumped too. So did my companions. It was all miraculous but the greatest miracle of all was I had acquired four close friends as if four magic wishes had come true: Lalw, Hannah May, Delyth, and Bessie Maud. A treasure-trove in a tent. Miss Prydwen had declared we were good companions and that was what we were resolved to be and the tent pole was our Round Table. We were like the wild flowers we collected and looked up their pretty names: maiden pink, forget-me-not, meadow-sweet, wild rose, lady's mantle, lords and ladies and goodness knows what. To live for ever in honesty and loyalty.

For the first time in my young life I reached out my hand before going to sleep and another hand took it. Lalw's hand was harder and stronger than mine. She helped on the farm after school. Her father won prizes at ploughing matches and her mother used a butter stamp with an elephant's head carved into it. Lalw had a birth mark on her neck. Hannah May lived in the police station at Nantygroes and had red hair. The policeman won prizes for singing at eisteddfodau. Bessie Maud had a lady's bicycle and let me learn to ride on it. I fell off I don't know how many times and we all laughed. Delyth was the minister's daughter but she didn't hold it against me for being church. We were both great readers and we exchanged books. What a time we had. The whole world seemed love and loyalty. Around the camp fire, or in the barn when it was raining, Miss Prydwen told us marvellous stories that made us sigh and shudder. We had our names and we had our roles and our games and our stories. This was heaven.

Then I had to return to the house of long silences governed by a climate of likes and dislikes impossible for a young girl to iden-tify. The kind of atmosphere you find yourself still trying to analyse sixty and seventy years later. [My goodness how could a modern forward-looking miss like my great-niece Non ever understand it, with or without her microphone and electronic marvels?] It became clear that my father had acquired a dislike of the Rector. This was an evident change of heart. That I could understand sufficiently to make a sequence of rapid adjustments. Inspired by Prydwen Parry's glittering example, the Rector had launched a scout troop for boys and enrolled my brother Tom in a senior position. This would not have been too bad. My brother looked impressive in his brand new uniform, which my parents resented having to pay for. He displayed his mastery of all the appropriate accoutrements and they could have been pleased about that. I was. My father said the Rector was very much an amateur and had a hell of a lot to learn about discipline and order. 'Just look at his wife.' That sort of cryptic comment.

The Rector's real offence came when in collaboration with Prydwen Parry he started a branch of the Urdd. 'It's a conflict of interest,' my father said. 'What does the man think he is up to? He could have left all that namby-pamby mish-mash to the nonconformists for God's sake. What does he think he's doing? It's not his job to go about fostering separatism. I don't know what the world is coming to.' In fact worse was to come. In the summer of 1930, the Rector and Miss Parry decided to celebrate the fifteenth-hundred anniversary of the Alleluia Victory by staging a pageant that would involve the children of two parishes and a few adults as well. My father thought the scheme ridicu-lously ambitious. And when he learned that the pageant would involve a sequence of the knights and ladies of King Arthur's

Round Table he poured scorn on the anachronism and the unholy mixture of history, legend and myth. It was at this time in my life that I became aware that there existed a category of information that was secret and confidential: a range of matters of which I had knowledge but about which I should never let on. This was an intuitive rather than a rational process, and it may account for my present inability to get to grips with chronology beyond a primitive 'before' and 'after'. I knew, for example, that the Rector wrote a script in verse and that Miss Prydwen Parry corrected it in red ink. I knew this because I was sometimes assigned the role of courier. It was quite a traffic of messages and they were sometimes secreted in the most exotic places; such as the wardrobe in the vestry or under the Rector's hassock. It became a game and Bessie Maud and I were let into the secret. There may have been others, but I hardly think so.

In spite of my father's caustic comments all might have gone well until Prydwen Parry executed what one might call a reversed version of the judgement of Paris. For the coveted role of King Arthur there were my brother Tom, one would have thought the obvious favourite, Jac Plas a powerful lad who bordered on the illiterate, and Lalw's brother Iorweth. For some obscure philanthropic reason which I never understood but out of love and loyalty never questioned, Miss Parry chose Jac Plas. My brother Tom never forgave her.

III

'Your grandfather had a brilliant career, Non!' Miss Probert said. 'I suppose you've heard about that.'

It was a gentle probe that seemed to have embarrassed Non a little. She was here to ask questions rather than answer them. She had been advised that interrogation was a technique that required patience as well as persistence.

'Tom had a scientific mind, you see. Right from the beginning. Determined to find out things. You could say he had a gift for detection. Not a nosy parker. Just an urge to find out things for himself. And one day I suppose he realised that the process worked better in physics and chemistry than with human beings. And of course that kind of knowledge was much more in demand: especially when war came. Mind you he had to fight all the way to get ahead. Against father mainly. Father said there was no money for university. Tom could get a good job in Mog Rees's brickyard. On the managerial side of course. If he did well one day Mog Rees might make him a partner. He had no children of his own. But your grandfather studied day and night and won a State Scholarship. So that put paid to the brickyard. My father was furious. Didn't even congratulate him. Didn't really believe in education. The truth is I don't really know what he believed in. Except the hereditary principle. Order and discipline and that sort of thing. They never got on.'

Non waited politely while her great-aunt pondered the mystery of family relationships. In her notebook there were subject headings she would like to follow up: social deprivation in the rural environment; the decline of religious observance; mechanisation on the farms; depopulation; the arrival of piped water, indoor sanitation, electricity. Her great-aunt had first-hand knowledge of the manifold processes of transformation.

'Tom was never easy. *Your* father didn't get on with him all that well, did he?'

'I suppose not.'

Non was caught in possession of facts her great-aunt would love to know about. There needed to be an exchange: a trade off. The old lady was playing her own game. She would pick up details to fill in a picture: hints at least of those hidden discords that had the power to govern the emotional climate. She would like to savour them in the seclusion of her sheltered accommodation.

'There are patterns that recur, you know. That's one thing that old age teaches you. The Proberts are very like the Hanovarians. A royal succession of conflict between the reigning monarch and the heir apparent. It's still going on isn't it? My theory is it won't come to an end until we abolish male primogeniture. And who's 'we' you may ask? Women of course. You could call me an early feminist. Except I had to keep it all to myself of course.'

Elsie Probert peered more closely at her great niece in search of a sympathetic response; a smile and a laugh perhaps that they could share.

'Do you remember your grandmother?'

'Not terribly well. They lived in Oxted which was a long way away.'

The great-aunt did not find this excuse very convincing.

'She thought I was weak in the head.' she said. 'Staying home to keep house for my father. She thought he was a disagreeable old man and she said so. I thought so too, but I didn't say it. She said I should have put him in a home. Maybe she was right. She was tough. A nursing sister from Ballymena. Lalw's brother said her voice sounded as if she were gargling pebbles. That was Iorweth. He took me to the wedding. A big church in Finchley. Lalw gave me clothing coupons for a new suit. The year after the war. Or was it two years after the war? She had nursed Tom when he had sandfly fever in India. She was very bossy as you would expect with a nursing sister in those days. Still she was devoted to Tom and he was difficult enough so we can't ask for more than that can we?'

Non's hand was hovering about the recorder uncertain whether or not to leave it on.

'They're both gone now, so we may as well speak frankly. Tom took a job in South Africa because Maureen your grandmother, bless her, couldn't stand the sound of Welsh. That's what he told me anyway. When it came to it she didn't like the sound of Afrikaans either, although she didn't say that out loud. It could have lost him his job. They were glad to get back when he was appointed head of Meriweather Technical College. She had to wait a bit longer before he became a Vice-Chancellor or what-ever they call it of a University. But what I wanted to ask was about your father, Duncan Probert. What was it that brought him back to Wales?'

Unobtrusively Non switched off the recorder.

'It must have been my mother,' she said.

Miss Probert's eyes widened with avid interest.

'They were never very keen on talking about it,' Non said.

It did not appear that she herself was keen on talking about it either. A qualified understanding had to be reached. The old woman would only talk freely if she were fed tit-bits of inside family information.

'I think Duncan had been sent down after some student protest in London at the end of the sixties. Or even later. He found himself living in some squalid student commune where the Marina is now in Swansea.'

'You call him Duncan.'

Miss Probert seemed to find this mode of address between daughter and father strange and somehow entrancing.

'That's what he likes,' Non said. 'He wants to be young for ever. I call them 'ti' too. Both of them. That's the way it always was.'

'You are very close.'

Miss Probert held her breath as she waited for confirmation of this insight.

'They're just conventions aren't they?' Non said. 'Speech patterns. Fashions in modes of address.'

'But how did they meet?'

Miss Probert spoke as though this first encounter had to be the crux of any romantic relationship.

'In a police cell,' Non said. 'A whole bunch of them. That's what they always said. Duncan had an old van and he carried a dozen language protesters to a trial in Cardiff. My mother shouted her protest in Welsh and they were all jailed for contempt of court. He had no interest in the language before that. Then he said he became obsessed with it. The rebel had found a cause.'

'And a wife.'

Miss Probert was eager to add this.

'How romantic.'

'Up to a point,' Non said. 'They've been divorced now four years.'

'Oh dear. I didn't know that.'

Miss Probert shook her head as if she had just been given bad news. She was ready to extend sympathy. They were related and if there was grief involved, she was there to share it.

'That must have upset you..?'

Non showed no inclination to expose her inner feelings.

'Oh I don't know. I suppose they are entitled to live their own lives in the way they want to.'

Miss Probert fell silent. This seemed a concept she had never encountered before.

'You think we have too much choice? In this day and age?'

Non was smiling at her.

'I don't know what to think.'

Although she couldn't find appropriate phrases to express an opinion, Miss Probert showed she was prepared to keep an open mind on the subject and be as frank as her great niece might wish.

'You could be right,' Non said. 'It's all a bit of an illusion. This business of freedom of choice. And it's pretty obvious that most people are not equipped to deal with it. It's a bit of a responsibility being free. Anyway, Auntie Elsie, could we get back to Llannerch before the war?'

Miss Probert sat up straight in her large armchair and began to laugh.

'My trouble my dear, is that I've never left it.'

IV

It haunts me even in my sleep. That white stallion in the Rectory field prancing about tossing its delicious mane in a wild expression of freedom, and Lalw pinches my arm and giggles because the horse's male member is hanging down at such length. There is a white railing to protect us as we hurry down the drive. Stallions can be dangerous. We can't run because we are carrying a fruit cake in a basket. We have a key as well in the basket. Dorothy Justin Jones locks all the gates and all the doors. My father has said Dotty Jones is dotty. Living under siege. Outside all the nonconformist denominations are doing an Indian war dance outside the stockade. He thinks this is enormously funny and he and Mog Rees sit in his study wreathed in tobacco smoke and chuckling away at his inventions: the Wesleyans are Dancing Dervishes; the Baptists have a minister called Sitting Bull. The Methodists he calls Mohicans.

I just have to make a greater effort to recall exactly what happened. Dreams are irrelevant. Facts are more fantastic. Miss Prydwen Parry had baked a birthday cake for the Rector's wife. What could be kinder. Lalw and I had been deputised to deliver it and we felt the responsibility was an honour. That was one of Prydwen Parry's many gifts, to give each one of us the sense of being singled out for the honour of carrying out her will. There was definitely a tinge of religious devotion as we executed any duty allotted to us. We had been advised not to go to the front door. It was large and white and locked except for such ceremonial occasions as a visit from the Bishop. The key in our basket opened the double door also painted white that led to a rear yard between the outbuildings and the kitchen. There was a bell to pull and we pulled it. Dorothy Justin Jones's face appeared in the kitchen window. Her hair, as Girlie used to say, was on top of her teeth. A steel comb stood out above it like a crested crown. Her face was red and her thick lips were trembling with either fear or anger. We couldn't be certain which; but either case made us exceedingly nervous.

She had to hold on to the open door as she swayed in front of us.

'Many happy returns of the day, Mrs. Justin Jones.'

We recited this together. And then I spoke since I was church and Lalw was chapel. Lalw took the basket and I held out the cake.

'Miss Prydwen Parry sends you this birthday cake with her very best wishes.'

The Rector's wife was glaring at me as I held out the cake. Suddenly she snatched it from me and hurled it across the yard. Lalw and I gazed in horror at the ruined cake, as though we had witnessed an earthquake. Should we go on our knees and gather what was left in the basket?

'Where did you get the key of that door?'

I stared at her pointed finger. I could see the tobacco stain on it. Her anger made her cough. She pushed a clenched fist against her breast and her voice croaked like a witch's curse. I was very frightened. It couldn't have been many days later that I saw the Rector standing in the doorway of the large shadowed kitchen of Gelli Wen, talking to my mother in a low voice. This was clearly in order that my father in the study should remain unaware of his presence. There was pleading going on. I knew adults, like children, were enmeshed in a perpetual pattern of bargaining, except in the adult world the object of desire remained so obscure and difficult to understand. One time Dorothy Justin Jones and my mother had been friendly. They used to visit Llandudno together. That had stopped and from what I was able to pick up, my mother had been offended because the Rector's wife, on some unspecified occasion had insisted on taking precedence over Mrs. Probert of Gelli Wen. It was something to do with Dorothy Justin Jones being the daughter of an archdeacon and incapable of forgetting it. In the solitude of her self-imposed eminence, I saw the Rector's wife sink slowly into an alcoholic abyss. Were the Rector's whispers from the open door directed to some emergency rescue? It was something to do with asking my mother to accompany Mrs. Justin Jones to some church women's guild at Oswestry. They would need to change trains twice. I don't think my mother ever did.

Miss Prydwen Parry had given my brother Tom the role of Sir Lancelot. He said it was a consolation prize and he wasn't really in charge. Miss Parry gave us to understand that the Knights of the Round Table were carrying on the good work of the Alleluia Victory: defending civilization with a capital C against the onslaughts of pagan savagery and social disorder. We listened to her with our mouths open but afterwards on the way home Tom snorted it was a load of rubbish. He was so dismissive I grew quite afraid of him. At first he kept his inside knowledge to himself. Then he came to feel he had not sown sufficient seeds of doubt in my innocent mind. He had to prove my idol had feet of clay. One day when there was a rehearsal in the Memorial Hall, he went in search of the wooden sword he was supposed to flourish, and saw in a dark corner of the cloak room Miss Prydwen Parry in the Rector's arms. 'They were kissing' he said. I suppose in our house this verged on forbidden fruit. I knew he took to spying on them. I know as much because in my own circumscribed fashion I took to spying on him. Spying must be infectious.

Much to my father's disgust the higgledy-piggledy pageant was a great success. There were blurred pictures in the local press and the parish acquired an unexpected fame that surprised and pleased all the inhabitants. Would the world expect a Llannerch pageant as an annual event? What other burning topics could be resurrected from her hallowed past? We had never imagined we had so much history to be proud of. My friend Delyth the minister's daughter, the great reader, and Bessie Maud were dressed up as the two virgin martyrs Gwenffrewi and Eleri. I don't recall the legends that Miss Prydwen Parry was embellishing. They were saints certainly. And I have remained a virgin for the whole of my life. No bad thing to be in this sex-obsessed age. In the sixties Delyth had a lot of trouble with her children. Bessie Maud died in the seventies and I've no knowledge of what became of her family. I know she had joined some evangelic sect and went from house to house selling tracts. All I've done is survive. I go to chapel clinging to my hymn book in the hope of salvation. One isn't all that much use without the other.

Lalw and I rode in a decorated waggon lent by her father, the genial Mr. Bellis of Caemerch. We were dressed as native maidens and Iorwerth as a Cymric chieftain. He held the reins and he had a drooping moustache stuck to his upper lip that kept coming off. Lalw carried a horn of plenty and I had a great bunch of flowers. I can feel them now in my arms. I was worried about them withering so I watered them. And then I worried about them wetting my dress. It was the rehearsing I enjoyed. In the field below the house at Caemerch. Tumbling about in the waggon as Iorwerth tried to make the old carthorse, Cyrnol, break into a gallop. I was allowed to spend the night at Caemerch and share Lalw's bed. My best friend. I was never happier.

It could have been an excess of drama that turned that summer into a disturbed troubled season in Llannerch y Marchog. A petition was set in motion to restore our full name on signposts and for postal purposes. My father wouldn't sign it. He wouldn't let my mother sign it either. It was as if he were looking for an awkward position to take up. He no longer approved of Prydwen Parry. She wasn't a fairy princess, only a pantomime demon in disguise intent on awakening a sleepy but contented village with a poisoned kiss. Out of the wreath of tobacco smoke in the seclusion of his study he even muttered things like, 'pride going before a fall.' I was already primed with anxiety and apprehension before the catastrophe happened.

Miss Prydwen Parry's Austin Seven could pick up the Reverend Justin Jones and transport him to rendezvous and locations well out of my brother Tom's reach, however hard he pedalled. He turned his detective attentions to Dorothy Justin Jones. He confirmed his suspicion that the Rector was now feeding her addiction with tempting variations of alcoholic beverages. He said the outhouses where once he had been allowed to play when he was smaller, were filled with an exotic assembly of empty bottles. Perhaps spurred on by the success of the pageant, or rather stung by it, Dorothy Justin Jones took to visiting the parish church and putting on performances of her own. Tom lurked behind the tombstones and watched her unsteady progress from the Rectory through the little gate to the vestry door. There in the vestry she would put on vestments which he said she had no business to do, and perform rituals of her own devising in front of the altar. These sometimes involved dancing. He saw the sunlight pierce the stained glass and glitter on the tines of the steel comb in her hair. What could a solitary woman do to praise the lord except like King David dance and strip in front of the ark of the Lord. And indeed, according to Tom, she had started to strip. He was crouching down in the rear pew where my father always sat and saw the Rector's wife, drunk as a lord he said, trying to dance and divest herself of her voluminous old fashioned vestments. She was making such an effort she slipped on the altar steps and fell, and the steel comb penetrated the back of her skull. She lay there either in a drunken stupor or dead. In either case he fled.

The Llannerch I loved, far away and hidden in the friendly hills, had lost its innocence. It wasn't really hidden any more. Only bathed in an unholy light. Familiar natural features stretched towards me with a fearsome sharpness. And people too. Bobby Backward who used to wink at me when he tugged at the bell rope before the evening service now seemed to leer knowingly every time I glanced at him. How could the church ever be the same? Or the world outside. Ifan Lemuel, the roadman I always talked to on my way to school, said his thick moustache was made of the same bristles as his cane brush. If I gave him a kiss he would quickly prove it. It was an old joke but now I fled from him in terror. Ifan was quite hurt. He shouted after me 'you'll live to be an old maid if you don't look out,' and his threat echoed for hours like a gong in my head.

Nothing that had happened was my fault but I seemed to take the responsibility. I was woven into a hypocritical web. Poor Mrs. Dorothy Justin Jones. Such a terrible accident. And in church too. Before the Table of the Lord. And poor Mr. Justin Jones who had been obliged to live with a deranged woman. Everywhere there was the hush of things being hushed up. If I had to walk down the main street of the village there were always women standing in the open doorways with their arms folded staring at me. Awful things had happened and I was part of the conspiracy.

Nobody would ever love me any more and it was all my brother Tom's fault. He kept telling me things and adding to my burden of guilt. Why should he want to specialise in being knowing and dropping hints? He wanted Elfed the gardener and Girlie the maid to appreciate how much more he knew than he was prepared to let on. With me he had a habit of waving his hands like a magician on a stage. Even my parents frowned as they looked at their son and heir and wondered what made him smirk so much. Only with me could he afford to make open boasts about how much he knew because he knew I was too scared ever to betray him. The more intensely visible the world around me, the more hidden and terrible the truth.

The affair between Prydwen Parry and the Reverend Justin Jones leaked out. Had my brother Tom gone around the parish dropping hints? Vague sympathy transformed into mounting indignation. How long had it been going on? 'Under our very noses.' Out of the depths of his tobacco smoke screen my father's sarcasm intensified. 'For God's sake, the man can't just hang on here.' I heard him urge Mog Rees to agree with him that it was too indecent. Somebody should have a word with the Bishop. The least the man can do is emigrate. And take the woman with him. The delightful Miss Prydwen Parry had become a fallen woman. They fled I thought just as Tom had fled from the scene of the crime. The Reverend Justin Jones found a parish some-where near Hadrian's Wall. My father made a joke about it. They could keep the pagans at bay. I missed her so much. Just before the war broke out we heard that she had died in childbirth and something froze inside me.

IV

'Did you mean it, that you never left Llannerch, Auntie Elsie?'

Miss Probert took time to answer, allowing an old lady's sweet smile to break before she spoke.

'I never wandered all that far,' she said. 'Unlike your grandfather. He couldn't get away far enough. What you could say is I took it with me wherever I went. Most of the time I had to. My land of heart's desire was Caemerch just inside the next parish. Caemerch kept me sane.'

'That was a farm, was it?'

Non concentrated hard. There were many threads to pick up without breaking them by asking too many questions.

'Lalw's home. A wonderful place. The happiest family you

ever saw. Her mother and father were so kind. Like figures in a fairy tale. And they ate so well. Gwilym Bellis had a glass eye. Bright blue to match his own. Such good food. They always said I needed fattening up. You should see me on the old bicycle I bought for ten shillings pedalling over the stream and up the hill as far as I could go without getting off. Three miles it was from Gelli Wen to Caemerch. Before she had a bike Lalw used to walk to school. In all weathers. Miss Parry had a cupboard in the changing room next to the infants. She kept a change of clothes there for Lalw. And for her brother. They used to get soaking wet. I remember the smell of their clothes drying in front of the headmaster's fire.'

'So you really never left?'

'Oh yes I did. The war came and it was a chance to get out. See a bit of the world. Lalw and I went nursing. A children's hospital in Liverpool. It was bombed. I was frightened out of my wits. And then my mother died. So I was quite glad to go home and look after my father. That's how it was in those days. War or no war. A daughter's first duty was to look after her father. And the same thing happened to Lalw more or less. Her mother fell off a ladder in the stockyard and hurt her back. There was a war going on and farming was terribly important. Shall I tell you why your great-aunt is a fussy old maid?'

Non showed she would be a willing listener.

'Do you really want to know?'

'Of course I do.'

'We are related after all, aren't we? Not that I'll have all that much to leave you in my will. This place is quite exclusive. Only maiden ladies. It was all Lalw's fault, bless her.'

When Miss Probert chuckled Non managed an uncomfortable smile.

'It wasn't so bad, looking after my father. Things had changed after all. He could grumble as much as he liked but he was under my control instead of me being under his. Around his basic needs I could arrange my life much as I liked. I started going to chapel with Lalw. This was a great relief in itself. It didn't matter any more what my father thought. He depended on me. Chapel responded to my needs and allowed me to give the church a wide berth. I loved the vigorous congregational singing. Such an emotional release. People need an emotional release, don't they? Especially in war time. And especially old maids. I liked long sermons. Especially when they were humane and intelligent. We had a new minister. Raglan Thomas. Very handsome. He came from South Wales. He must have had polio as a child because one leg was thinner than the other. He had a slight limp which we found quite charming. You know how young people follow pop stars nowadays. Icons and idols they call them. Raglan Thomas was our pop star. But such a quiet one. With such a soothing voice. And those sermons seemed to have such a depth of meaning. I don't remember them at all now, but I remember how I felt. It was wartime and we were so preoccupied with the problem of suffering and pain. There was so much talk of death in the world, life seemed infinitely precious.

Lalw and I were quite fascinated by him. I would catch myself in the garden earthing up the potatoes or feeding the chickens – in wartime I seem to remember chickens all over Llannerch – and counting the days before the next service. And there was the W.E.A. class. He had a class on Church History and you would be surprised how much I read up on the subject. I managed to get a photograph of him and I kept it in my dressing-table drawer. I would open the drawer to take a peep at it and then pull a face at myself in the mirror.

Anyway he chose Lalw, not me. In spite of that birth mark on her neck. Or maybe because of it? All that was left to me was rather forced expressions of delight. The chapel and the family were so happy about it. Even then I think I found it difficult to distinguish between disappointment and relief. And the war was over. Within a couple of years Raglan was given a call to a prosperous Presbyterian Church in Pennsylvania. When they'd gone I think I missed Lalw much more than I missed him.'

Miss Probert was scrutinising her great niece too closely for comfort. She needed a response.

'Is she still alive?'

This gave the old lady great amusement.

'Some of us still are, you know,' she said. 'Whether or not we should be is another question.'

'I meant are you still in touch?'

'The Reverend and Mrs. Raglan Thomas, Sunset Valley, Santa Fe. Sheltered accommodation. What more can we ask for? Once a year I get a circular letter. She always calls Llannerch her Garden of Eden, and always vows to come back. I don't think she ever will. Still we were only good friends. We are related, aren't we?'

'Yes, of course we are,' Non said.

The Man in the Mist

I

Glyndwr Brace and Gwyndaf Rondel. Glyn and Gwyn. We go
back a long way, Glyn and I. It was never a matter of choice. As
it happened our mothers were in college at the same time. I say
'at the same time' rather than 'together': acquaintances, my
mother gave me to understand, rather than close friends. The
wheel of fate gave a brief turn and Mrs. Brace and Mrs. Rondel
found themselves sitting on district committees concerned with
a range of subjects from public health to cultural wellbeing. Mr.
Brace was the headmaster of the Primary School at Penybont.
The Reverend Griffith Rondel ministered to a dwindling flock in
the quarrying village of Llanbedr further up our charming valley
which was no more than twenty miles from the border. Our
mothers were constantly on guard against barbaric intrusions.
Our whole area had a reputation to maintain for cultural
achievements and an affable gentility. Their husbands were less
worked up about the threats and perils of the situation. Mr.
Brace loved the choir and his game of bowls. My father was a
man who had learnt to stifle the quick reply and take satisfaction
from a thoughtful silence. He wrote an occasional column in the
local paper: 'Bygones and Reminiscences' and studded it with
gnomic verses declaring the Past was a stagnant pool and the
Present a lively torrent of bright water running past too quickly
to his taste. The two men got on well and left their wives to cultivate their separate frustrations.

We were only sons and we had this in common. Our mothers
were earnest and well intentioned. In an earlier age they would
have been devout women who expected their piety to be fittingly
rewarded. Great things were expected of us from a surprisingly
early age. We were thrust into eisteddfodic competition and since
Glyn had a voice like an angel and also looked like one even

when his mother made him wear a bow tie, he invariably won and I had to count myself lucky to come second. I could sometimes beat him in written competitions but that was never more than a tame consolation to my mother or indeed to me. The applause and the public glory came from ringing the treble rafters. It may seem long ago and in another world yet I can still hear a distant echo. Glyn was always amiable and when the Urdd district competitions came along we were safely on the same side. I wouldn't say I bathed in his reflected glory but I recollect I was strangely warmed when I succeeded in standing next to him in a group photograph.

My research work has long since taught me that we all step out of a context: and this elementary fact governs our interior being to a greater extent than we realise. Where you come from has a special relationship to where you are going. Our consciousness is permanently imprinted with the surroundings of our childhood. You could say as soon as we learned to walk we were made aware of the beauty of our valley and of the inestimable value of its language and traditions: these primeval tropes were woven into even our complaints about the weather: wind and rain were an aberration from an ideal norm where Welsh speaking nymphs and shepherds cavorted in refreshing sunlight.

By dint of unremitting labour I won my scholarship to Jesus College. I was so intent on my efforts that I never discovered why exactly Glyn went off to Cardiff to pursue a course in journalism. It is more than possible that our mothers weren't speaking at the time. Something political. Vague accusations of an unreliability that was little short of a betrayal. There was certainly a distancing and a prolonged silence. It came as a shock when Glyn and I next bumped into each other on a Saturday night at a London Welsh Club in the middle of the sixties. There he was in all his glory, a centre of attention, exuding an aura, clearly the best looking and most impressive chap in the place. There were girls there falling over themselves to meet him. He had become Glyn Brace, a face on the television screen, reading the news and making himself amazingly agreeable to the world in general. All that had been going on while my nose was fixed to an academic grindstone and I had been gratefully obliged to every single person who helped me on my way from my infant school teacher to the head porter at Jesus College. Who would ever want to know about me and my painstaking researches? Glyn had floated to the top by some mysterious feat of levitation. He was just there, all smiling good looks and good nature. I acquired instant kudos simply through knowing him.

II

While I was doing a year's research in the Public Records Office and the British Museum, Glyn gave me two rooms in the basement of his flat in Bayswater. He was reluctant to accept the nominal rent I insisted on paying. Living in the same house was enough to add to my status. Sharing an address may have led people to assume that we were more intimate than was in fact the case. In those days Glyn radiated friendliness: there was no real difference between his screen persona and his cheerful attitude at home. The way he hosted programmes of all shapes and sizes seemed to chime in with the mood of the times. He would cope with even the most obstreperous participant as though he were helping an old lady to cross a busy street. In those jolly rooms in Bayswater I first acquired a taste for the company of artists and writers. If they were all up and coming so in my own modest way was I. I gained confidence and I began my modest career as a connoisseur and collector. As I told my father and mother, to acquire taste you must rub shoulders with the very people who create it. In retrospect I can't claim that it all had the same abiding effect on Glyn.

In fact I know that he does not see those far off bachelor days in the same rosy light as I do. When I see him I never mention them in case he thinks I'm stuck in a time warp. I can still derive a quiet pleasure remembering those promising young people passing in and out of the flat. Time warps are not all that bad. After all, successful historians live by them. I could mention

Felicity Forbes. So rich and well-connected. She provided a significant moment. More than a moment. A significant transition. She was besotted with Glyn and assumed his natural geniality and warmth was inspired by her riveted attention. She always called him 'Brace' in a manner that implied he was her particular property. When he had gone out, I suspect, deliberately to avoid her, I would sit there and have to listen to her rattling away. 'He has no idea of his own potential,' she would say. 'He really hasn't. There's no knowing where he could go from here. He could become a national figure. I try to tell him there is no limit to the wonderful things he could achieve if only he took himself in hand...' To maintain her equilibrium I suspect, when she spoke to him she affected to be brutally frank. 'Look here, Brace. There's one thing wrong with you. You've simply got to iron out that Welsh accent.' I could have told her she was making a mistake. He flushed in a way I'd never seen before. 'Oh bugger off, you silly woman,' he snarled. This was so unexpected and so different from his normal discourse that she fled the house in tears. I've no recollection that she ever returned. I read in the newspapers some years later Felicity Forbes had married a pontificating politician almost twice her age.

Now that I'm pushing sixty and enjoy a personal chair I can afford the time to sit back and consider what exactly it was in those halcyon days that made Glyn such an attractive figure. He enjoyed exceptional good looks. I was always aware of that. And in those Bayswater days that shimmering translucent coating of fame that was in itself a medium of elevation. And he seemed so carefree. He looked at you as he looked at the world with a sympathy and understanding that you instantly took for affection. I remember my mother whispering enviously 'Glyndwr likes people,' as though it were an unaccountable defect. From an acquaintance of his mother she learned that a languid Head of Programmes had said 'I just had to promote the dear boy. What does it matter if he's young and inexperienced. He's so beautiful.' You could say in the candy-floss world of broadcasting a man was over qualified if he appealed so much to male and female alike.

I suppose it was Glyn I have to thank for bringing my professor's daughter within my orbit. At the age of eighteen Valerie Pritchett was sent to the Guildhall School of Music, as she said, to learn a bit of everything and to see if they could make anything of her voice. When Pritchett gave me an extension to my research fellowship he more or less suggested I should keep a neighbourly eye on her. This I did most assiduously. It may well have been my connection with Glyn that brought her and two or three of her most intimate girl friends to the flat in Bayswater. The joke we share is, it was only when her singing career failed to take off that she agreed to marry me. And maybe the added inducement that Glyn had agreed to act as best man. For the second time in my life I was happy to be photographed at his side. It seems sometimes that I am under a lifetime's obligation to admire him. Not that I have done so badly myself. After all I married Principal Pritchett's daughter and acquired a personal chair. An academic career, like research itself, is a long term project.

III

Valerie and I attended Glyn's wedding in a smart London church. I was disappointed that he hadn't invited me to be his best man. I was less hurt when I saw that function performed by his Head of Programmes. And for the first time in my life I felt a little sorry for him when I encountered his mother-in-law. Glyn and Maria could have posed for ever as the ideal couple and their images reproduced in illustrated magazines all over the globe. In her own Italianate way Maria was every bit as beautiful as Glyndwr Brace. At the reception the mother of the bride was everywhere: a raucous bedizened Central European clearly glorying in her English title – Lady Alma Coates-Argent. Her husband the Brigadier, a tall distinguished figure not altogether steady on his feet held on rather too tightly to the wheelchair of an aged relative and engaged at intervals in polite conversation with Mrs. Brace who had taken refuge in the same corner of the room. I could see them watching with varying degrees of apprehension the peregrinations of the Lady Alma. She seemed to want to talk to everyone.

'Well now... are you anyone important?'

Her black coiffure was in some disorder as she stood before me, her jewels flashing in the light of the chandeliers. For a moment her prominent teeth looked as aggressive as a crocodile's. The breadth of the smile was intended to indicate she was making a joke. In her emphatic Central European accent it sounded more like an accusation. It did occur to me that she might well have insisted that the Head of Programmes should be best man. Her daughter was under her thumb and Glyn would be under her daughter's thumb: it seemed an ominous portent. She was trying to make a further amusing remark about orders of precedence in the old Austro-Hungarian Empire. It seems her mother had been the daughter of a Duke and therefore took precedence over a sister-in-law who had only married a Baron. I had a distinct impression that the woman was temporarily deranged by alcohol and the excitement of the occasion.

Valerie took a far more sanguine view. In the Powder Room she found Lady Alma's eccentricities fluctuating cheerfully between the outrageous and the delightful. With Glyn and Maria, she assured Valerie, it had been love at first sight – Lady Alma was concentrating on her cosmetics as she spoke. 'The first thing that comes into her head,' Valerie said. 'I like that about her.' It seems that she and Valerie were staring into the mirror as she said it. 'There they were,' she said. Maria was making him up before transmission. It wasn't her usual job. Their eyes met in the mirror... and that was it. 'Like a clap of thunder,' Valerie said. Lady Alma paused to take it in and then gave a raucous laugh and clutched Valerie in her arms as though they had on the instant become friends for life.

I can understand now why Valerie and Lady Alma had so much in common. It is as though her music studies have given Valerie an operatic view of life: romantic and high pitched and at the same time underneath that surface-glitter, something of the tough and disillusioned professional who quaffs a consoling pint in the half-light of the back-stage bar. Lady Alma's background was so operatic she was able to change the plot at her own convenience to accommodate whoever happened to be listening to her. By one account she was sixteen years old when she and her mother fled from Vienna for fear of being raped by savage invading Russian hordes. Another version was a different flight: in the back of a cart, her mother clutching a shopping bag with her jewels wrapped in a woollen scarf to smother any tell-tale tinkle they could make. This time they were being pressed by Tito's communists and had been obliged to cross the Julian Alps in the snow and the ice.

While she became so absorbed in Valerie who so enjoyed her rambling anecdotes, the Brigadier began to take a polite interest in me. According to Valerie he was her third or even her fourth husband. There seems to have been a clandestine marriage in the American Zone which gave her her first British passport: this was not always included in the total. She told Valerie she could not help having an aristocratic disdain for mundane detail: but the truth was, in her youth her beauty exceeded her daughter's and her mother, the Duke's fifth daughter, had her hands full driving off unsuitable men.

To me the Brigadier's patience and forbearing were a revelation. This was a much decorated leader of men, famed, I came to learn, in his early career for daring and iron discipline. As we got to know each other better he would take me to his club where he would drink whisky and water and regale me with tales of his service days that centred not so much on exploits of derring-do but on the strange habits and customs of the natives in various corners of the globe: and particularly on the adventures of some of his brother officers. The late Bertie Peckingham, for example, was a character he liked to talk about. He got trapped in a harem in Saudi Arabia, did a spot of gun-running in South America, and lived for several weeks with a gorilla in the forest of Burundi. I listened attentively. The Brigadier was kind enough to propose my father-in-law, Professor Pritchett as he was then, for membership of the club and in the fullness of time I became a country member myself.

IV

An objective evaluation of our respective careers would have to admit that Glyn's peaked too soon. I don't say this with the complacency of a long distance runner. My upward path was far from smooth. I had to wait uncommonly long for a senior lectureship. When it at last arrived our third child was on the way and I suspect Valerie brought some pressure to bear on her father. One of the pearls of worldly wisdom Glyn and I used to share on the pleasant occasions when we had lunch together was that merit alone was never quite enough. I had two sources of information concerning Glyn's professional progress. Glyn himself and my wife Valerie – she and Lady Alma played duets together regularly once a week. Repartee and revelation were a stable part of their exchanges: with the help of pink gin Alma becomes increasingly imaginative and loquacious and my wife Valerie is a tenacious listener. She claimed she had sufficient material to write a series of libretti based on Alma's colourful life stories. For my own part I was more interested in sifting the chit-chat to surmise what was happening to Glyn's brilliant career.

Glyn had concluded a man couldn't go on reading the news for ever. It was indecent exposure he said: a person condemned to age and dwindle in front of the world's eyes. He wanted an Arts Programme that could be popular and accessible and yet battle through the pedestrian and mundane to find something worth saying. I caught the light of battle in his eye and realised that somewhere under that calm and comforting exterior there were smouldering fires. I thought I knew him. He was at least as familiar as the view of the hills from the bedroom window of my childhood and yet I didn't know him at all.

My understanding of Glyndwr Brace's character was probably flawed: but at least it was grounded in some aspect of reality. At least I know where he came from. Lady Alma's view of her son-in-law, as transmitted to me by Valerie, amid much giggling, headshakes and raising of eyebrows, stemmed direct from cloud-cuckoo land. He was a golden boy destined for great things. Because he was Welsh, Alma deduced he would have the patronage of the Prince of Wales, and at one time she had a clutch of anecdotes that gave support to this theory. In her perspective, the day would not be all that far distant when Glyn's name would appear high on the Honours List. It amused us, Valerie and myself, to contrast Lady Alma's view with that of her husband. At the club, when his distinguished features were flushed with yet another whisky and water, he would question me. 'He gets so damned serious about everything,' the Brigadier would say.

'Why is that do you think?' I tried to enlighten him on the subtle effects of a Welsh nonconformist background. He didn't really take it in. 'No sense of humour,' he concluded. 'That's his trouble. He's a proper bloody Puritan.'

Glyn took his work just as seriously as I took mine. I admired his dedication. He sounded like a communicator with a mission. 'We are in business to inform and educate and entertain in precisely that order.' As I looked across the table I felt I could be in the presence of a leader of men. I had to admire his manifest integrity: this was a quality that would outlast any boyish good looks. But of course he had a mother-in-law to contend with. As the years passed she became restless when his name failed to appear on the Honours List and her daughter Maria failed to present her with a grandchild to spoil. Glyn was philosophical about this.

Maria was creative in the sense that she painted. She was just as creative as he was pedagogic and what, he would ask me across the luncheon table, what was wrong with that? I appreciated the interest he took in our children. He was delighted when we sent them back to my parents to become properly aware of their roots. He said we shouldn't be sitting around in metropolitan settings polishing our roots. Roots should be buried deep in the native soil so that plants could derive nourishment and create a fresh flowering. He made play with the word 'plant' too, which seemed very witty as we sipped our wine.

He had a disappointment to contend with in this connection. The beautiful Maria had nothing to say to our valley. 'Provincial' with her was a term of abuse. The views that had so entranced us as we grew up meant nothing to her. 'All that perpetual green,' she said. 'And the grey skies. Where the hell is the sun?' And of course over and above that, she didn't get on with Mrs. Brace who had become gloomy and introspective in her widowed state. From the first she had nothing but profound misgivings about the Coates-Argents. She came to believe that her ambitions for her beautiful son had landed him in courts of licence and luxury where vice was bound to lurk. In her younger days Mrs. Brace had been a stalwart of the Powys Women's Temperance League. There was a lingering possibility that a flaw in her own nature could be held responsible for some impending corruption of her perfect son.

When I was elevated to a chair in Cardiff, Glyn's congratulations were warm and sincere and possibly tinged with envy. I have to admit my chest expanded an inch or two at the thought that it was a promotion gained purely on merit. My father-in-law made one of his jokes to say that the place was too far away for him to pull any wires. In any case he had retired. At our next lunch, still glowing with the sensation of success I put it to Glyn that it might be time for him to consider returning to the land of his fathers. It was an inopportune moment. His handsome face suffused with a dark flush and he muttered something about his womenfolk being eager and even impatient to see how far he could go.

They didn't have all that long to wait. I have been told by specialists that there was a moment in the 1970s when the tranquil sea of British broadcasting became shark infested waters. This, the specialists argue, was due to an acceleration in technical developments, a decrease in the level of public intelligence due to a passivity – created by a combination of material prosperity and a surfeit of viewing, and the increasing interest of multinational finance. Whichever way the situation was analysed I could see Glyn and his innate idealism were on a losing wicket.

Thrusting up-and-coming young men and fierce young women seemed to swarm into the studios from all directions. It was an encounter with one of these, over a programme for which Glyn himself in his mellifluous baritone provided the commentary, that did the damage. A trivial matter it might have been; the programme went out and was rated satisfactory. But the row initiated a crisis. A whispering campaign grew in volume. Glyn Brace's voice was too deliberately melodious and his manner too ingratiating for contemporary taste. He was a has-been covered with an evangelical mildew. He looked too pleased with himself and the public had no desire to be preached at and certainly not by a fading Welsh *jeune premier*.

I was bedding down nicely in the Cardiff Faculty. My number of committees of wider interest had steadily mounted and I was invited to take a seat on the Broadcasting Council. Valerie integrated comfortably into the musical life of the city. Our house on the edge of the golf course was the envy of my colleagues. It combined the virtues of a semi-rural vista with all the amenities of a prospering city. In my old and trusty Mercedes I could arrive at my reserved parking space on the college campus within twenty minutes. In the course of my committee duties I learnt of a new job that seemed to me to suit Glyn down to the ground: an assistant head of programmes with special responsibility for development. I had to tell him about it. Valerie advised me not to. She even went so far as to accuse me of developing into a busy-body. This stung me, I have to admit, and I informed Glyn about the new post without delay.

He was very interested. Maria and her mother however were furious. This was no route for a man of so many qualities to take. It led nowhere but to the Sticks. The impenetrable Welsh back-woods. How could he even think of it? Where would they be, mother and daughter without their regular diet of concerts, theatres and private views and parties. Who would see them and who would they see? And what was that humdrum Professor Gwyndaf Rondel about, trying to drag their man of infinite promise and abounding qualities down to his own mundane provincial level? I could see Glyn was about to withdraw his candidature. In his role as an unselfish and noble husband he had to be prepared to set aside his own inclination in order to please his wife and her mother.

It was at this point that nature intervened in the most spectacular manner. I have often pondered the circumstance as a striking example of the unaccountable chaos of existence. It was no surprise to me that the Brigadier was conducting what could be called a romantic friendship with an old flame of his youth. A man who resorted as often as he did to the refuge of his club had to be in need of some form of extra-marital comfort. They were sheltering together under a tree on Hampstead Heath, out of a chivalrous concern I would imagine for the ladies hairdo. The tree was struck by lightning. It was rumoured that the elderly lovers were found stunned and smothered in each other's arms.

Rumour had it but not the Press. The lady belonged to a family with influence and ranks were quickly closed. It was all hushed up, but not of course within the home. Glyn had to confess he had never in his life witnessed such an unquenchable blaze of fury and hysteria. He had to confide in someone and I was at hand and so he turned to me. As I listened and as I watched him I felt that the whole sorry business was transforming his outlook on life for ever. More than that, it shattered his cultivated façade of confidence and calm. In his news-reading days he used to tell me how he would alter the wording of a bulletin in the interests of clarity and how much the hacks in the newsroom resented such interference. What order could a habit of clarity impose on so much irrational emotion and confusion? Broadcast news bulletins were news from nowhere when pierced by the lightning of the mystery of random existence.

Even to the women the despised job in the Sticks suddenly took on the glow of a heaven-sent solution. Would this be a happy issue out of all their afflictions? Only if swift action was taken. And I have to claim some credit for having taken it, and in more than one direction. Valerie said she was amazed at my unaccustomed decisiveness. The broadcasting committee were given to understand that Glyndwr Brace was returning to his native land for the highest possible motives. At the same time there was the problem of finding women who claimed aristocratic descent, some kind of spacious dwelling where they could feel themselves appropriately at home.

Graiglwyd was a manor house of medieval origin that needed modernising. It was a place that they could become attached to. And that was exactly what happened. I found out about it from an architect friend but Valerie got the credit. Her duets with Lady Alma were resumed on a weekly basis. Maria converted an outhouse into a studio. Glyn travelled the twenty miles back and forth to Broadcasting House without a word of complaint, and I could enjoy more than a hint of satisfaction at having stage-managed the immigration.

V

It was Gwyn and Glyn again and this time on a genuinely creative footing. We weren't pacing each other any more: we were collaborating. I wouldn't go as far as Valerie to say that Glyn Brace entered our Broadcasting House on a cloud of metropolitan glory. I would say he managed the transition with discretion. There were plenty of prickly people about but they were soon won over by his obvious devotion to Cymric history and culture. He said he had a mission to make the viewers take a deeper interest in their own square mile and a series he initiated called *The Genius of the Place* gained a fair amount of critical acclaim. *The Parish Pump* was a popular quiz he initiated. He developed a taste for documentary film making, and from time to time he invited me to lurk in the background as a consultant in charge of research and content level. His greatest triumph in which I can claim a small part came about virtually by accident.

Before moving to a retirement home at the seaside, his mother discovered in the attic the personal diary of a Welsh itinerant preacher caught between contending armies in East Tennessee during the American Civil War. This mid-nineteenth

century Elijah Brace was involved in an amazing variety of enter-
prises; bookselling, pamphleteering, emigration schemes,
escaping slaves. Glyn persuaded a distinguished actor to play the
role. There was filming in Tennessee. Early stills were unearthed
and there were enactments in both languages and some critics
called it a piebald production: but it was shown twice 'on the
network', as they say, to the delight of the Controller. My
connection with the programme did me nothing but good. I was
invited to lecture at colleges in the United States. Valerie came
with me and enjoyed the lavish hospitality.

The impact of notable television programmes however brilliant, seems to fade with depressing speed. When the conveyor
belt speeds up it becomes that much easier to fall off it. The post
of Head of Programmes fell vacant. I strongly advised Glyn to go
for it. On grounds of seniority and experience I argued, the job
was his for the asking. He was so enamoured of film making by
this, all he did was express contempt for the power game and
administrative ambitions. A new Head was recruited from the
fiercer fringes of the commercial world in the hope, I suppose, of
boosting the ratings and tightening up production practices. This
was Kenneth Crosby-Jones who already bore the nickname of
Skull 'n' Bones before he arrived. This I assume was due to his
skeletal appearance and menacing manner. When he bared his
teeth it could be a snarl or a smile. He was a tall man with a roll
in his gait that was sufficient to alert his staff that he had not taken
on his new job in order to make their lives more comfortable.

'Glyn Brace! I remember you.'

There was an underlying threat never far from the jovial
surface.

'That mellifluous voice set to quieten the nation's nerves.
Nicely tucked in between Children's Hour and the Regional
Weather Forecast. Now that gives my age away, doesn't it?'

At the first or second Programme Board under the new
regime Glyn was enlarging with enthusiasm a project he had
been working on for a series on the United Nations Charter of
Human Rights. This was a Bill of Rights and an International

Covenant and there were unique television techniques that could bring it all more closely to the people. Crosby-Jones chaired the meeting. He allowed Glyn to run on. When his enthusiasm was showing signs of petering out he spoke.

'Nice idea. Pass it on to Schools.'

When he told me about it Glyn said he had a definite sensation of being brought to heel. This made me aware of that quality of innocence in Glyn's character that tallied all too easily with the role of sacrificial lamb. In the name of our friendship I felt I had to do something to support him. I said as much to Valerie and it was she who offered what she called a social solution to what I was sure would be a growing problem. I heard Glyn repeating Skull 'n' Bones's more outrageous phrases such as: 'Hasn't anyone told you, Glyn boy. The age of exhortation is over'... or... 'We're not here to make people think, comrades. We're here to make their flesh creep.'

When Glyn came up with an idea on the travels of Welsh missionaries he dismissed it with a joke about dressing them up as Tellytubbies. He was bent on making himself a difficult man to work with. He was a man of means who didn't give a damn. Valerie's social solution, as she called it, was for Maria and Alma to invite Skull 'n' Bones and ourselves to dine at Graiglwyd. (Glyn had had to fight with his wife and his mother-in-law to prevent them tacking the word Manor on to Graiglwyd on their headed notepaper.) There was a mischievous gleam in Valerie's eye as she spoke of letting the monster loose so that they could clasp him in their pseudo-aristocratic embrace. She took as much pleasure as ever in listening to Lady Alma's vacuous chatter. They still met to play duets although arthritis was stiffening Alma's fingers. In a raucous whisper she told Valerie that Maria was the daughter of a man named Banish and he came between the second and the third husband and may well have been the love of her life. It appears he fled to South America after wounding a fellow officer in a duel and was still alive and living in Chile. Maria was all she wanted to remember him by: a devoted daughter. Valerie went to great trouble to retell the things the old woman said and amused herself endlessly trying to disentangle fact from fiction. If I ventured to rebuke her for wasting her energy on the subject she would point out how colourless my career had been in comparison. 'Llanbedr meets Penybont', she would say. 'What an enchantment. The Glyn and Gwyn story.'

At Graiglwyd Lady Alma made the garden her special responsibility. When her arthritis worsened she engaged a retired gardener who listened patiently to her voluble instructions but never altered his steady working pace. Alma was given to insist that there were corners of the garden that reminded her of some-thing or other in her grandfather's estate in Dalmatia. She said as much to Skull 'n' Bones when she took his arm to visit the Rose Garden. To my surprise he accepted her social pretensions without question. It was out of character. In the office he would have taken particular pleasure in deriding so much exaggeration and titled name-dropping. He liked to boast that he was the son of a miner and an elementary school teacher famous for her socialist vehemence. He expressed a deep admiration for Maria's paintings. Such vivid colours, he said, were life enhancing. The pronouncement was so emphatic and came from such an unex-pected source that Maria could not prevent herself from blushing with pleasure.

During the dinner Valerie seized the first opportunity to enquire demurely whether or not there was a Mrs. Crosby-Jones. Indeed there was, he replied. But best described as the ex-Mrs. Crosby-Jones.

'Candice Speaker by name,' he said. 'Speaker by name, speaker by nature. She came over from Canada in search of celebrities. Very disappointed to discover I was only a back-room boy. She has ended up editing a women's magazine and lives on a weekly diet of the rich and the famous. Hard as nails, the fair Candice. I was never nearly famous enough for her. Not like Glyndwr here. Glyndwr Maldwyn Brace. Now there's a name to conjure with.'

Light-hearted banter in the best possible spirit. Maria and

Alma laughed appreciatively. Glyn was less amused. On the way home I asked Valerie what she thought of Skull 'n' Bones. Was he jealous of Glyn did she think? Could that explain it?

'I've no idea about that,' she said. 'But I can tell you one thing. He's a womaniser.'

'Good Lord. He's such an ugly bastard. Obsessed with power I would have said.'

'Ugliness has got nothing to do with it.'

Valerie sounded uncomfortably knowing.

'He's got antennae,' she said. 'Very quick on the uptake in these matters. He could see Maria was panting for the oil of admiration so he poured it all over her painting.'

IV

I accompanied Glyn to his mother's funeral. I felt it was the very least I could do. She was buried in her husband's grave in the old cemetery attached to Capel y Cwm. There were a great deal of pietas involved in the obsequies even though the number of mourners were few. The historic little chapel only opened for services four times a year and the graveyard was suffering from neglect. I assumed there were no funds allocated for upkeep. Subsidence caused headstones to tilt at crazy angles and they were covered with patches of white lichen that obscured the inscriptions. It was a breezy day of sunshine and high clouds. Out on the moorlands there were curlews calling. Together with the ragged singing they added to the melancholy of the occasion in the isolated graveyard.

Maria was not with us. She saw no reason to interrupt a painting holiday in the Charente. She had paid for it in advance and she was going to get her money's worth. Lady Alma claimed infirmity and the need to be pushed around the garden at Graiglwyd in her new wheelchair. A more expeditious ceremony could have been arranged in the Crematorium at Colwyn Bay: but Glyn was intent on carrying out his mother's last request to the letter.

After the funeral he was determined to climb Foel Wen so that we could gain a panoramic view of our valley. He was oddly cheerful like a man who has learnt the worst and decided he could live with it. He said he was keen to look down at the Bwlch Pass where an eccentric old shepherd who called himself ap Berwyn, claimed to have seen the ghost of a man on horseback disappear into the mist. It was a favourite story of his father's. Ap Berwyn couldn't decide whether it was Hywel Harris he had seen or Williams Pantycelyn: but he was quite certain it was one or the other.

As I puffed my way through the rocks and tufted grass I began to regret having agreed to follow him. He would have gone in any case and left me getting more and more bored sitting in the car. We weren't properly shod for this kind of scramble, and we weren't boys any more setting out on an adventure to see what lay on the other side of the mountain. We were middle-aged men and in my case too fat and out of condition. As I crossed an unexpected strip of wet marsh I felt like a tame rabbit pushed out of his hutch to suffer a taste of soggy freedom. There he stood on the top, like a statue against the sky. He was the image of a man resolved to be in tune with the familiar earth and its seasons. He was still an imposing figure. All the same the perfection of his youth had blown away for ever. Gone those golden curls Maria first saw in the mirror of the make-up department. All he had now was thinning grey hair blowing about his skull. I was panting when I reached his side to look back the way we had come.

'You know what we've been doing?'

I wasn't sure whether he was talking to me or to himself. The stiff breeze was carrying his words away.

'"Let their habitation be desolate and let no man dwell therein"... We've been going up in the world and leaving an empty desert behind us...'

I wasn't entirely certain what he was referring to. Looking down the valley there were several ruined farmsteads that had been abandoned in our lifetime; and two quarries closed. I couldn't see how we, he and I, Glyn and Gwyn, could be held responsible for that. Economic and social forces. Global forces at work like the mills of God grinding out change. He was of course being affected by his mother's death. As he spoke he sounded inconsolable. When a man is overcome with grief he reverts to the affections of his childhood. I knew that from my own experience. He was in a mood to rebuke himself. And in order to do that he had to take the responsibility for the decay of our valley and our traditional way of life on his own shoulders. I could hear him muttering to himself, 'What the hell have I been doing? Just one mistake after another. Is that all it amounts to?' It wasn't the time or the place to argue that ageing men had no choice except to come to terms with historical necessity.

We scrambled down the short route to the Bwlch. Glyn led the way. There were moments when he leapt about like a youth pretending to be a mountain goat. I couldn't do it myself but it brought back a memory of our past like a snatch of a forgotten tune. We reached the narrow road suitable for single lane traffic with passing places at intervals. There was the road south and the lake in the distance: the view that used to intrigue us in our childhood as the ordained limit of our little world. Below us on the opposite side of the road the grim spruces of the forestry commission grew in tighter ranks than Chinese terracotta soldiers.

On our way back Glyn turned up a short lane to show me an empty cottage. It had a garden choked with weeds and a row of crumbling outhouses. He leant against the stone wall and pointed at the damp and dismal buildings. He took some pride and pleasure in the scene.

'Bryn Bach' he said. 'Ours. We bought it for next to nothing.'

'We' meant Glyn and his mother. It was a strange thing to do. She could never have lived there. I could only imagine it was a gesture of defiance.

'You can tell your kids,' Glyn said. 'They can stay here whenever they like.'

They were hardly 'kids' any more, our offspring. I had to thank him on their behalf, although I couldn't imagine any one of the three taking up the offer: one teaching English in Vienna, one in Australia and one coining it in the computer rat race. It was an effort for them to contact Valerie and me, let alone tramping up the lane to this dilapidated cottage. All the same I warmed to Glyn for acknowledging my status as a parent. It suggested I had something that could be envied.

VII

At Broadcasting House, Glyn had a devoted secretary called Angela Welyn. She was a large woman who wrote poetry in the strict metres in her spare time. Her services had been invaluable when we did our series on *The Genius of the Place* and the *Parish Pump*. (I say 'we' because my name appeared on the closing titles as consultant.) She was modest about her metrical accomplishments and said she enjoyed it more than knitting or doing crosswords. In a world where first names were freely bandied about in abbreviated form and frequently tacked on to 'darling', Miss Welyn persisted in calling Glyn 'Mr. Brace.' I have to say that to me these lingering formalities underpinned a rock-like working relationship: but Angela Welyn and her devotion, her heavy accent, and her large feet were a source of constant amusement to the ladies of Graiglwyd Manor.

On Glyn's fifty-seventh birthday Miss Welyn was the first person to read an abrupt memo from Personnel inviting Glyndwr Maldwyn Brace to consider the advantage of early retirement. Her first inclination had been to hide the offensive missive so as not to spoil his birthday. She was appalled and offended by such bureaucratic lack of consideration.

'When I think of the services you have given the Corporation, Mr. Brace.'

Her indignation brought tears to her eyes. 'All those years,' she kept saying. It was possible she was keeping in mind also her own long service. There was the upsetting consideration that if he went, she would be consigned to work for someone else and there was no one really in the organisation that could compare with Mr. Brace.

'Its disgusting,' she said. 'It's as if everything you stand for is being betrayed. Public service, Inform, Educate, Entertain.'

She repeated the well-known phrase like a mantra.

'I don't know what public broadcasting is coming to. I really don't. All they seem to want to show is an endless flow of tits and bums.'

Glyn looked at her in astonishment. He told me that the slang phrase in her slow Meirionydd accent sounded like a malediction in some obsolete language.

'It's alright Miss Welyn' he said. 'You mustn't worry. I'm more than ready to pick up my P45.'

This was no consolation to her. He went on to discourse on the sense of false security individuals could acquire if they snuggled too closely into the tentacled embrace of a corporate institution. This was no comfort to her either. Like many men with a devotion to duty, Glyn was strangely impervious to the impact his presence and his casual remarks were liable to make on people.

It was duty to his wife and her mother that restrained him from seizing the early retirement offer. Sir John's inopportune demise, Lady Alma often explained, according to Valerie, was barely enough to keep her in gin and cosmetics. When Glyn informed them of his possible early retirement they became very agitated. A change in financial circumstances could seriously affect their lifestyles. Their Graiglwyd was an establishment in need of generous funding. How could they possibly contemplate giving it up? Lady Alma worked herself up. 'Does it mean I shall have to end my days in some shitty little bungalow?' It seemed to Maria that there were problems involved that her husband, the thinker and dreamer, was incompetent to deal with. The best solution was to invite Ken Crosby-Jones to dinner and seek his support and considered advice. When Glyn said 'good God, no!' she affected to be taken aback by his vigorous refusal.

For some time before the memorandum from Personnel, Glyn had been stricken with a period of prolonged idleness. He had been condemned, he felt, to mooch about his office trying to conceal the fact that he had very little to do. It was as if he were being given time to contemplate a position that was increasingly isolated and vulnerable: and why colleagues who had been consistently affable now seemed to be making deliberate efforts to avoid him. Was he to believe that the Head of Programmes, the eminently sociable Skull 'n' Bones, was taking subtle steps to get rid of him? To allay these misgivings he drove himself to work on new programme suggestions. There was one on great Welsh politicians and another on great Rugby players but both were rejected. It came as something of a surprise, therefore, when Skull 'n' Bones called him in to discuss the possibilities of a film on an item Skull 'n' Bones had picked up when glancing through Glyn's old project on Missionary Journeys. 'I read the stuff you know,' he said. 'More than once if it comes to that.' He sat back with his knee against his desk to make a few lordly gestures as he expanded his notion. I could imagine my old friend watching him with a curious mixture of dutiful suspicion.

'It was that word *Tahiti* that alerted me,' he said. 'This chap Davies making a dictionary and the war between the islands and the French trying to muscle in. There's the making of a film there. In a documentary sense of course. Could you do me a project paper on it? And a budget maybe? I think it's something we could push. A special project. Mind you I'm not asking for a *Mutiny on the Bounty...*'

He was being uncommonly cordial. Glyn took him at face value. Preparing such an exciting project would renew his enthusiasm to what he could still consider his calling with a capital C. Maria invited us to join the dinner party at Graiglwyd. It was a jolly occasion. Skull 'n' Bones was indulging in that degree of forthright frankness that can only be exercised by those whose power base is unassailable. He was among friends. He could be as frank as he liked.

'I tell you this, Glyn boy. When you get back you snatch that early retirement. Screw the bastards for all you can get. Golden handshakes and all.'

Lady Alma clapped her hands unable to contain her excitement.

'Screw the bastards!' she said in her best Central European accent. 'That is beautiful. I like that. "Screw the bastards!"'

Everyone around the table burst out laughing. And even Glyn was forced to smile. Wine of excellent vintage flowed and joy seemed unconfined. Crosby-Jones' gestures grew more expansive and stretched to include me.

'Gwyn boy! Why don't you go with him? Consultant. All expenses paid. Hold his hand, man! Make sure he doesn't get seduced by sultry south-sea maidens.'

I tried to look sceptical, but it was a tempting prospect. We worked well as a team: a happy combination of research and technical expertise. Together we could complete a 'recce' in half the time. If I made the trip during the vac I could easily spare ten days to a fortnight.

'The Rev. Glyn and the Rev. Gwyn!'

Crosby-Jones' skeletal face was flushed with more imaginative inspiration.

'You could both go dressed as eighteenth century missionaries,' he said. 'Think of the reception you would get. Dressed in shorts and a dog collar and living on coconuts!'

I don't know whether he was deliberately scraping the gilt off an impulsive offer. Too much admiration from the women may have compelled him to go beyond the bounds of his authority. He waved his thin hands about as if he were conducting a display of his own coruscating wit and enjoying the sound even more than Lady Alma who gasped and croaked and clapped her hands as though she were a vital part of the orchestration.

In the car on the way home Valerie was ominously sober.

'Don't you dare take up that offer, Gwyn Rondel.'

I assured her I had taken it all with a pinch of salt but I wondered why she was so adamant.

'He's up to something. That's why.'

She concentrated on driving and whetted my curiosity by remaining thoughtfully silent – an old habit to which I had long grown accustomed.

'There's a Television Film Festival the end of next month.

Somewhere like St. Tropez. I'm not sure where: but he wants mother and daughter to accompany him. He's booked rooms for them in the Beau Rivage. She wasn't supposed to tell me. But you know what she's like when she's tanked with gin. She can't stop talking. And I'll tell you something else, Professor Rondel. He is after Maria.'

My heart sank. At first glance it appeared unbelievable.

'He's very well off,' Valerie said. 'Far more than he ever lets on. His shares in commercial television doubled in value the day after he was given them and he's more or less a millionaire. That's what Alma tells me and she's got a nose for cash that can smell money several miles off. For years now she's been hinting that Glyn has been a great disappointment to her and by extension to her beautiful daughter who's worrying about getting thicker around the waist.'

She shook her head pityingly when she heard the depth of my sigh.

'You've been mollycoddled Professor Rondel. You don't know what goes on in the real world. It's a proper jungle. The old witch says he's bought a mill near the Abbey of Saint-Hilarie where her delightful daughter will be able to paint to her heart's content. And who are little bourgeois people like us to stand in the way of genius fulfilling her potential?'

VIII

I never went to Tahiti. We went to Australia instead. Our second daughter had given birth and there was a rough and ready clan of in-laws to attend to. I was worried about Glyn when we left, but Valerie was quite firm. She said misfortune was like an infectious disease: it was wiser, if you could manage it, to give it a wide berth. She didn't share my feeling that it was necessary to warn Glyn about what was going on behind his back. With a rather knowing smile she repeated an old adage that warned the passer-by never to come between warring husband and wife. 'Besides,' she said. 'Remember those wedding pictures of the charming couple in the smart magazines!'

All the same one morning when she was out I rang Glyn's office. He wasn't there. I spoke to his faithful secretary Miss Angela Welyn. She told me he had gone north to his cottage at the top of our valley to concentrate on preparing a project about missionaries. Her enthusiasm for the project made me uneasy. She seemed to be claiming a share in a fresh vision that had vouchsafed itself to the unique talent of Glyn Brace. It made me curious to know more about it. Whatever it was, it hardly tallied with the ironic attitude of Crosby-Jones towards a missionary journey. I was torn between my habitual discretion and a desire to warn such innocents about Skull 'n' Bones's machinations. When I said nothing I felt helpless and in some sense guilty by association.

Valerie enjoyed our visit to Australia far more than I did. It was too hot. There is a bond that exists between mother and daughter that the male of the species is not designed to share. On top of that I was forced to endure a plague of boils on my backside. I was convinced they were caused by the interminable flight and some bites that I sustained in the hotel in Bali. For almost a month I lived in dread of the long journey home.

To my eyes when we came back we arrived in another world. For some reason I began whistling to myself as though a benevolent providence had provided me with an opportunity for a fresh start. This was absurd since I was a man pushing sixty. Nevertheless I approached my duties in the Faculty and the College with a fresh burst of energy as if some sprite or spirit on my right shoulder had whispered in my ear that there was still time for me to make a mark. And indeed there was a prestigious invitation waiting my return: to deliver the biennial interdisciplinary lecture on *The Individual and the Institution,* 'a perspective for the twenty-first century'. There were six or seven months to prepare it. I need hardly add that the subject soon began to occupy all my waking thoughts and disturb my sleep. I had to make a good job of it. No 'ifs' and 'buts'. My enduring reputation would depend on it.

Glyn of course was a case in point. Early in my researches I visited the vast new building of Broadcasting House and asked at the desk to see Mr. Glyn Brace. The young woman must have been new. She looked at me blankly and admitted she had never heard of him. I looked around the echoing hall and had to conclude the place thereof knew him no more. And there was no sign of Miss Angela Welyn. Had it become a place to escape from? In the car park I turned around to view the imperturbable impersonality of the massive building. When I was on the council I remember a weighty administrator jangling coins in his pocket and declaring the building was already too small on the day it opened. Like the Kremlin or the Empire State Building in its own way it was a symbol of something. But exactly what was not so easy to define. Clearly I needed to talk to Glyn about it. We were friends after all and friends were always happy to enlighten one another. At the first opportunity I headed north for Penybont and Llanbedr and that isolated cottage, Bryn Bach, off the mountain road to the Bwlch.

I knocked more than once. No one answered. The door was unlocked. I went in. It was clean enough. There was a white disinfectant powder sprinkled on the bare floor-boards. I was shocked by the lack of comfort. Just a table, three wooden chairs and an oil lamp on the window-sill. Not even a clock on the wall. Bryn Bach had two rooms and an empty kitchen and two bedrooms; one also empty. By his bed there were a few books and the flute I could remember him playing as a boy. The solitude of the cottage suddenly gripped around my heart and I could hardly breathe. I was an intruder. I could no longer bear to look around. I only came to my senses when I closed the door behind me and rushed out to the road.

At the run-down village shop I made enquiries. It was kept by a rotund Lancashire woman called Mrs. Culshaw who surveyed the world in which she had found herself moored with a scepticism you could almost touch. About Mr. Brace she knew everything and nothing.

'He calls himself a shepherd,' Mrs. Culshaw said. 'All he does is keep an eye on Ysgubor Fawr sheep.'

She pronounced the name 'Skipper Ffawer'.

'If you want to find him you'll need to go wandering the mountain. You can tell him if you like his order is ready, and for him to come and get it. He seems to live on tinned food. I tell him he needs to eat more. He says he doesn't want to get too fat for fear of frightening the sheep. He's a funny old thing I can tell you.'

My visit was a failure not just because I failed to get hold of Glyn. It disturbed me greatly. What in the end did I have to say about 'The Individual and the Institution' that was worth the length of a lecture? I stood alone on the mountain road and I was overwhelmed by the sheer emptiness of the formidable landscape. My presence added nothing to it. So what did Glyn find there as he wandered those interminable hostile slopes in search of lost sheep? Freedom and independence for all were all very well, but what about the monotony? Had he somehow gained access to a reservoir of inner resources that I knew nothing about?

There were of course obvious clues to his behaviour. Valerie informed me, with a calm that bordered on indifference, that Graiglwyd was up for sale. Her detachment amazed me. I wanted to ask if she would miss her duets with Lady Alma that had been a feature of her life for almost thirty years. How had my wife established a new range of interests and acquaintances with such ease? Clearly she did not miss the Graiglwyd women anything like the way that I was missing Glyn. It wasn't merely a question of boyhood friendship. How could people pass in and out of your life and leave so little impression? Was the social order designed not to bolster but to diminish our existence?

I came to feel that Glyn had some specialised knowledge about all this, and that it had to be key to the lecture I was struggling so hard to prepare. I would get back to Bryn Bach at the first opportunity and this time I would take the quicker route from the South, past the lake and yet another quarry that had closed and then up the single track with passing places to the Bwlch. It was autumn and I could count on there being few tourists about.

As the road went higher, the mist came down and I switched

on the fog lights of my car. I was of course apprehensive. If anything came to meet me I would have to reverse and that wouldn't be easy. When I reached the top of the Bwlch there was a limited parking space and I moved off the road to take a breather. I was taking a drink from the thermos flask when I saw the dark shadow of a man enlarged to giant proportions against the white mist. He was moving with the calm and confidence of a man who could see the unseen. I thought it was Glyn. I called out his name and I could hear the echo of my own voice.

'Glyn! It's me, Gwyn! I want to ask you something.'

There was no answer. I wanted to run after him. I couldn't because there were pitfalls and crags and hollows all around us. I knew the treachery of the terrain and I couldn't take the risk. I sat in the car with my forehead on the steering wheel overcome with my own helplessness. All I could do was turn back. When I reached home I took to my bed. Neither Valerie nor our family doctor could account for my condition. My lecture had to be cancelled.

The Arrest

I

A short stocky man stood in the middle of a room lined with books. He was in his shirt sleeves. His clenched fists inside his trouser pockets pressed down hard so that the tough elastic in his braces was fully stretched. He shut his eyes and breathed deeply. When his tight lips expanded with the conscious effort of subduing his excitement, he looked pleased with himself. He opened his eyes. They were a piercing innocent blue. A beam of the morning sunlight caught the framed photograph of his college football team hanging above the door. He saw himself picked out plainly in the back row, his arms folded high across his chest a tight smile on his face, his head crowned with golden hair cut short at the back and sides and brushed back in close even waves. It was a head of hair to be proud of. A blackbird in one of the cherry trees at the bottom of the garden burst into a prolonged cadenza. His hand opened and passed softly over the trim white waves that remained to him, still cut close in the old style.

His wife appeared in the study doorway. Her grey head was held to one side. She dry-washed her long white hands and smiled at him winningly.

'I don't think they are coming today, Gwilym.'

Her voice was quiet, a little tremulous with anxiety and respect.

'Cat and mouse.'

His thumbs planed up and down inside his braces.

'It's obvious what they are up to. Cat and mouse. Trying to break my will. Trying to make me give in.'

His wife lowered her head. Her concern seemed tinged with guilt.

'Let him stew a bit longer. You can hear them say it.'

The room reverberated with his resonant nasal baritone. He was a minister who enjoyed the art of preaching. His wife's attitude of troubled and reverential concern urged him on.

'The magistrates were very polite. Very gracious. The narrow iron hand in the thick velvet glove. A month to pay. That month expired, Olwen, ten days ago. And still they have not been to get me... That's the way things are done in this little country of ours. It's all persuasion, moderation, compromise. As I said yesterday, an entire population is guided, herded like a vast flock by the sheepdogs of the communication media into the neat rectangular pens of public obedience. And we still don't realise that those pens are process machines and that we have all become units of mass government analogous to units of mass production: uniformed wrapped and packaged products of the state machine.'

She closed her eyes before taking a step into the room. Her hands spread out in a gesture of pleading.

'Gwilym, she said. You've made your stand. The congregation understands and admires you. That's something a minister can be proud of. Why not pay now and have done with it!'

He lifted a warning finger.

'I have forbidden any member of my congregation to pay my fine! I have made a legal statement to the effect that all our property, such as it is, including our little Morris Minor, is in your name, "Mrs. Olwen Dora Ellis". They can come when they like to arrest me.'

She moved to the window and looked forlornly at their narrow strip of garden and the circular rockery they had built together. The aubretia was already in flower. The north wall of the chapel was faced with slates that looked less austere in the vibrant sunlight. The minister ran his finger lightly along a row of volumes on a shelf.

'The role of the church in the modern world et cetera et cetera,' he said. 'How readily we take the word for the deed. It's deep in our psyche. What we need is more preachers in prison.'

'Yes, but why you, Gwilym?'

The question was intended as a humble appeal: but she could not prevent it sounding sulky. He waved it aside.

'Yes but where are the young ones? You are a man of fifty-six,

Gwilym. You have certain physical ailments sometimes...'

'Piles,' he said.

He spoke as one at all times determined to be frank.

'Otherwise I'm extremely fit.'

'It worries me. I can't bear to think of you going to prison for a month.'

'Twenty-eight days.'

'It really worries me. I don't think I can stand it.'

They both stood still as though they were listening to the uninterrupted song of the blackbird in the cherry tree. He wanted to comfort her but her distress embarrassed him too much.

'We've been over this before,' he said. 'Somebody has to take a lead. Our language is being driven out of the homes of our people and our religion is being swept away with it. We must have an all-Welsh television channel. That's all there is to it. That's what our campaign is all about. When words fail, actions must follow. Stand firm, Olwen.'

At last he moved closer to her and put his arm over her shoulders.

'Now what about a cup of coffee?'

II

It was while they sat in the kitchen drinking it, the police arrived. Mrs. Ellis glimpsed a blue helmet moving above the lace curtain.

'They've come,' she said. 'Oh my God... they're here.' She stared so wildly at her husband, she could have been urging him to run away and hide. He sat at the table, pale and trembling a little. He spoke in spite of himself.

'Didn't think they would come today,' he said. The peremptory knock on the back door agitated Mrs. Ellis so much she pressed both her hands on her grey hair and then against her cheeks.

'I've got fifteen pounds in the lustre jug,' she said. 'Do you think they'll take them, Gwilym, if I offer them?'

The colour began to return to his cheeks.

'They don't really want you to go. The prisons are too full

anyway. I read that in the paper only a week ago. They're too full you see. I meant to cut it out to show you. They won't have room for you, when it comes to it...'

The minister breathed very deeply and rose to his feet.

'It's not a place for you anyway. Not a man like you Gwilym. This is your proper place where you're looked after properly, so that you can do the work you have been called to do. A son of the Manse living in the Manse. There isn't a man in the Presbytery who works half as hard as you do...'

'Olwen! Pull yourself together! Be worthy.'

A second series of knocks sent him rushing to the back door. He threw it open and greeted the two policemen with exaggerated geniality.

'Gentlemen! Please come in! I've been expecting you and yet I must confess I'm not absolutely ready to travel, as you can see. Won't you come in?'

He led them into the parlour. The room was conspicuously clean but crowded with heavy old-fashioned furniture. It smelt faintly of camphor. In a glass-fronted cabinet there were ceramic objects Mrs. Ellis had collected. Two matching Rembrandt reproductions hung on either side of the black marble mantlepiece. The minister invited the policemen to sit down. The senior policeman removed his helmet. A dull groove encircled his thick black hair. Sitting in a low armchair he nursed both the charge-sheet attached to a clip-board and his helmet on his knees. His companion stood at ease in the doorway until he realised that Mrs. Ellis was behind him. She recoiled nervously when he turned and pressed himself against the door so that she could pass into the room. He was a young policeman with plump cheeks and wet suckling lips. When she saw how young he was she looked a little reassured. The older policeman twisted in his chair to speak to her. His voice was loud with undue effort to be normal and polite.

'I don't expect you remember me?'

She moved forward to inspect his face more closely. His false teeth flashed under his black moustache and drew attention to his pock-marked cheeks and small, restless eyes. The minister's wife shook her head a little hopelessly.

'I am Gwennie's husband. Gwennie Penycefn. You remember Gwennie.'

'Gwennie...'

Mrs. Ellis repeated the name with affectionate recognition. She looked at her husband hopefully. He was still frowning with the effort of identification.

'You taught her to recite when she was small.'

Mrs. Ellis nodded eagerly.

'And Mr. Ellis here confirmed her. I don't mind telling you she burst into tears after breakfast. When I told her where I was going and the job I had to do. "Not Mr. Ellis" she said. "He baptised me and he confirmed me." Poor Gwennie. She was very upset.'

The minister nodded solemnly. He stood in front of the empty fireplace, squaring his shoulders, his hands clasped tightly together behind his back. The armchair creaked as the policeman lowered his voice and leaned forward.

'What about paying, Mr. Ellis? You've made your stand. And we respect you for it. It's our language too isn't it, after all. I don't want to see a man of your calibre going to prison. Honestly I don't.'

'Oh dear...'

In spite of her effort at self-control, Mrs. Ellis had begun to sigh and tremble. The policeman turned his attention to her, gruff but confident in his own benevolence.

'Persuade him, Mrs. Ellis bach. You should see the other one I've got waiting in the station. And goodness knows what else the van will have to collect. The refuse of society, Mrs. Ellis. Isn't that so, Pierce?'

He invited a confirming nod from his young colleague.

'Scum,' Pierce said in his light tenor voice. 'That one tried to kill himself last night, if you please.'

'Oh no...'

Mrs. Ellis put her hands over her mouth.

'Younger than me too. Now he needs a stretch. Do him good.'

'Officer.'

The minister was making an effort to sound still and formal.

'This man you say tried to kill himself. What was his trouble?'

'Drugs.'

The older policeman answered the question.

'Stealing. Breaking and entering. Driving without a licence. Drugs.'

The policeman spoke the last word as if its very sound had polluted his lips. His colleague had managed to tighten his wet lips to demonstrate total abomination. He made a strange sound in his throat like the growl of an angry watchdog.

'Will you give me a moment to... dress... and so on?'

The policeman sighed.

'You don't need anything, my dear Mr. Ellis. You go in wet and naked like the day you were born.'

Mrs. Ellis moved into the crowded room. Even in her distress she navigated her way between the furniture without ever touching their edges. Her arms floated upwards like a weak swimmer giving in to the tide.

'I'll pack a few things,' she said. 'In your little week–end case.'

Her eyes were filling with tears and it was clear that she had not taken in the policeman's last words.

'Wear your round collar, Gwilym,' she said.

She spoke in a pleading whisper and made a discreet gesture towards her own throat.

'There's still respect for the cloth, isn't there?'

'I go like any other man who has broken the English law,' he said. 'Get me my coat, Olwen. That's all I shall need.'

The younger policeman looked suddenly annoyed.

'Look,' he said. 'Why cause all this fuss for nothing? It's only a bit of a telly licence. Why don't you pay the fine here and now like any sensible chap and have done with it?'

The minister looked at him.

'You have your duty,' he said. 'I have mine.'

III

The rear door of the van opened suddenly. The minister had a brief glimpse of men out in a yard smoking and enjoying the May sunshine: they were plain-clothes men and policemen in uniform. They paid little attention to the van, even when a bulky youth in frayed jeans was lifted bodily and pushed into it. He collapsed on the cold metal floor near the minister's feet. His large head was a mass of uncombed curls. When his face appeared his lips were stretched in a mooncalf smile. He was handcuffed and there were no laces in his dirty white pumps. His wrists were heavily bandaged in blood-stained crepe. His nose was running and he lifted both hands to try and wipe it. A plain-clothes detective bent over him, still breathing hard.

'Now look, Smyrna,' he said. 'You promise to behave yourself and I'll take these off. Otherwise you'll be chained to the pole see? With a ring through your nose like a bull.' Smyrna was nodding and smiling foolishly.

'You've got a real minister to look after you now. So you behave yourself and I'll bring you a fag before we leave.'

His boots stamped noisily on the metal. The slamming of the rear doors reverberated in the dim interior of the police van. Smyrna, still sitting on the floor raised his arms to stare at his wrists. The minister nodded at him and moved to make room for him on the narrow bench. Smyrna's tongue hung out as he searched the pockets of his jeans for a cigarette. He found a flattened stump, rolled it between his dirty fingers and stuck it between his lips.

'Got a match?'

The minister felt about in his pockets before he shook his head. He looked apologetic. The young man sucked the wet stump. He lifted his bandaged wrists so that the minister could observe them.

'You know what he said?

'Who?'

'That sergeant. That detective sergeant. "Didn't make a good job of it, did you?" '

The minister leaned forward to scrutinise the lateral scratches ascending both the young man's strong arms.

'That's sympathy for you. I was upset. It's a terrible thing to happen to anybody. Eighteen months in prison. And that was all the sympathy I got.'

The minister gathered up the ends of his clerical grey macintosh and leaned forward as far as he could to show intense sympathy.

'How did you do it?'

Smyrna's lips stretched in a proud smile, the cigarette stump still in the corner of his mouth.

'Smashed my arms through the glass. Thick it was. Frosted. Too thick really.'

He mimed the act of scratching his arms with pieces of broken glass. Then he pulled a face to indicate his pain. The minister was distressed.

'Is it hurting now?' he said.

'Aye. A bit.'

Smyrna's head sank on to his chest.

The van lurched abruptly out of the yard. Through the small window the minister caught a glimpse of familiar landmarks warmed by the brilliant sunshine: boarding houses, a deserted slate quay, a wooded corner of the island across the sandy straits. Smyrna was on his knees communicating with the two policemen who rode in front. A plain clothes man the minister had not seen before, lit a cigarette in his own mouth and then passed it between the bars to the young prisoner. Smyrna settled at last on the bench, enjoying the luxury of the smoke, staring most of the time at the bandages on his wrists, lifting first one and then the other for a closer inspection.

The minister asked him questions. He wanted details of his background. As the van travelled faster the interior grew colder and more draughty. Smyrna's eyes shifted about as he tried to work out the ulterior motive behind Mr. Ellis' probing solicitude. He pulled his tattered combat jacket closer about his body and sniffed continuously to stop his nose running. His answers became monosyllabic and he began to mutter and complain about the cold and the noise. His eyes closed. He sagged in his seat and his large body shook passively with the vibrations of the uncomfortable vehicle.

The van turned into the rear of a large police headquarters. It reversed noisily up a narrow concrete passage to get as close as possible to a basement block of cells. Smyrna jerked himself up nervously and called out.

'Where are we then?'

The minister tried to give a reassuring smile.

'I've no idea,' he said.

The van stood still, the engine running. There were shouts outside and the jovial sounds of policemen greeting one another, Smyrna's mouth opened and his eyeballs oscillated nervously in their sockets as he listened.

When the doors at last opened a smartly dressed young man jumped in. He wore large tinted spectacles and his straight hair was streaked and tinted. He wore his bright handcuffs as if they were a decoration. He sat opposite the other two, giving them a brief nod and a smile of regal condescension. There was no question of removing his handcuffs. His escort examined the interior and then decided to ride in front with his colleagues. As soon as the doors were locked the van moved off at speed. Smyrna unsteadily attempted to wipe his nose, first with the back of one hand and then the other. He stared at the newcomer's handcuffs with a curiosity that made him miss his own nose. His mouth hung open. A fastidious expression appeared on the new prisoner's face.

'You're a dirty bugger aren't you.'

A modish disc-jockey drawl had been superimposed on his local accent. The effect would have been comic but for the menacing stillness of his narrow head. It was held in some invisible vice of his own making. His eyes, pale and yet glinting dangerously, were also still beyond the grey tint of the thin convex lenses.

'I don't like dirty buggers near me. I can tell you that now.

What do they call you?'

Smyrna's jaw stretched out as he considered the quiet words addressed to him. Was this a new threat forming itself? Had his environment become totally hostile? The well-dressed prisoner was handcuffed after all. He was a man of slight build. He looked down unhappily at his own powerful arms and began once again to examine the bandages on his wrists.

'Smyrna,' he said. 'Smyrna. That's what they call me.'

'What's that for Christ's sake. Some bloody Welsh chapel, or something?'

He bared the bottom of his immaculate teeth in an unfriendly smile.

'Now look here...'

The minister felt obliged to intervene.

'You must understand that our young friend here isn't at all well. You can see for yourself.'

The cold eyes shifted to examine the minister for the first time.

'Who the hell are you? His old dad or something?'

He directed the same question to Smyrna with the slightest nod towards the minister. He was amused by his own remarks.

'Your old dad, is he? Come for the ride?'

The minister made an appeal for sociability.

'Now look here,' he said. 'We are all in the same boat. In the same van anyway. Let us make an effort to get on together, and help each other.'

The handcuffed man studied the minister with the absorbed but objective interest of an ornithologist examining a known if unfamiliar species in a wholly inappropriate habitat.

'How long you in for, Moses?'

'A month. Twenty eight days that is.'

The minister was prepared to be relaxed and jovial.

'Oh dearie me. That's a very long time isn't it? What about you snotty Smyrna?'

'Eighteen months.'

Smyrna's large head sank on his chest. His jaw began to work. In the depth of his misery he seemed unaware of a trickle of mucus that ran from his nostril over the edge of his upper lip.

'Wipe your snot, you dirty bugger.'

The handcuffed prisoner's voice rose sharply to assert itself above the noise of the engine taking a hill in low gear.

'I bet you're one of those miserable sods who grind their bloody teeth in their sleep. Aren't you?'

Smyrna smiled rather foolishly. He had no defence except to try and be friendly.

'How long you in for then?'

He put the question with amiable innocence and waited patiently for an answer. A pulse began to beat visibly in the handcuffed man's tightened jaws.

'Nine.'

He spoke at last, but so quietly Smyrna leaned forward as though he were about to complain he hadn't heard. One of the police escort shifted in his cramped seat to peer back at them through the steel bars. The scream of the engine subsided a little.

'Nine months did you say?'

Smyrna was smiling inanely.

'Nine fucking years you snotty piece of crap. If they can hold me.'

He lifted his handcuffed hands to the breast pocket of his smart suit and let them fall again.

'Here...'

He was ordering Smyrna to extract a packet of cigarettes from the pocket. Smyrna glanced apprehensively at the broad backs of the policemen in front.

'Never mind them, snotty. When you're inside you do as I tell you. You may as well start now.'

Smyrna was permitted a cigarette himself. He was instructed to sit alongside his new master to enjoy it.

'You sit there mate, and then I won't have to bloody look at you.'

Smyrna settled down, inhaling deeply and giggling. He blew on the end of the cigarette and pointed it at Mr. Ellis.

'He's a minister,' he said.

'Is he now? Well, well. He should be sorry for us.'

He held out his handcuffed wrists and nudged Smyrna to do the same. When he understood the order, Smyrna shook so much with silent giggles that he had difficulty in keeping his bandaged wrists level and close to the handcuffs.

'We make a pair. A pair of Jacks. Isn't that so, Snotty? A pair of Jacks.'

Smyrna laughed delightedly. He let his arms drop but a glance from his new companion made him raise them again.

'What is it then. What is it you're in for?'

The minister cleared his throat. He straightened his back.

'For refusing to buy my television licence,' he said. 'On principle.'

'Oh my God. One of them language fanatics. I tell you what I'd do, Moses, if I was in charge. I'd stick the bloody lot of you up against a wall...'

'You don't understand,' the minister said. 'I'm not blaming you. You've never had a chance to understand.'

'Do you hear that?'

The man in handcuffs elbowed Smyrna again to show him he could lower his arms if he wanted to since he had decided the joke was over.

'He's a fucking Welsh hero. That's what he is. In for twenty days and then out for a fucking laurel crown made of leeks. That's him. I tell you what we'll do, snotty. We'll be in the same cell tonight. And I won't be wearing my bracelets. How about knitting him a nice little crown of thorns?'

Smyrna inhaled cigarette smoke to the bottom of his lungs and nodded gleefully.

Sisters

I

We won't be bullied, my sister and I; either by each other or by anyone else: especially our large and lumbering brother, the ferocious Francis. If anyone asks, we just say we get on better, Eira and I, with the width of a street between us: Eira is sweet and willowy; I am a five foot nothing battering ram. The street is tree lined, which is pleasant except for a brief period at the end of autumn when the pavements can become slippery with fallen leaves. From my bedroom window I can keep an eye on Eira's house further down on the opposite side of the street. There's a car parked outside there now and I have to make an effort to stop wondering who can be calling on her. It's none of my business. As we both agree, steady work keeps us on the rails. When you're pushing sixty the world doesn't get any less confusing or less frightening. At least we have each other to rely on. Our father used to say that Lucy's feet were just a few centimetres closer to the ground than Eira's: as dutiful daughters we accepted his verdict on most things. Now I know that the dicta he liked to intone were rarely more than glib assertions to ease and facilitate his abiding obsession with making money.

In his own way he was proud of his daughters who painted. We were still young and reasonably presentable when we discovered we preferred to paint than be painted. We began with landscapes in watercolours. Father used to say Lucy and Eira devoured landscapes: which we thought an unhappy figure of speech since it was he, aided and abetted by our ferocious older brother Francis, who did the real devouring. He owned quarries, some slate, some limestone, some granite and he was astute enough in the late fifties to get rid of his railroad shares and buy more derelict quarries and carry off whole mountainsides to catch the great boom in motorway building. Our guilt was never assuaged by the Trust established in our favour. We moved further West to a small town between the mountains and the sea: but the Trust still has us tied up in knots. And the ferocious Francis is still around to make sure we never escape.

We agree that is a melodramatic way of putting it. What it amounts to is Francis can't help being bossy and he's always ready to fiddle with that Trust to his own advantage. And he has a nasty sense of humour. 'Just pretend you are artists starving in a Paris garret, instead of a pair of painting birds each in her own gilded cage.' That sort of thing. 'I have to be a cynic to be able to afford your fancy idealism!' What he calls idealism is no more than an inconvenient combination of being both shy and fastidious.

I look through the bedroom window at regular intervals to reassure myself that the world is something more than a frightening illusion; and of course ascertain that the car is still parked outside Eira's house. Living alone for long stretches at a time can undermine your conviction of the immutability of places and people. That boy down there kicking an empty tin can. Why should he feel compelled to look up at me and put out his tongue? He sees an old woman frowning and doesn't appreciate I am no older than he is inside the bubble of this moment. Now he vanishes and there is nothing left in the street to react to, except that car outside my sister's front door which might as well not be there. It is certainly not an object I could consider painting. I am aware that the skulls of the world are nothing less than a multitude of universes: but that brings me no comfort. It accounts for the fact that I live alone and sleep with an eye on the night sky through my large skylight. I lie awake often considering what my painting should be about. It is a mistake to believe love inspires art. Certainly the art that I aspire to. Or Causes. And I have always been a one for causes. A cautious protester you could call me. An anonymous subscriber. But my art such as it is centres on the contemplation of stone walls. If I walk far enough I will always come across a dry wall where the stones lean against each other like rugged individuals dressed in green moss or white and grey and yellow lichen. It took at least twenty years for my lemon and lilac period to be superseded by an obsession with brown and black and the spatial relationship of rocks and gullies.

Little of this interests my sister Eira and we are too close to each other for her not to say so. That is why we avoid the discomfort of sharing a house. My luxury is to listen to Bach while I'm painting. Eira has more moods. She wants silence one day and a blaring Berlioz the next. She has an enthusiasm for things mythological and is easily influenced by the last exhibition to take her breath away. We are forthright with each other, so we never feel any overwhelming need for public criticism or even recognition: that is not to say a little genuine appreciation would not go amiss.

In the course of our lives I have had more than one occasion to tell my sister that her manner with men can verge too easily on the flirtatious. I can't help it if she attributes the reproof to some subliminal form of jealousy. I was never that interested in handsome young men. At the same time I freely acknowledge that I do not have a dimpled smile or the coy look that lurks under long eyelashes. I know that and I accept it and I am always grateful when she bestows a smile on me and laughs at my sharp remarks. She knows, even against her will, that it is her welfare that I have at heart. It is that more than any vulgar curiosity that makes me want to know whose car that is, parked in the road outside her demure front door.

II

I never accused her of flirting with the Reverend Heilyn Hughes. From the first I regarded him as a rather pathetic figure. He was thin and he smoked and his hands trembled and he was in awe of a large wife who did everything for him. She would even tie his shoelaces out of respect for his exceptional poetic sensibility. He may have won chairs and crowns but I suspected his strict metres of being melodious clichés. He had been minister of a nonconformist church in an industrial district where the membership included the descendants of the participants in a general strike of over a century ago that had lasted two terrible years. Academic sociologists had a range of rather dusty metaphors to chronicle the lasting effect on the community: as far as Heilyn Hughes was concerned he had to cope with a simmering vendetta that traced back directly to the families in favour and against continuing the backbreaking strike. It seems that the day after his inaugural sermon on Christian harmony two of his deacons came to blows in the street outside the chapel. His wife maintained that it was the strain of trying to keep the peace in a divided church that brought about his nervous breakdown. For my own part I found the man distastefully complex. If he lacked the inner strength he should never have taken on the job.

Eira, however, was all sympathy and understanding. It was Mrs. Hughes that suggested to her that she might care to paint a portrait of Heilyn. After all he was an artist and he had recently composed yet another winning poem at a crown Eisteddfod. Heilyn Hughes was deep into the composition of an epic poem based on the third book of the Mabinogion. It was to be his masterpiece. In order to deepen her appreciation of his efforts, Eira attended evening classes in medieval Welsh. I had nothing against that: but when she got to work and I viewed her efforts my comments were not welcome. I said he looked like an emaciated King Lear caught in a rain storm on a blasted heath. It found its way to the attic where Eira kept an entire roomful of canvasses to be reused.

Her most successful effort was a portrait, against a quarrying background, executed in the pointillist manner: I began to suspect the style could have been adopted in order to prolong the length of the sittings. The poet and the painter had discovered they were soul-mates. They had the same mildly ecstatic way of contemplating their sensibilities. They shared common spurts of enthusiasm. They fed each other sweets to fill the emotional vacancies in their lives. I told Eira that I found these prolonged sessions unsavoury. He read long extracts from favourite poems while she lingered over corners of her canvas.

The fact that he had so few physical attractions made it all the worse really. They were turning her studio into a spiritual laundry where they took in each other's washing.

It was when Mrs. Hughes – I always called her Mrs. Hughes, I have no idea of her Christian name – caught a glimpse of her husband's portrait hanging halfway up the stairs to Eira's bedroom, that she called a halt to their burgeoning elective affinity in the most practical way possible. They moved away. She bought a house in Tywyn, Meirionydd. That was more than forty miles away and in those days Eira hadn't learned to drive. Not that she drives all that well now. If we make a trip together I prefer to take the wheel myself. Eira was distressed, but I wasn't sorry to see them go.

III

I suspect it was Heilyn Hughes's flights of poetic fancy that were responsible in the first place for Eira's enthusiasm for the work of Marc Chagall. It never appealed all that much to me, but Eira was unhappy and I tried to be sympathetic. She went on at length about the parallels they had discovered between Celtic and Jewish mythologies. She bought a whole set of Hastings' *Encyclopaedia of Religion and Ethics*, second hand, to pursue her researches. They took a lot of room in her cosy little sitting room. She pored over them for a whole winter and began to scribble notes instead of painting. Things like 'All I possess is the land within my soul where all the natives hover in the air. I give them all the food and shelter they need. They inhabit my thin street...' That sort of thing. Fortunately our street was wide rather than thin: but I worried about her. It seemed as we advanced inexorably towards the frontiers of middle age she was becoming more fey and myself more truculent. I felt we needed each other more than ever.

Eira discovered that Marc Chagall was alive and living in the South of France. A great museum was being built to house his works in Nice. What was to prevent us pulling up sticks and moving to live somewhere convenient down there? We had the money and in another country we wouldn't need to conceal how much money we had. It was more than possible that if we hung around the museum long enough we might bump into the great man himself. Just to see him from a distance would be enough to light the touch-paper of her inspiration. And so on. This must have been in the seventies and Eira could have been suffering still from the absence of her soul-mate.

I had difficulty in restraining her. And there were the furious Francis's suspicions to be allayed. There were always papers he would require either one or both of us to sign at very short notice. My plan was to move for a month or so to a pleasant pension in Haute de Cagne. It was a compromise that kept the peace. I could cast an eye on Renoir and Leger and Matisse while Eira got herself worked up about the ineffable Chagall. I was impressed by my own cautious wisdom. It would give Eira time to work the worship of Chagall out of her system: either discover a new enthusiasm or recover her sense of proportion so that we could return to our terrace houses and resume our own modest aesthetic explorations.

All went according to plan until our second visit to the new museum. A handsome young couple stood close together in front of 'Le Cirque Bleu'. The young man was whispering into the young woman's ear and she was smiling with such calm content that I found myself transfixed by her fragile beauty. His protective arm was around her shoulders and his lips close to her ear. Her eyes were wide open as she listened to his voice tracing the swerve of the unearthly female acrobat watched by a blue fish, a green horse and a yellow moon. As I stared at them I realised that in spite of the luminosity in the girl's bright eyes, she was blind.

Eira had also noticed the young couple. She was taken with the dark good looks of the man. It was a chiselled smooth face with a wide mouth that could exhale melodious whispers. His sun tan was as evenly spread as a marble pallor and his black curls were carefully groomed. I could feel Eira's arm tremble as she took mine. The presence of the young couple made the pictures in the gallery even more vivid and alive. Eira began to mutter something about 'The Marriage' in my ear until I became embarrassed and insisted on moving away.

Later in the modest restaurant near the Gare du Sud, by a coincidence that transfixed us both, the young couple settled in the next table to ours. We heard the man's assertive tones ordering their luncheon. It was French with an American accent. He looked after her so well. They were a devoted couple. Eira and I began to murmur to each other as though we were in church. I could not help myself watching as the handsome fellow cut up the meat on the girl's plate to make it so much easier for her to eat. I remember thinking that if angels ate, this is how they would do it: the movement of her jaw was so delicate and discreet and her beautiful lips in no way distorted. He caught me watching. I blushed and he nodded understandingly. In his clear voice he asked us had we enjoyed our visit to the exhibition. Eira and I almost choked in our anxiety to reply suitably to that rich confident American voice. You felt immediately that he belonged to a benevolent ruling class that moved easily through an interesting world that was all theirs to examine and if necessary manage.

Eating in the same place becomes a form of intimacy once you start talking. He was so polite and reassuring. In no time at all we learned that he was a doctor but without a practice and that he had a habit of starting to write books without finishing them. His name was Jean-Pierre Bermont and he came from Atlantic City, New Jersey, of all places, but we were not to hold that against him. Luciana, his wife, came from Laveno on Lago Maggiore which she considered the most beautiful spot in all the world, and for that reason they made their headquarters in Stresa so that they could look across the lake at the islands and the Alps and her birthplace and admire them all. The truth was she could see a lot more than you would think. The wind across the water could speak and that meant that Luciana knew more than most people. She was absolutely still as he spoke and the slight smile on her face was as calm as a Ghirlandaio Madonna.

What they learned about us came from Eira who did most of the talking. I could hardly take my eyes off Luciana. Where did all that calm and inner strength come from? Whatever the extent of her blindness, she seemed to turn it to positive advantage. He was intrigued to learn that both the Welsh sisters painted, but in totally different styles. As he and Eira talked they seemed to be building with amazing speed a commonality of interests and reactions. Eira didn't fail to bring in the *Mabinogi* and he took such a close interest as more and more information flowed from her excited lips. At last Luciana made the slightest move with her hand on the table and instantly Jean-Pierre jumped to his feet. He gave the impression that he existed chiefly in order to respond to his wife's unspoken wishes.

While I was still contemplating the gracious style of Luciana's movements, Eira had given Jean-Pierre our address in Haut de Cagne. We had no car and he said it was absolutely essential that we should visit Vence. He was in fact descended from one of the lords of Villeneuve which if you cared to count made him a distant relative of a Queen of England and an Empress of Austria! But all that was nothing compared to the Matisse chapel which was a symphony in white and a complete masterpiece. There was just colour enough he said to make us aware of the overwhelming importance of that precious commodity.

I sensed at least two things. My sister Eira was smitten. If you touched her arm it seemed to vibrate like a string wound too tight. And the handsome Jean-Pierre knew it and had already begun to feed on it. He was an admiration addict. It was the drug that kept him going from one uncompleted project to another. As for myself, my feelings were frozen by the haunting beauty of Luciana. Because of some mysterious condition she seemed a being preserved against the ravages of time: a painting come to life. Alongside her Eira, my pretty sister was already a flower that showed the first signs of withering even when the presence of Jean-Pierre made her smile and sparkle. Within a matter of days, in my sketch book, Luciana's perfect features began to haunt my geometric abstractions.

IV

Our Franco-American friend turned up in some style outside the gates of our pension. The hood of his tourer was down: all very cinematic. But no sign of Luciana. My disappointment was instant and deep. Eira was ready to be swept along between a blue sky and a blue sea like the heroine of a woman's magazine illustration. She wore a diaphanous yellow silk scarf to keep her wayward curls in place. She was the princess and I was her faithful attendant. I sat in the back.

'My Luciana is resting,' he said. 'She sends her love and commands me to take special care of you both.'

It was only a form of greeting but the idea of the perfect creature sending us her love gave me a special pleasure. How much could she see as she rested in her darkened room? It was impossible to measure, but how much more I would have liked to be sitting alongside her bed. What I envied most as I sat in the back of Jean-Pierre's tourer was the privilege he enjoyed of looking after the wonderful girl.

Outside the Mairie he pulled up unexpectedly and while we waited with bated breath he began to pick a posy of red carnations growing in the municipal flower beds. He left the door of the car open as he did it. He presented the posy to Eira.

'From the land of flowers,' he said, 'to the lady made of flowers.'

Eira gurgled with excitement and said how remarkable he should remember. On the steps of the Mairie somebody in uniform had started shouting. He managed to turn and apologise to me before we shot off at an alarming angle and the car door slammed shut.

'There stands a bureaucrat,' he said. 'Not a drop of poetry in his make-up. Can't wait to arrest me.'

As we drove on he claimed to be much more Provençal than American.

'I have an anarchic nature,' he said. 'Like the troubadours. So it's just as well I have Luciana to keep me in order. My duty to her is absolute.'

These kind of protestations I knew only served to intensify Eira's infatuation. It wasn't so much a man she needed as an idol before which to prostrate herself in worship. As she geared herself to contemplate this selfless paragon, the world around her would become hypnotically beautiful. By such a means her painting would attain a fresh peak and at last she would do herself justice.

We went swimming in a private beach to which Jean-Pierre had access. At least they did. In the blue water among the porphyry rocks. I sat between lentisk and lavender in the shade of a wild olive nursing my own thoughts. What does absolute mean? He was frolicking in the water with my sister. Her bathing costume was too loose and her breasts were being exposed and she didn't seem to notice. So what did it matter? Absolute only becomes absolute when the word need no longer be spoken. When you come to conclusions you usually land in a territory just outside the reach of words. Perhaps that is why I spend my whole life struggling to be a painter.

As the days passed in a dream Chagall might well have painted, many an afternoon, Jean-Pierre took us sight seeing and Luciana stayed home to rest. One of the few jocular things I still remember her saying was that she had developed the siesta into a state where therapy became a fine art. When she chose to speak we all fell silent: intent on whatever she might be disposed to say. Her English was limited and her fluttering accent wholly delightful. On our expeditions without Luciana, Jean-Pierre and Eira seemed to grow much more interested in each other than in the churches or the ancient hill towns we were supposed to be visiting. As I stared at some splashing fountain built in the form of a giant urn covered with mysterious patterns, they wandered off, absorbed in each other. When we returned to our pension I listened to Eira with unusual restraint and patience because I wanted to piece together the fabric of life that surrounded and protected the delicate Luciana. I surmised that her infatuation with Jean-Pierre Bermout was deeper than any she had enjoyed, and of course suffered, before. He seemed to exist for her on an altogether higher level than the emaciated bard Heilyn Hughes. All her life of course Eira has been eager to approach good-looking men. I used to catch her gazing eagerly at some stranger or other as if he would be the bearer of a message she had been waiting all her life to hear. We sat out on the terrace drinking coffee after dinner under the starlit sky, and she told me in an excited subdued voice, sharing a deep secret, that Luciana had a weak heart. They could not sleep together because the noise of her pacemaker kept him awake. She was as delicate and as precious as a piece of rare porcelain. It was an illness that preserved her in an appearance of perpetual youth. Jean-Pierre felt guilty because of his own robust health: and the dear girl was more than ready to forgive him because of the care he took of her and the depth of his dedication and the overwhelming unselfishness of his love.

I listened and said little. Eira was perfectly aware of the characteristic behaviour patterns that governed her life: she lived across the street, just out of my hearing in order to foster them. She once declared it was more than an inclination, it was a necessity: and she closed my front door before I could level any criticism at her. On the Cote d'Azur she gave me to understand that this was more than an adventure. It was life – and therefore art – enhancing. I could only wonder how far they went and what she allowed him to do. All around us there were mass communications blathering on about the permissive age. I felt I had been born old-fashioned. I wondered in the schoolgirl parlance of my sheltered youth whether they had gone 'all the way', and for various reasons I concluded they hadn't. On the other hand I could have been wrong. I had thoughts of my own and I never subjected the two of them to twenty-four-hour surveillance. Eira could burble on openly about Jean-Pierre. My stifled obsession with Luciana was a deep secret.

Once I was able to sit alongside her dark blue day-bed and read to her in my imperfect French. I stumbled and I barely understood what I was saying, but Luciana smiled and in her quiet voice said my accent showed the poem in a new light. It went on at length about the mind struggling to free itself from the body. I didn't mind the length. It was a conflict between serenity and ecstasy and that was what I felt. She held out her hand. It was so soft. I longed to fondle it and put it to my lips.

V

One evening we dined with the Bermonts on the quayside of the old port at Antibes. I had seen a lot of Matisse and had fantasised at length about painting Luciana in a red interior, sitting behind a still life on a blue table: or with an anonymous female, representing myself, with a hand under my chin gazing at her image in a state of permanent enchantment. I knew it was a ridiculous day-dream but I indulged in it. Our days in the sun had become variations on a theme. Luciana sat demurely at the table and behind her there was a polite background of white yachts and fishing boats, and up the hillside, Jean-Pierre told us authoritatively, Josephine's villa.

'I have to tell you this,' he was saying. 'You are very remarkable. Both of you.'

I had noticed when Luciana was present he would include me in his discourse. No doubt to make up for ignoring me when he took us on one of his outings.

'Both of you. Two sisters living across the street from each other and dedicated to painting in styles that are even further apart. And yet pretty devoted to each other. Honestly we can't wait to have a look at your work, can we Luciana?'

She listened to him with a detached intentness as though she were a spectator at a play that needed close attention to be understood.

'I'm such a hopeless amateur myself. Such a lightweight!'

I could see Eira's lips forming a silent protest. She didn't speak for fear of interrupting the oracle.

'I just flit from one subject to another. I could learn so much from you. About persistence. And dedication.'

I thought I knew what Eira was thinking. Her hero was too

richly endowed, too gifted in too many directions. And he had sacrificed a range of brilliant careers in order to dedicate himself to the care of his fragile wife. My sister looked blissful in the pale light from the interior of the restaurant. She could have been listening to music just outside the reach of my hearing. There had to be something exquisite about imagined illicit love which I assumed she was enjoying and I was determined not to envy her.

A tall black man in a white turban approached our table with a tray of gold and silver rings and bracelets. To Jean-Pierre he appeared to be a familiar figure. They smiled at each other and were cordial in elementary French. The man moved at his leisure, clearly licensed to circulate the tables. I felt suddenly emboldened. His wares must have been genuine and did not seem unreasonably priced. I had an unusually large amount of money in my leather purse. With a particular calm I selected a gold bracelet so that I could reach sideways and clip it over Luciana's thin wrist. There was a discreet round of applause. Everybody was impressed. No one more than I myself.

'It's far less than what we owe you,' I said.

Eira agreed vehemently. Luciana kissed me on the cheek. I will never forget the cool touch of her lips. To me it was more than a benediction. When we reached the pension that night we were in agreement that we had never been happier: each in her own way.

VI

It couldn't last. These transports never do. We began to receive urgent messages from our brother Francis. It was time to return home. There were urgent documents that needed signing. Eira was determined not to move.

'He can't bear to see us enjoying ourselves,' she said. 'If there are papers to sign let him send them out here.'

We had established a way of life and as far as Eira was concerned it could go on for ever. I ventured one evening to ask her what she was hoping for when she said nothing more than what we had already. I couldn't fault her reply. Francis however, grew more furious than ever. The documents could not be allowed to leave the lawyer's office, and if we did not return within a matter of days we would be faced with a financial crisis that would change our lives for ever. He said we might even be obliged to sell one of our houses and live together under the same roof. It was as bad as that.

'He's bluffing,' Eira said.

I had never seen her so resolute or so bold. Usually I was the one designated to face our brother's fury and make an effort at answering back.

'It's the same old thing,' Eira said. 'He thinks of us as a pair of parasitical butterflies. All I can say is we do a damn sight less harm in the world than he does.'

Then to my amazement she lit a Turkish cigarette. Or at least that was what it smelt like.

I took Francis's threats more seriously than did Eira. Perhaps my attachment to Luciana was a degree less euphoric than her ongoing flirtatious infatuation with Jean-Pierre. After all, her excursions and escapades were high adventure: all I seemed to be doing was assembling an archive of Luciana's smiles. The most intense sensation I was left to cherish was the day when we sat waiting together on a bench in Princess Pauline's Garden and she touched my hand and said:

'Lucy. Luciana. We are the same? Daughters of light?'

She spoke as though the thought had been in her mind for some time.

'We are part of the same poem? Do you think?'

I had to breathe deeply in order not to burst out into tears. Within a day or two after this our problem was solved. Jean-Pierre arrived at our pension with the news that he and Luciana had been summoned back to Stresa. Luciana's mother who lived in Laveno was dangerously ill. And that was that. Nice and environs were as empty as the wastes of the Gobi Desert without Jean-Pierre and Luciana. After a trough of depression Eira declared there was so much to be salvaged.

'They'll be coming to see us,' she said. 'Next spring at the latest. Jean-Pierre will stay with you and Luciana with me.'

She turned her mouth down in mock disapproval before giving one of her silvery laughs. We left for home in reasonably good spirits.

VII

I cannot imagine what possessed Francis to bring that man Solomon Wickens to see us, apart from his habitual weakness for showing off. Francis wore brown boots to underline that he saw himself as a countryman: a large and would be jovial farmer wearing a raincoat down to his ankles and a battered soft hat, with his hands in his pockets and his unprotected stomach sticking out, presenting his sisters to this stranger as though they were prize exhibits of his in a cattle pen.

'Here they are,' he said. 'My sisters I was telling you about. Busily engaged in painting the inside of a bushel.'

The Wickens creature shook his shoulders obligingly although I doubt whether he had much idea what Francis was talking about. We were given to understand that he was Flashlight Films and that Francis had bought himself a seat on the Governing Board. This was the end of the seventies and there was much talk everywhere of the burgeoning television industry and a host of opportunities of making easy money. Francis was clearly determined not to lose out: but why drag us into it? He was just showing off. Apparently at a Board Meeting he had claimed to have a special interest, even an inside knowledge, of the visual arts. Wickens had a way of prancing about and rubbing his hands like an actor taking too much pleasure in his own performance. He had woolly hair and a red face and staring eyes that seemed to insist you should agree with everything he said.

'It's such a wonderful set up, isn't it?' he said. 'Two delightful sisters living across the street from each other and painting in totally different styles. Where do you exhibit? I can just see it. Mix ever so slowly from the exhibition to the separate houses and the separate studios.'

He was making expressive motions with his large hands, making a picture frame. I had a distinct feeling it was all getting out of hand like a vehicle careering down hill. Francis had said something about a television company needing cultural credentials.

'We don't,' I said.

'I beg your pardon?'

He raised his bushy black eyebrows in an actorish idea of courtly enquiry.

'We don't exhibit,' I said. 'And we definitely don't make a spectacle of ourselves in front of the cameras. Do we, Eira?'

'No we don't'.

Her agreement was so half-hearted. I suspected she would really have liked to. After all she was pretty. It would have been like looking in a mirror for a little reassurance. But I wasn't having any of it. And without one of these two sisters Mr. Solomon Wickens' fancy concept would not work. He didn't entirely give up. He begged to have a look at our stuff. Eira gave in: so I had to too, or appear churlish. His praise was lavish and I am quite sure excessive. It was obvious to me that he had no idea what he was talking about. Eira's work is as different from mine as chalk from cheese but he kept insisting that he saw what he called a generic relationship. He even talked about a family style. I had to restrain myself from blurting out that he was talking piffle.

'You know...'

He put his hand on his brow as though a startling new idea was fermenting inside it. He addressed Francis first and then the two weird sisters.

'You know, Judith should see these. Judith van Linz. A very dear friend of mine. She runs the Obelisk Gallery in Muswell Hill. They have a gallery too in Leatherhead. But Judith *lives* in Muswell Hill when she's not in her place in Minorca.'

I kept so quiet they had no idea how fiercely I resented their intrusion. I had acquired a rare elixir of life and I needed peace and quiet to mix it with my narrow range of paints to give them a quickening luminosity. And I needed solitude to explore. A fallen wall could be an intense experience suspended in space. That's what the connection between an individual life and the natural world was all about: exploration and reinvention in artistic form. How could I spare any time or strength on any other activity and how else express my debt of love to Luciana? Into my own familiar world I brought her presence: the paths I took through the rocks and the woods her spirit took with me: and that was something that could never be said.

'Well now then girls...'

I was always on my guard when the furious Francis began to make friendly noises.

'I've managed to pick up two nice little wodges of commercial telly shares for you both. We can expect them to treble in value over the next few months.'

He rubbed his hands with an unconcealed glee that seemed to me to verge on the obscene. We had signed too many papers. We had handed over to him too many powers. He was able to do what he liked with the Trust, and short of going to law, and some almighty rumpus, I, and certainly Eira, could not even begin to contemplate, there wasn't much we could do to stop him. No more signatures I said to myself: knowing it was probably too late anyway and Eira would be soft enough to give in yet again for the sake of a quiet life, or as she would say herself, 'so as not to hurt Francis's feelings,' which I would dismiss as stuff and nonsense since I knew Francis had very few feelings for anything or anyone except himself and his untiring efforts to make more money.

'I can't understand why you don't sell any of your pictures, girls. Honestly. There must be some bloody fool somewhere who would be ready to buy them. At the right price of course.'

He still believed all our efforts and explorations were nothing more than subsidised self-indulgence. I contemplated the grim reality. In more than twenty years he had never made the slightest effort to try and understand what it was Eira and I were about, because he didn't have the slightest desire to know. To him we were just a pair of silly women allowed to play about with paint on condition we signed the proper papers at the proper intervals. We could have been a pair of mentally deficient patients housed in separate shelters of secure accommodation. So long as we signed what he asked us to sign, it suited him that we were neatly locked up in our own absurd concerns.

VIII

I regarded Judith van Linz with deep suspicion when she first arrived. What was she after? It was a wet and windy October day and she wore a grey cloak as wide as a ship's sail that threatened to blow her clean away. Her affectation of breathless sincerity was rendered genuinely breathless by the weather. She said she couldn't bear it and I restrained myself from saying in that case why did you bother to come? As the weather got worse there was an expression of horrified amazement on her face which suggested she couldn't make out why my sister and I had chosen to live and work in such a clouded dismal dripping hole. I did remark quite sharply that bad weather was bad weather wherever you found yourself on our planet; and in any case that as far as I knew lots of human creatures prayed for rain: none as far as I knew ever went on their knees to beg for drought. This made her laugh and in any case I gathered it was her intention to please. The fact is, after an initial coolness, we became quite friendly. She studied my pictures through those large owlish spectacles of hers and I studied her ear rings and bracelets and pouting red lips with a certain disapproval until I realised she was genuinely interested.

'This is an agony in a rocky garden,' she said, 'but do I detect an unseen presence?'

She spoke all the time as though she was aware she was treading on delicate ground. She was able to demonstrate a wider vocabulary than I ever could as she spoke of planes and the recognition of space and three-dimensionality and the opaque and unopaque eloquence of my browns: how their relationships varied and how sometimes they seemed positively to be singing to each other. I began to listen to her quite greedily and I could feel myself ready to slip under her influence.

What held me back was the way she tried to probe into my relationship with my sister. This put me on my guard and kept me back from open and frank communication with a woman who nevertheless clearly understood the creative process and may have been the very person ordained to tell the world what my painting was all about: a recognition of the depth of understanding that came from struggling to explore the depths of one particular place.

'There's much sorrow here,' she said. 'Something of the intensity of unstinting love that a mother can give an autistic child. Or am I saying too much?'

She could say what she liked. She responded with such spontaneous feeling to my pictures, I was able myself to study them in a fresh light. In the end it came to what she was after: an exhibition in her gallery in Muswell Hill. She talked it up so much that I got quite excited, until I thought of Eira.

'What about my sister?' I said.

There was an unusually long pause. Her pouting mouth opened and closed with hesitation as her mind raced ahead to prepare an acceptable formula before she actually spoke.

'Ah well,' she said. 'Therein lies the rub.'

'What rub?'

I was anxious and insistent on plain speaking.

'I can't find a way of saying this without hurting somebody's feelings. Artistic integrity is a hard taskmaster. How can I put it? Quite frankly Lucy, Eira's work is not in the same league as yours.'

This was a verdict that gave equal pain and pleasure. Maybe Eira's fantasies and romantic yearnings were of no interest to me: but she was my sister. We might have looked semi-detached or indeed fully detached to the outside world, but we depended on each other as on no other human being. Even in my most ecstatic phases I had to acknowledge that brilliant and inspiring as love and infatuation undoubtedly were, for everyday use there was no substitute for reliability. I didn't say as much then. It was a field of my existence that I wouldn't want Judith van Linz to peer at, let alone enter.

'I couldn't possibly exhibit without Eira,' I said.

There was much expostulation and talk of schools and influences and trends and traditions but I stood firm.

'We could have separate rooms,' I said.

I almost suggested one of us could be in Muswell Hill and the other in Leatherhead. It wouldn't have been any use. Judith made it clear that my sister was a lovely person but she didn't have any interest in her work and had no desire to sponsor it.

We left the matter like that. On the table as they say. And I didn't tell my sister anything about it.

IX

My little house contains my little life. I was working intently on a large canvas when the knock came on my front door: four short taps meant it was Eira. I was furious. At that very instant I was keyed up to conjure sparkle and glow out of a juxtaposition of black and white rocks with streaks of luminous brown of my own making. It was a delicate difficult operation and my thoughtless sister had no business to interrupt my concentrated effort so early in the morning. I tried to keep her waiting but the experiment collapsed, the inspiration evaporated and I was compelled to unlock the front door.

She stood there holding a sheet of paper in her hand. Across the street our lethargic postman was still delivering letters.

'Dreadful news,' she said. 'Luciana's dead. I can't believe it.'

I stood there glowering at my sister, unable to speak or to move or even blink. I was growing so cold inside I could believe I was dead myself. Whatever she was saying washed over me. It was a frozen moment of my life. I couldn't tell Eira that her words were turning me into a pillar of salt. I could see the tears coursing down her cheeks. Who was she crying for?

'He looked after her so well,' she was saying. 'Poor Jean-Pierre. He must be devastated.'

Where did she get that word from? Was he a ruin then? A brick with too many straws in it? I seem to have passed my life standing in my bedroom window wondering about it. Outside is the street: a dry river of life on which I provide myself with a running commentary. Inside the studio is still the heart of my existence. There is always a cloud of menacing dust that threatens to settle in a thick film over everything. I have to paint ever more vigorously to dispel it. My brush will renew Luciana's existence, although she remains invisible. This is my way of life since the day I lost her. It's all to do with the profundities of asking what is the point of everything. If she is dead how can she still be the light of my life?

Jean-Pierre turned up within a year or so just as Eira hoped, from the very moment she knew that Luciana was dead. I don't blame her. I only stood as I'm standing now and saw his American motor car parked outside her house: as strange and as outsized it seemed to me as a decorated elephant. After all he was the object of her affections: and as always her sentiments are so much more voluble than mine.

Judith van Linz was visiting me. We had come to an arrangement. She had begun to spirit away my pictures in twos and threes: on the strict understanding that Eira would know nothing about it and that my authorship was confined to the semi-anonymity of the letters LB, scribbled discreetly in the right hand corner of the frame. The secret grew into a bond between us. Judith had plans to cultivate a clientele: more than that she said, to create a cult. 'There's nothing like a cult,' she used to say. 'You can watch it grow like a plant in a hot house to quite exotic proportions.' We confided in each other a great deal. We discussed profundities as well as prices. As they say in those stupid films I watch on television when I'm too tired to go on working, Judith was 'straight with me.' All the same I never told her about Luciana.

We had a quiet laugh together about Jean-Pierre. He was so transparent. So obviously a moth. A male flibbertigibbet. He always turned up as though the whole world would be delighted to see him. He barely looked at Eira's pictures and never even glanced at mine, but he assumed we were totally flattered by his admiration and attention. 'You clever ladies,' he would say. 'If only I had half your vision and persistence I'm sure I would be a happier and more useful man. Where shall we go today, do you think?'

Trips were still his thing. Eira said that when Luciana died he had applied for a post as a flying doctor in Australia. He was quite resolved to make a new life for himself. Then something happened that quite put him off. Eira couldn't exactly remember what, and I restrained myself from wondering aloud would it have been hard work by any chance? She said somebody or other had been nasty to him.

It was my idea that we all went for a climb together. The four of us. There was this myth about spending a night on Cader Idris: you came down either a madman or a poet. Jean-Pierre was very intrigued. We wouldn't spend the night up there, Judith and Eira weren't willing, but at least we'd go and have a look. The day we went started bright with watery sunlight. To cheer Judith up I said it was a light you would never see anywhere else: a magic balance the earth demanded: water and sunlight, mist and magic. And when we reached the summit the mist descended. I wasn't worried, but Judith and Eira were terrified. And then the mist turned to rain and their terror to moaning misery. Halfway down Judith slipped and twisted her ankle. Jean-Pierre suddenly remembered he was a doctor and became unbelievably brisk and efficient. He bound her ankle and she weighed on him for the rest of the way down.

I have to admit I was really enjoying it. I even went as far as to say that to be a success a trip needed to be taxing. We took refuge in an inn and the rare comfort of drinking beer in front of a roaring fire. I ventured to raise my glass and declare we should do this more often. I got little support. Jean-Pierre was ready to launch on a new enthusiasm and we had to hear about it. We were a captive audience in front of the log fire while the rain poured down outside. Willing captives to a great extent: Eira with her eyes glittering with admiration in the firelight and Judith apparently listening in spite of herself. 'California,' he said. That was the place to be. We should all make a big trip to California together.

'That's where it's all happening,' he said. 'We need to see it as it unfolds. Sense that atmosphere. With the greatest respect, dear ladies, Europe is finished. Except as the ultimate dreamscape of course. A cultural theme park. That's all it is. Okay. Okay. I love it just as much as you do in my own barbaric and wayward fashion. But it's all past with a capital 'P'. Monuments and museums. Folk dancing and fancy dress. A tail-end mish-mash of nostalgia and tourism. Over there the future is just getting into its stride. It's all invention and enterprise. The dawn of new ideas. We've got to go there. Get the smell of the place. See what it's all about.'

All that eager eloquence depressed me. He declared himself a cosmopolitan as though that was the ideal, the only and the ultimate. If that was so, where would it leave me? A lichen on a stone. A fossil underfoot. Something to be ignored and blithely trodden on. I was isolated because Eira was listening to his flawed gospel message with rapt attention: and so, to my dismay, was Judith.

X

She rang and she wrote. She wrote and she rang. But she never came here again. The last time was from Heathrow.

'Don't think badly of me, Lucy. Explain things to Eira. He's such fun to be with. That's my only excuse. He says he finds me irresistible. Of course I know that's rubbish. And he's insisted we get married. For his folks' sakes and for heaven's sakes. I don't know. My head is spinning, that's all I know. I'm signing my independence away and its goodbye to my lovely galleries. What on earth am I doing? It won't last. I give it five years at the most. Honeymoon in Tahiti and New Zealand and a new life in California. Can you believe it? Dear Lucy. You know I love your work. Don't give up. And don't think badly of me.'

I hardly thought anything of her by then. Heathrow indeed! I could barely make out what the woman was saying. There were voices everywhere: desperate noises as though a whole species were threatened with extinction and struggling for survival. I had to be concerned for my sister. Was her heart broken? If it was she would never admit it. She was tougher than she looked, my sister Eira and I was very glad of that. She was hurt. There were occasions when I heard her give a deep sigh for no apparent reason. And she would pass unexpected remarks such as 'You live for a minute or so and spend the rest of your life thinking about it.' Or, 'Could it have been as wonderful as all that? It couldn't have been'. There was such a tinge of sadness in her voice I used to think of ways of giving her some fresh zest for life and banishing that romantic illusion that was clearly still haunting her.

I drew her into a prolonged struggle with the furious Francis and that nauseating firm of solicitors he employs in Clwyd. At least disappointments sharpen the wits: with a little effort they can also stiffen the will to resist. The steps he wanted to take would increase his income and reduce ours.

'You don't need so much, girls.'

It was such a bare faced presumption: as if he were talking to a pair of schoolgirls instead of two women on the verge of the menopause.

'You've got a nice little way of life and nothing at all to worry about. You've no idea what it's like in the financial jungle where I have to make a living. You talk about the world learning to live on less. So why don't you practice what you preach? Set an example, for God's sake.'

We would never have had the nerve to preach. But his taunts were enough to push us further into the ranks of the activists. We refused to sign his papers. Instead we increased our subscriptions to a range of good causes. Eira was just as determined as I was. She was even more active. Everything we did and said seemed to make Francis more furious and he stopped coming to see us. We only communicate these days through two sets of solicitors. Which is absurd to the point of being ungodly. But that's the way it is.

Protesting, we agreed, brought us into contact with a better class of people. We were drawn into a world of cells and societies. What the young people were calling the battle for the language involved a steady sequence of protests against developers and authorities and principals and powers, what Eira and I referred to between ourselves as 'The Silent Plague.' Once you looked at the world from this angle they seemed to pop up all over the place. We never got as far as Greenham Common. Our excuse was there was more than enough to look after in our own little corner of the world. The Chernobyl explosion gave us all a nasty shock and for the first time Eira and I summoned up the courage to join in a protest march. To be quite honest we admitted that we both enjoyed it. However it was no more than a brief cheerful respite.

You can make an impressive picture with brush and colour on a primed canvas: but you can't build a nuclear power station with just a pick and shovel. Twenty years to build and a thousand ages to bring them down. The silent plagues that threatened the planet were governed by invisible powers. In our own quiet way Eira and I became seasoned protesters. We were at it so long we saw student leaders of the most ardent and idealistic kind succumb to the power of the silent plague and start swimming up the only channels the superstructure left open, to greater wealth and importance. It didn't take all that many years for them to mutate. We have such an impossible society to try and change in any way for the better.

For the first time in our lives we agreed to hold an exhibition. It was to be in the old Parish hall at Penymaes and the proceeds would be in aid of the families of the coal miners' strike. Not that it would buy them much in the way of provisions. It was a symbolic gesture, Gwenfron ap Hywel said, a demonstration that solidarity mattered. She was a tall strong girl from the hills driven to a permanent state of indignation, she said, by having to put blue spots on the backsides of her sheep to show they were contaminated through nibbling radioactive grass.

Our pictures were hung in different rooms. Eira's were more popular than mine even though her prices were higher. She had titles on hers like 'Dawn' and 'Aber Falls' and 'Sighs and Wishes' and goodness knows what. All I could think of was numbers and dates. For the sake of appearances I put up my prices. Gwenfron held the canvas as I did it. She conspired with me to allow me to buy them back myself.

This was when Heilyn Hughes turned up again. He had given up smoking and put on weight. I might well not have recognised him since most of his hair had gone and two front teeth had become more conspicuous and made his smile even more ingratiating. He said he was on our side. How could he not be; being both a poet and a preacher. He stood there dry-washing his hands and wishing I would move away so that he could enjoy a more intimate conversation with Eira.

Gwenfron's hill farm was called Hafod y Gedol. I was made welcome there and there were cairns and outcrops and prehistoric remains on that land that gave my painting a new impetus. Her husband was a little prehistoric himself. He looked strong enough to wrestle with a bear. He said very little but you could tell by the way he looked at his wife that he adored her. After all she was a graduate who had chosen of her own free will this way of life, which to a spoilt town dweller like myself appeared austere and at times isolated and uncomfortable. Fine for sunlit picnics. Tough when the sheep were buried under the snow and the tractor was the best hope of bringing in supplies and the children home from school.

For me it was a pleasant place to visit. I took care not to impose myself. I wondered what would be the best way I could express my affection and my admiration for that outpost of independence. We were part of a group outside the County Hall protesting against a diabolical plan to dispose of nuclear waste in a disused quarry not six miles from Hafod y Gedol. We were stamping our feet and sipping hot tea and chatting to pass the time when I suggested to Gwenfron that I would like to do something to help with the education of two of her boys, Arwel and Owain. A Trust fund perhaps in their name. Something towards their later education. She shook her head vigorously. She was so emphatic about not needing it I feared I had hurt her feelings and even damaged our friendship. I resolved never to mention the subject again. All I did was draw up a will in her favour and deposit it with our lawyer. It amused me to imagine what a pleasant surprise she would get when this sterile spinster's time was up.

XI

I paint. I go on protests. I write letters to the local press under a variety or pseudonyms: "Seithenyn, Disgusted, One of the People, A Friend of Glaslyn, Gwynedd/Llŷn... 'Name and address supplied.'" They are as full of facts and figures as fruit in a Christmas pudding and Gwenfron sees to it I am supplied with data that is accurate and up to date. She has a team of correspondents who fire away at her direction. I smother any sombre inclination to compare myself to King Canute and Maelgwn Gwynedd and plod on as hard as I can to please her. She is such an admirable woman. And I like to imagine what is left of my life is still suffused with that trace of love that Luciana left me.

I spend too much time in my bedroom window wondering what my sister is up to; and, maybe, waiting for a wonder. Eira admires Gwenfron too, but she is also scared of her. Somehow she has succeeded in keeping out of the letter writing rota. She has a tendency to pose as a preoccupied genius. It is a reputation she enjoys among our protesting sorority and I can't say to what extent she has cultivated it. Eira is meditating a new work. She must not be disturbed. Have a word with Lucy. She's not as fierce as she looks.

She was always a delicate flower. Somebody started that rumour. That sweet little creature does not enjoy Lucy's rude health and iron constitution. Nonsense really. She's just as healthy as I am and even more determined. We have to live inside the roles assigned to us. It's quite a mystery to know who does the assigning. It is a fact that she is more attached than I am to home comforts. She collects vegetarian cook books and claims to enjoy cooking. I just think it's a waste of time.

I must have blinked. The car outside her house has vanished. The street and even the world seems suddenly empty without it.

If I wait, will it come back? Across the street a man I know by sight moves between the trees, walking with two sticks. I feel a momentary concern. The last time I saw him he was using only one. I cannot tell how long ago. The street and the trees display the ageing process. And if I stand in the window any longer I shall be covered with cobwebs.

I was preparing myself the simplest of nourishing suppers – bread and milk followed by black coffee and two Aberffraw biscuits – when I heard Eira's four sharp raps on my front door. This was most unusual. We rarely eat together and if we do it's in her house rather than mine. She scurries in as if she were escaping from a pursuer. She is obviously the bearer of bad news.

'Rebecca has had a stroke.'

I snatched the pan of bread and milk off the gas ring, struggling hard to recall who Rebecca might be. To my sister this was obviously a calamity. It took a few seconds for me to grasp that she was talking about the imposing figure of Heilyn Hughes' wife. The large woman had been struck down and Eira was deeply affected. Of course she had been in closer touch with the poet than she had ever let on. I wasn't blaming her. It was in order for each to mind her own business that we lived in separate houses. Eira always had a wider social circle.

'She's in a wheelchair,' she was saying. 'It's very hard on him. He's not so strong himself.'

I offered her some hot bread and milk. She waved it aside. She was deep in thought and decision making.

'He wants me to go to them. Help them out. He wants me to move in. It's a large house. On the sea front. He could never manage by himself.'

I was taken by surprise and I had to restrain myself from making sarcastic comment. Housekeeper. Home help. Cook and bottle washer. Mistress? What was she supposed to be, for heaven's sake?

'You're not going?'

How could I be anything but unsympathetic to such an absurd proposition. My tone of voice immediately put her back up.

'Of course I am.'

'You can't possibly...'

'Why not?'

'What about your painting?'

This made her smile.

'Since when have you been worried about my painting? The poor things are desperate.'

'It's that Heilyn creature. He's taking advantage of you.'

'That's just what I want him to do,' she said.

'But he's such a feeble creature. He's not much of a poet either, if it comes to that.'

'You don't like him,' she said. 'You never did.'

'It's not that. Not at all. I tell you the truth. As I always do. It's the Truth that matters.'

In spite of my irritation I could not help being impressed by her calm.

'Affection and warmth are more important than the truth.'

She spoke with such conviction my irritation turned to anger.

'That's rubbish,' I said.

'I'm going,' Eira said. 'I'm going where I'm most needed.'

She stood up and I realised it was her last word on the subject. I shouted in an attempt to detain her.

'Do you think I don't need you?'

She turned to smile at me before closing the door.

An Ethnic Tremor

A girl at the steering wheel and her grandmother shrinking in the passenger seat. The impatient traffic behind them, another hairpin bend ahead, and at this altitude the leaves of spring not grown enough to conceal the chasm and the rocks and the foaming torrents below them. The girl's hair was tied back by a white head band and her manner was resolutely jolly.

'Come on now Sirikins! Think of it as an adventure... oops!'

She clutched at the wheel as if it could also function as a lifebelt. Her grandmother appeared too small for the slack safety belt limp across her lap. She gripped each side of her poorly sprung seat muttering to herself and plainly wishing both the road and the adventure out of existence. A grandmother was entitled to dote on her grand-daughter and give her anything she asked for and enjoy the mere process of giving in. This extended essay on the German occupation of Slovenia was the lynch pin in the girl's course work, and a first class in the course work was vital to the final assessment. And who would enjoy basking in her reflected glory more than her grandmother and in the end it was enough to persuade a doting grandmother to cross the Karawanken Alps and visit a past she had spent the best part of her adult life trying to forget. She had been pretty little Sigrid Ungart once, and she had inbred childhood prejudices to contend with: south of the mountains lurked an uncongenial people who didn't try to speak German properly: a disloyal disaffected thoroughly unreliable race. This quondam Yugoslavia, this Slovene province, was a place to avoid not revisit.

And yet the girl was delightful and to have her to herself at any time was one of life's most pleasurable privileges, but this journey was already proving to be anything but pleasurable. What she took to be an ominous knocking in the diesel engine of the ancient Mercedes, which they had hired so impetuously in the garage at Obergratschach, set her teeth on edge.

To reach the top and the Austrian customs and the mouth of the Loibeltunnel was no relief.

'This car is not fit to go any further,' Siri said. 'There's enough room to turn back here, Meg. I can tell you all about it. We don't have to go there.'

'Onward and upward!'

The girl was too pleased with herself and too determined to take any notice.

'The worst part is over anyway.'

She leaned over to give her grandmother one of her most winning smiles. They were supposed to resemble each other in looks and character. Everyone in the family said so and Siri had taken to believing it religiously. Much as she wanted to she couldn't pull back now. She couldn't disappoint that charming smiling face.

Inside the Loibeltunnel, she found everything including the noise of the engine, even more menacing. She decreed all tunnels to be unnatural, a crime against nature. Where was all the water supposed to go? The Alps were created to protect us and the tunnels were undermining them.

'Protect us from what Siri Parry? The lesser breeds without the Law?'

Siri's objection to tunnels became more vehement. They were unhealthy. And the roof could fall in. They were artificial. Her voice became plaintive. That was the trouble with the world. Men just couldn't leave anything be. Endless male aggression. Yet another symptom. At the Slovene control point, still blinking in the sunlight she handed out their American passports without looking at the uniformed officer. *Sigrid Parry and Megan Parry-Rutger.* Useful vacations in search of antecedents, forebears, ancestors. There had been a nineteenth-century immigrant named Anton Rutger. The Swiss Rutgers were a wild goose chase. Looking for possible relatives in the Zurich telephone book... Siri seemed trapped in her seat. She sulked and relied on her white hair to mask her identity and allay any suspicion. The frontier policemen were more interested in the girl at the wheel:

blue eyes and black hair and the kind of frank open smile with dimples that men everywhere find encouraging. If there were any delay in being waved on it was due to their interest in Megan rather than the US passports.

Austrian cars behind them turned into the car park of the new supermarket and duty-free shop. Going down to Trazic, Siri transferred her disapproval of tunnels to checkpoints and frontiers.

'Who needs them?' she said. 'What are they good for in the modern world?'

'You are an awful rebel, Sirikins,' Megan said. 'You really are. The trick is I've got to put myself in your place.'

'Well you can't, can you.'

Siri sounded cross. 'You are you and I am me. I had to stay here. I had no choice. I hated it.'

Megan was confident enough to look around as though in search of some quality she might also dislike. She was too pleased with herself for having conquered the pass on both sides of the Alps. She began to feel an affection for the old Mercedes and petted the wheel as if it were the head of a faithful steed. She had to take in the lofty magnificence of the surrounding mountains. They towered into the blue sky with snow still streaking the jagged peaks.

'Here we are,' Megan said. 'This is fairy land. And I have to know what it's like to put myself in your place, Sirikins.'

'Well you can't, can you?' her grandmother said. 'I don't know that I can either. I was nearly twenty then and I'm nearly eighty now. And two inches shorter. So there you are.'

'But still the same underneath. That's what I'm saying.'

'Frayed around the edges. That's true enough. But still the same 'me' inside. Whoever that may be.'

'That's what I'm saying. Sigrid Ungart. Siri Parry. And Sirikins. And still the same old rebel.'

'Old world' Megan insisted on calling it. Coaching inns alongside the road should have horses and carts not motor cars in their courtyards. Village streets were hemmed in by houses with roofs leaning forward like gossiping neighbours. Megan was keyed up to absorb everything. In the meadows stretching along-side the open road women were making early hay. The long grass hung out on racks under narrow roofs in the middle of the fields. Megan was intrigued by the women in their scarves and their pinafores working with wooden rakes and pitchforks with what looked like age-old patience.

'It's like a children's picture book,' she said. 'Does it all look the same?'

'It seems so. And yet it can't be. I used to wonder what they had to eat.'

'They?'

'The local population. I knew it couldn't be as much as we had. We took our rations for granted. Like the Army. '

'The Wehrmacht.'

Megan was eager to sound knowledgeable.

'The Army. What else. Armies are always armies. They get the best food.'

'The master race though. You learnt it all in school. Social Darwinism. Part of nature and all that. Breed for the best and produce the perfect German race.'

'Horrible rubbish.'

Siri gripped her stomach as though she were enduring a spasm of nausea.

'You said it penetrated a whole education system. You said it lingers on.'

'Did I? Well there you are. Old people say all sorts of things.'

'What was your job exactly?'

'My job?'

The old woman could have been considering the meaning of the phrase for the first time.

'You don't have to tell me anything unless you want to. I don't want to pester you with questions.'

'You couldn't pester me if you tried.'

The closeness of their understanding was the most agreeable thing left in the world. The grandmother's eyes shone and her smile was all encompassing. She wanted her Megan to shine: to be so brilliant that she would live to see the day of her triumph and she would embrace her and bask in her reflected glory. Siri became stern with herself.

'Mind you we shouldn't look too far ahead. Or too far back either. The present moment is the one that really counts.'

It was pleasant to amble along through the tranquil country-side and ponder the nature of time together. Megan thought hard and came up with her own conclusion.

'If there weren't a past there wouldn't be a present, would there? What did you do?'

'Do? I just sat in the front office and looked decorative.'

This was a a joke they could share.

'This was part of Austria. All this. And Austria was part of Germany! "Two eyes of the same head." That's what Uncle Franzi used to say. Because Hitler said it. But it wasn't. It's just this. Somebody else's fatherland to sing about. Slovenia. They must have a national anthem. Their own money. Their own flag. And once it was Yugoslavia with Serbs crawling all over it. That's nationalism for you. The scourge of the world.'

Megan slapped her right hand over her heart and carolled 'God Bless America'. Siri was less inclined to be frivolous.

'Why can't people just be people?' she said. 'I'll never understand it.'

'In that office. What did you do all day?'

'They were governed, so I suppose we did the governing. So boring typing all day. There were raw materials passing through for the war effort. Copper from Serbia. Bauxite from Croatia. Why on earth do I remember that? All those figures on those reports. I don't know what they meant. I wasn't very good at it.'

'But you were so decorative, you got away with it.'

'I used to sing a lot in my head. I remember that. I used to dream about being an opera singer.'

'I meant to ask you what happened to that?'

Siri's fingers fluttered above her head.

'Melted into thin air,' she said. 'The smoke of an enchanted cigarette. An empty dream.'

She warbled a snatch of an unrecognizable aria.

'But it kept me going.'

'Until the gallant Welsh captain came along and proposed to you on the Vienna express. When it was all over.'

In a puzzled silence the old woman appeared to be having difficulty in connecting up separate elements of her past.

'Something like that,' she said.

She heaved a deep sigh before shaking herself free of her tangled thoughts.

'And if it wasn't, my girl,' she said. 'You wouldn't be here.'

It was a pleasant conclusion to arrive at. Megan grasped the steering wheel more tightly as she confronted the mystery of relationships and the furtive nature of time. This frail old lady in range of her touch had once been as young and more beautiful than her own robust self. And they were linked indissolubly together. There was chance and there was destiny and somehow these conflicting concepts had combined to send them wandering in an old Mercedes somewhere west of Trazic.

'But you helped them, Sirikins.'

Megan smiled at her grandmother with affectionate pride.

'Helped who?'

'The Partisans. And that handsome Partisan doctor. What was his name?'

'That's your mother's myth-making.'

Siri looked resolute and determined to face facts.

'A High School girl trying to make up for her mother's buttered Austrian accent.'

'You've got a lovely accent, Sirikins. I adore it and so does everyone else.'

'"Buttered" your grandfather used to say. The Welsh fancy themselves with adjectives. He had an accent himself. He never really got rid of it.'

'Why should he?'

Megan was quick to respond.

'The whole world doesn't have to be ironed out.'

Siri began to chuckle to herself.

'As long as he lived he used to correct my pronunciation under his breath. Not to mention the bad grammar. I can't think why you are not writing about him. Much more edifying. As a subject. A coal miner's son from Bargoed rising to be head of one of the best colleges in New York State.'

'With all due respect, grandmamma, that's just worthy.'

'He was a wonderful man you know.'

'Of course he was.'

'He saved my life, you know. In all sorts of ways. He gave it a new meaning. I miss him so much.'

'Of course you do.'

'He had to emigrate to be appreciated. At home he couldn't get promotion because he didn't have Welsh.'

Siri's eyes watered as self-pity merged into indignation.

'Look at the place. Everything in Slovene.'

She pointed at new road signs.

'How on earth are we expected to find our way? You can't even read the adverts.'

She swivelled about in her seat searching for recognisable landmarks. She pointed at what appeared to be the highest peaks.

'Is that the Triglav or the Mittagskogel? How am I supposed to know. And look at all these yellow signs. I can't tell you how much I hate nationalism. It' s all so petty when you get down to it. Yugoslavia indeed. Hotch-potch. Croats and Serbs and Slovenes and Albanians and god knows what else all at each other's throats. Things were much better here under the Empire. That's what they used to say.'

'The Austro-Hungarian Empire? Before the first World War?'

Megan spoke with careful precision. She had to keep her extended essay in mind. Part of her work plan was to record her grandmother in full spate on tape and then edit the result back in Buffalo.

'When you live in the shadow of history you are never aware of its presence.'

The sound of her grandmother muttering mystic formulae caused Megan immediate concern.

'Listen. We've got to stop somewhere and have a recording session. Strike while the iron is hot. And maybe have a bit to eat. Save up these pearls, Sirikins. They can go straight into my thesis.'

'We were important then, you know. This part was well governed. Milos said so and he knew what he was talking about. An oasis he called it. The still centre in a warring world. That sort of thing.'

'Milos. The Partisan Doctor?'

The recorder and the picnic lunch were in the boot. Megan had to find a pretty spot where they could park and record and eat.

'Uncle Franzi was mad about law and order. We won't have any *Behördenkrieg* here he said.'

'*Behördenkrieg*? What does that mean?'

'Bureaucratic infighting. Different agencies fighting for power and prestige. Officials lining their pockets. It went on you know. A war is not a musical comedy in spite of all those uniforms. If there are any perks and privileges going, people usually grab them. Mind you Uncle Franzi was a dedicated National Socialist. Swallowed the lot. A dyed-in-the-wool Nazi.'

'Wow.'

The car almost ran into the ditch as Megan wobbled off the road, determined to find a place to park. Her grandmother shouted in her fright. What in the world did the girl think she was doing. They would be marooned in a dead-end and no-one would ever find them. Lost for ever in a foreign land. The lane widened abruptly, much to Megan's relief and delight. Her instincts were justified and they had found the ideal retreat: a generous patch of green sward, a ruined mill by a swiftly-flowing stream and all round them the shade and concealment of the trees. Megan hummed and sang Schubert's *The Trout* as she dragged out folding chairs, a picnic basket, a blanket, a camera and a tape recorder.

'Here we are Sirikins. Armed to the teeth!'

Siri grew morose and even suspicious as she watched the girl's activity. Megan hummed away as she set the recorder on the lid of the picnic basket. She had to tap the flow of reminiscence the moment it resumed. Siri became perversely silent. She twitched her eyelids as if to indicate she was lost in her own thoughts and not inclined to share them. Megan was visibly scratching around to regain her grandmother's attention.

'What did he look like, the Partisan doctor?'

Siri sniffed dry amusement.

'If only I could remember. Fair hair, blue eyes. Like a Nazi recruiting poster. He spoke perfect German. Medical school in Berlin.'

'And he fell in love with you at first sight.'

'Did he?'

'He must have done.'

'I had a bicycle. I used to meet him by the lake. First thing in the morning. We used to swim together. I could swim better than he could. He said funny things. He said keep it a secret. Like a little box in your heart. I was so silly and stupid. Putting flowers on my desk. It must have given him away. They only grew in the high mountains.'

Tears gathered in the old woman's eyes as she watched the girl switch on the recorder.

'He was my Tristan,' she said. 'But I was a rotten Isolde. Trust me to make a mess of things.'

Siri struggled to her feet to survey the territory as if they were being observed by unseen eyes.

'I've got to relieve myself. You keep a look out, there's a good girl.'

Megan watched her grandmother wander across the road like a figure in a landscape continuing an interminable journey. Her limp seemed to underline an indomitable will. A survivor could not be classified as a victim and yet there were the burdens of a lifetime the old woman had been condemned to carry. There was so much to record if only she could coax her into a forthcoming mood and hold her there, discoursing like an oracle, distilling the wisdom of a lifetime in that accent her grandfather had described as 'buttered'.

No sooner had Siri gone out of sight behind a screen of fir trees than her sharp cry echoed through the glade. Megan raced across to the point where her grandmother had disappeared. She found her confronting a larger than life bronze statue of a young male striking a death-defying attitude. He was unarmed, his idealised head raised and his broad chest bared to receive the bullets of a firing squad.

'A Partisan.'

Megan was excited by their discovery. They were standing in a semi-circular memorial graveyard. Marble blocks instead of headstones were scattered in groups in the modest amphitheatre marked out by a low stone wall and a formal planting of evergreens. The grass was mown and there were withered wreaths still lying at the base of the statue. On a tall marble slab red letters spelt out a poem or a declaration in a language that had to be Slovene. There was the same red lettering on each truncated triangular block giving a name and a date of birth and the dates of death all between 1941 and 1944.

'This is a dreadful country.'

Siri moved to sit on the low wall and recover her composure.

'I should never have come back here.'

She was muttering to herself.

'I never wanted to see it again.'

Megan was absorbed in studying the names and the inscriptions. She tried to pronounce the names and collate the ages. Behind more than one she found gutted candles in transparent red containers: the living continuing to pay their respects to the dead with anniversaries and withering flowers.

'They were all young. Cut off in the prime of life. Executed. Each stone represents the base of a tree of life that has been cut off.'

Megan ran back to the car to fetch her camera. There was so much she wanted to record. Siri sat in the shade and watched her grand-daughter click away as close as she could to make a record of the inscriptions to be interpreted later.

'It's from Tito's time. All this!'

Siri was deeply disgruntled.

'Putting up things like this in the middle of nowhere.'

'Perhaps it was a place of execution.'

Megan was prepared to speculate.

'You said there were SS trucks that went out in the night.'

'This is the Balkans for heaven's sake. The SS were not the only gang to go in for executions. In this part of the world it's a way of life. Outside civilisation. You've only got to read the newspapers. Any day you like. They're still at it. It's a horrible place.'

'It's so peaceful now,' Megan said. 'Slovenia is peaceful. It's so green and peaceful. Your Partisan doctor said it was an oasis. Even then. Stand in the light, Sirikins. I want to take your picture. By the statue. Do you think it looks like him?'

'Don't talk rubbish.'

Megan was taken aback.

'I just thought,' she said. 'I meant no disrespect.'

'These are Communists,' Siri said. 'Reds. Can't you see for yourself? Put it away. I don't want my picture taken. Milos was a Chetnik. I told you about them. They hated each other. This appalling country. There is no end to it. They're still at each other's throats. Ethnic this and ethnic that. They're mad, the whole lot of them.'

'Not the Slovenes surely.'

'Everybody's mad if they get half a chance.'

Siri took refuge in being defiantly unreasonable.

'I'm hungry,' she said. 'Come on. Let's go and eat.'

The picnic was not a success. Siri seemed to disapprove of what she was eating. Megan presumed on her grandmother's affection to speak frankly.

'Are you in a mood?'

'Not with you, my love. Not with you. It's a poor look-out when a woman is dissatisfied with the food and the language of the land of her birth. It used to be music. And now sometimes it's like a tune being played backwards. A bad joke.'

She could see her grand-daughter holding her head at an angle in her anxiety to understand and sympathise.

'I was too young to understand anything,' Siri said. 'That's my excuse. And now I think I understand it's too late to do anything about it. It's always too late.'

Megan reached out to take her grandmother's hand. The old woman took to gratefully squeezing hers.

'I don't know whether he was a hero or not. I'm quite certain I wasn't. That's it you see. If you reject heroism in your youth, old age will be there to take a slow revenge.'

'How did he come and go so easily? In wartime.'

'That is a good question. He told me that he had two missions. Messages for Mihajlović and morphine to put people out of their pain. He had a bicycle. And a motor-bike. Once when I was swimming across the lake he was there waiting for me on horseback.'

Megan was ready to marvel at anything her grandmother said.

'He came and went,' Siri said. 'I can see now he had some kind of secret understanding with Uncle Franzi. Some form of collaboration. The reprisals down in Serbia were so savage. Mihajlović wanted to save the native population. And the price was passing on information about the movements of the Communists.'

'So your hero was playing a dangerous game?'

'My goodness I can see that now. But then it was normal. Unobtrusive. We had our own villa and my mother lived as though we were back in the days of the old Empire. She wouldn't have been surprised to see the Emperor rise from the dead to come and spend his summer vacation at Bled. She wrapped herself in ignorance thicker than cotton wool. It was safe to know nothing. Always look surprised.'

For the sake of Megan's thesis there was more to be done and more to be seen. Her grandmother was resolved to disregard her own unease and discomfort in the interests of the girl's thesis. Her youthful enthusiasm would blunt the sharper memories. On the road to Bled Siri suppressed her urge to mutter to herself by talking loudly above the noise of the diesel engine.

'I can tell you one thing. This landscape is empty! And I can tell you why. It has been replaced by the landscape of my other life. My dear husband, my children. All that. Women you see play these different roles. Do you understand? The child, the maiden, the wife, the mother. And the grandmother for goodness sake. Perhaps that's the one. You spend a lifetime aiming at it!'

Through the trees the road led to the lake. Megan found a place to park so that she could take photographs of the abbey on the small island, the castle towering on its hill, the villas built by the wealthy during the Imperial era. There was a Professor on Faculty mad keen on visual aids. 'Show! Show!' he would say. 'Put me in the picture.' Siri took out her elegant walking stick to contemplate the waters of the lake she used to swim so long ago. Megan joined her and clasped her arm.

'I waited for him here. My mother and Uncle Franzi had to drag me away. He was no longer of any use. The Communists were racing to take over. They wanted to grab Trieste and part of Carinthia. I wanted to wait so that he could escape with us. Back over the Karawanken and wait for the British to arrive. That's just what Uncle Franzi did. A born survivor. Burnt his uniform and took to his bed. And stayed there until it was safe to get out. He got a job in local government and became a fervent Catholic. I met your grandfather at a church concert. He spotted me singing in the front row. My heart didn't break. That's history for you.'

'What happened to him? Your hero.'

'He stuck with Mihajlović. They were hunted down. Caught starved and shivering. They were shot on the same day. July 17th 1947.'

'And where were you then?'

'In Bargoed. In South Wales. Carrying my first child and learning to be nice.'

Looking After Ruthie

I

Valmai chose to sit in the back so that she could stretch an arm behind little Ruthie without touching the child. As a primary school teacher, experienced and vetted, she had expertise in the handling of children, but on this occasion, Ruthie could only be nominally under her protection because her mother was at the wheel of the old Volvo estate car and, as ever, very much in control. Valmai's present status was that of Peris's best friend and it was incumbent upon her therefore to show a subsidiary eagerness for little Ruthie's welfare. Merely peering over her shoulder to reverse out of the coach house demonstrated Peris's competence and authority. She was a career woman with a host of concerns: a large house, an only daughter, a business in design and photography and picture framing: and a husband who at this moment was also a frustrated genius. Valmai was a divorced primary school teacher resolved not to spend time being alone and sorry for herself. Peris began to sing a little ditty as the car moved out.

'Never mind the weather, never mind the rain. Here we are together. Off we go again!'

'Off we go again!'

Valmai touched Ruthie lightly on the shoulder so that she could at least smile if not join in the chorus. The little girl exuded a degree of nervous impassivity that Valmai knew the mother often found disturbing. She shrank now inside her warm winter coat and the safety strap as if the whole world for some unaccountable reason was moving backwards.

'Off we go again!'

Valmai patted Ruthie's back and smiled vigorously to reassure her. Outside she caught a glimpse of the composer staring at the rain through the long window of the music room. The weather could be no inspiration. And nothing more to see than fields of potatoes stretching down to the Straits in need of harvesting.

'He's got to get it done,' Peris said. 'That's all there is to it.'

She was being resolute and unbending on her husband's behalf.

'I keep telling him. It's a matter of concentration. Gareth's got all the talent in the world but not the determination. Ruthless determination.'

Valmai kept nodding to express her appreciation of being taken into Peris's confidence. Gareth's lack of resolution could be a weakness she suffered from herself.

'We are ruthless aren't we, Ruthie?'

Peris paused briefly for her friend, and even her little daughter, to take in the humorous coincidence.

'If we weren't, we'd never been able to keep this ramshackle empire going. That's a fact.'

For most of the way Peris talked about her husband and his problems and Valmai listened reverently. The house was too large and proper upkeep was well beyond their means, but they lived there in order to accommodate his dreams. He wanted to have his cake and eat it. On good days the place inspired them both. She had plans to restore Caesengi and transform all the outhouses. But where would the money come from? And a wet afternoon in early autumn was no good. The roof leaked and that reminded them of all they had to worry about. How could he concentrate? But concentrate he had to. There was no other way. She had artistic aspirations of her own. They were more modest but they existed and they had a right to exist. She would have loved to concentrate on watercolour, but it was photography and framing that paid so she had to be content with being a craftswoman. Not that there was anything inferior in craft work. It kept the cash flow going. It paid the wages. It was all that inspiration business that gave them trouble. What was it? Where did it come from for God's sake? He wanted to write an opera. Very well. If that was the case he should get down to it.

The multi-storey car park filled up quickly on wet days so that Peris had to drive to the fourth floor before she found a parking space. The manoeuvring was difficult. Valmai stretched her neck this way and that in moral support, but Peris was in cool command of the situation. As they marched through the arcades, Valmai and Ruthie had to break into a trot to keep up with her. Peris continued, intermittently, to comment on the nature of the partnership that kept Peris and Gareth Garmon so firmly together in spite of economic hardships and temperamental differences. She was prepared to admit that there was a touch of the heroic about it and Valmai was eager to agree. When the opportunity arose she would like to contrast it with her own miserable matrimonial experience.

The women's fashion section on the second floor of the department store would never have been her first choice, Peris said. There was just not enough time to pop over to Chester. She had to have something new for the Private View and this was just about her only chance.

'Look at that lovely white rocking horse, Ruthie,' Peris said. 'You'd just love to ride it, wouldn't you?'

Ruthie showed no enthusiasm. Her eyes ranged around for avenues of escape.

'Of course you would.'

Ruthie stood stock still in front of the wooden horse. The play-corner was not to her taste. Other children were flitting in and out. If they lingered with nothing to do they could easily develop into a threat. As long as she delayed there was a hope that another child would mount the intimidating wooden image. The nostrils and the glaring painted eyes were a distinct threat.

'Perhaps she feels the heat. Should we take her coat off, Peris. I'll carry it.'

'Well if you want to be lumbered with it.'

The little girl sensed her mother's patience would shortly give out. Relieved of her overcoat she clambered onto the rocking saddle while Valmai held the horse's head. Once up, her chin settled into a coarse bed of white mane.

'You're a big girl,' Peris said. 'Enjoy it for heaven's sake.'

'We won't be gone for long, Ruthie,' Valmai said. 'When Mummy's found what she likes I'll buy you a goldfish.'

'And look after it, I hope!' Peris muttered as they marched through the regimented rows of frocks and dresses. 'She's so dreadfully timid.'

'I was terribly timid at her age. Because I was an only child I suppose.'

Valmai would have liked to have gone into greater detail.

'Well I'm not going to have any more, if that's what you mean. That's one thing Gareth and I are totally agreed about.'

She was examining the row of trouser suits with an expression of disdain on her precise and well made-up features.

'I don't know what it is about Ruthie. She has a way of looking at you that makes you feel horribly guilty. I suppose I must be. Gareth says one day the roles will be reversed. She'll be in charge and we'll be a pair of decrepit oldies. If that's the case I said, I'd better make the best of it while I'm still in charge.'

There was so much that Valmai would have liked to add about her own experience: in the interests of their friendship she had to be content with a sympathetic giggle.

'This might do. At a pinch.'

Peris snatched a suit and retreated purposefully into the nearest fitting room. Valmai's movements were less decisive. She settled in the solitary chair outside the fitting rooms, nursing little Ruthie's warm overcoat. It was a moment to meditate on the mystery of their relationship. It had begun in those early days in the college hostel when they had been two among six who shared the bathroom at the end of the corridor. Valmai, so plump and unsure of herself, had been in a tearing hurry to attend a seminar on the other side of the campus. Peris had been thoughtless enough to take a bath. She might well have been lying in it admiring herself when Valmai gave a wild scream and then trembled and burst into tears. Peris, so cool, forgave her, became her friend and established an emotional ascendancy that had grown with the years. There was a range of problems of her own –

'matters arising,' they used to call them in the old days – she needed to bring up with Peris when the appropriate opportunity presented itself. The trouble was Peris's activities and ambitions had multiplied at an alarming rate, not to mention those of her frustrated genius of a husband, and opportunities for relaxed and intimate discussion were becoming fewer and further between. She had to tread ever more softly when she attempted to win Peris's sympathetic attention.

'What do you think?'

Peris drew the cubicle curtain aside with a flourish and stepped out in a grey trouser suit that fitted her so well she could barely restrain herself from smiling. Valmai clasped her hands together and pushed them under her ample breasts.

'It's you, my dear,' she said. 'Absolutely. It's you to perfection.'

Peris examined herself critically from various angles in the full length mirror.

'There's olive green.' she said. 'Olive green would suit me better. Grey makes me terribly grey. But the olive green is a size bigger.'

This allowed Valmai to insist with dogmatic fervour, that cut was, in the final analysis, more important than a shade of colour, and that it was only a shade, after all, that they were talking about.

'There's no time anyway.'

Peris was decisive.

'This will have to do.'

Valmai was full of enthusiastic approval.

'You've got such good taste, Peris, honestly. And a perfect figure.'

Valmai clutched little Ruthie's coat more tightly. This could have been the moment to raise the subject of her own problems. From the perspective of Peris's perfection it should have been easy to slide attention towards her own shortcomings. The core of friendship after all should be an exchange of confessions. Peris was in too much of a hurry to listen. That was so often the case. Valmai restrained herself from resenting this fact of life. The degree of give and take was such a sensitive balance. She had once declined an invitation to move into a pair of spare rooms in Caesengi. Peris said quite frankly they could do with a bit of rent to help with the repair bills. It wasn't the most open-hearted of invitations and Valmai sensed that Gareth Garmon didn't at all like the idea. Somehow she ducked the issue: made a great thing about her love for the first floor flat she had found when she and Tim split up. She had a view of the harbour and she could gaze at it when she was washing dishes and compose her fairy tales for children of all ages which one day she was resolved, come what may, to publish.

'Would you just look at that!'

Peris stepped sideways to hide behind a rack of winter coats. 'Just look.'

They saw Ruthie lying on the rocking horse, deep in conversation with an older girl who held on to the bridle on the horse's wooden head.

'She's talking,' Peris said. 'She's talking her head off.'

'Is she?'

Valmai was being cautious. In such unexpected circumstances it was wiser to delay taking up a point of view.

'She never talks like that to me. Or to her father.'

'That's how they are. Children.'

After all she was a primary school teacher. This was a sphere in which she could generalise with a certain degree of authority.

'Once they hit it off there's no end to what they can find to say to each other. It's wonderful really. I've often noticed it. Two kids that had never met before. They stand there staring at each other. And out it comes. Whatever happens to come into their heads.'

'Look at her face. I've never seen her look so happy. Who is that girl?'

Dressed in shabby clothes, the girl holding the bridle looked remarkably calm and self-contained. She gave Ruthie her whole attention.

'Is she a gypsy?'

Peris was muttering to herself.

'Olive skin anyway. Indian perhaps? We'd better see what's

going on.'

The strange girl paused to take in their exuberant approach. For a moment she was as still as a photograph and they could take in the detail of her large eyes and soulful expression before she glided away and placed herself on the moving staircase.

'Well, who was that then, Ruthie?'

Peris was too purposefully cheerful. Her daughter looked at her and shook her head.

'She's gone,' she said.

Her eyes threatened to fill with tears. She seemed acutely aware of her loss. No sooner had she acquired a new friend than she had lost her. Or had these grown ups driven her away? Valmai stood by to pour oil on what could become troubled waters.

'I know,' she said. 'Why don't we go and have tea in the Crinoline Cafe? You know, where the serving ladies dress up. You'd like that wouldn't you, Ruthie?'

'What did she say to you? That girl. What did she say?'

Peris was becoming impatient.

'It's not a good idea you know to talk to strangers. She may look nice but we don't know her, do we? Somebody we've never ever seen before.'

II

Gareth Garmon admitted that his study was the best room in Caesengi. He said it gave him the space he needed to march up and down when he was working on a sequence, or, as he said, when he was furious with himself.

'It's not that I'm pining for recognition or anything like that. Those telly idiots can make programmes about Mari Emrys and her piddling choir until the cows come home. All I'm saying is, there is absolutely no point in writing music unless the bloody stuff gets played!'

'Well there you are,' Peris said. 'She's waiting for it so why don't you take it to her. And then she can get on with it!'

Gareth was reluctant to agree with his wife.

'It's not really finished,' he said. 'I really ought to go over it. I'm not pleased with it. It's just a piece for a girl's choir. But there's stuff in it that can be developed.'

'Take it,' Peris said. 'And take Ruthie with you. She can play with the rabbits. You like Mari's rabbits, don't you Ruthie? Better than Mari's ponies anyway. We must conclude that our daughter has very little to say to horses.'

Ruthie had tucked herself into a heap of soft toys in the corner behind the grand piano. It was the best place for her to spend time translating whatever her parents chose to say in her hearing. She could have been a rabbit herself peering out of her hole on an adult world that often appeared threateningly unintelligible. Her father was rubbing his chin as he stared at the music manuscript. There was no knowing what he saw.

'Let's hope there's something here beyond the quality of the ink!' he said.

'See what she thinks.'

'A spot of pain here... a splash of manufactured anguish...'

'I think she genuinely wants to help.'

'Of course she does. And grab a bigger slice of the credit. If there is any credit.'

'Oh come off it Gareth. Don't get yourself worked up. Don't waste your energy. You've got to concentrate on that piece for Cheltenham. Let her extract what she can manage with that choir of hers.'

'What does she know about it? They make a telly programme about her choir and it goes straight to her head. She's all paint and presentation.'

'Now Gareth. Don't be ungenerous. It's not like you. And it's not good for you either. A waste of spirit and a waste of time.'

'I'm sorry. But she gets on my nerves sometimes. She's so bloody confident. And that booming voice.'

Gareth held his hands over his ears in a gesture of exaggerated distaste. This made Peris laugh and Ruthie in her corner smiled with relief. Things were looking up. The prospect of some unspecified threat had passed over.

'We'll go rabbiting, shall we, Ruthie?'

She responded eagerly. Her father was sometimes ready to play with her and even take her out for walks. The reason, her mother had long given her to understand, was because he had more leisure. Peris had to work every hour that God sent to keep those imaginary wolves from the door. At the same time, Ruthie had to understand her father often needed time to brood. She should not pester him with questions, only respond as brightly as she could when he inclined to take an interest in her: which to be fair to him, he very often did. Childhood, he had been known to declare, was a massive mystery, and he needed to look closely at his daughter, particularly when he struggled to make musical sense of his own.

He was putting Ruthie's warm coat on when the doorbell rang. He had a way of opening the front door which suggested how much he resented intruders. When he saw it was Valmai holding a freshly baked sponge cake there was little welcome in his wan smile. He was clearly keyed up and the arrival of his wife's plump and unrelentingly amiable best friend did nothing to alleviate his nervous condition. She was obliged to divert her attention to Ruthie in order to generate a minimum of effusion to signal her arrival.

'I've come at a bad time,' she said. 'Would you like me to take Ruthie for a walk?'

'No thank you.'

The reply was immediate and brisk.

'Ruthie's coming with me. You'll find Peris in the darkroom. Where else.'

The darkroom door was open and Peris was about to close it. When Valmai held up the cake she was obliged to lead the way to the kitchen. Valmai's sponge cakes merited their due of praise.

'I've come at a bad time,' Valmai said. 'I can see you're busy.'

'When am I not? Shall we cut the cake and give ourselves a cup of tea?'

Valmai continued to express regret for the disturbance she

had caused. But she had to come. There was something she had to tell Peris. Not that she wanted to bother her but she had to tell someone.

'I've had a solicitor's letter from Tim.'

'Oh dear.'

Valmai was so distressed she had sunk down on a kitchen chair without making any offer to help.

'He wants half the money for selling the house. Otherwise he'll take me to court.'

'The bobby on the beat. P.C. Horen. I often wondered. What made you marry him?'

It was a cruel question. It showed how little aware Peris was of her friend's loving nature.

'My father used to say the trouble with policemen is that they're all frustrated barrack room lawyers.'

This was no description at all of her ex-husband. It was more amused curiosity than sympathy extended to a best friend.

'I must admit I never took to him. The little I saw of him. To be quite honest I thought he was too crude for you. After all you are a bit of a sensitive plant aren't you?'

This was the way with Peris. She specialised in being brutally frank even in regard to her own feelings. Unless Valmai took umbrage and decided to get up and go home to ponder the awkward question in greater depth, she had to look at her predicament with comparable objectivity. And in any case who else could she turn to?

'Why do we do anything?'

Even as she chewed the first modest portion of her own sponge cake, Valmai recalled the first time she had set eyes on her policeman: clambering up the steep school roof in order to rescue a cat stranded in the bell tower. It could have been something to do with her ambition to write and publish fairy tales: a some-day-my-prince-will-come nonsense transmuted into folksy fairy tales: or was it fairy-like folk tales?

He had a laugh she used to call wicked. This solicitor's letter seemed to prove it really was. He said he had watched her on

Friday afternoons sitting on a stool, without a book, telling a story and an entire class of eight or nine year olds, most with their mouths open, totally in thrall. That was the answer really. As far as she was ever concerned from the moment he rescued the cat, she was bewitched and she wanted to be his for ever: until she found out he was carrying on with Nellie Williams the blonde in charge of the check-out at Quix only six miles away from the terrace house her doting grandmother had given them as a wedding present. And now what he wanted was not her but half the sale price of the house.

She could still shudder at the boundless extent of her trust in the man. She never quite knew the exact hours of her policeman's duty. What he had the nerve to call his 'prowls' were all, he claimed, part of his drive for promotion. He was a born sniffer dog, he said, and he loved the night air and sooner or later he would transfer to the C.I.D. and help to save the world. His laugh was so infectious. She was lost with him and lost without him. When she threw his gear out of the bedroom window and it all landed in the snow, he kept on laughing. She could have died of her fury. And now he was demanding money with menaces. If this were a fairy story, he was both the villain and the hero and the horror lay in the fact you could never tell which was which.

'When it comes to selling and buying houses,' Peris said. 'People are less than human. They are at their beastly worst. You are telling me.'

While she struggled to follow Peris's heated account of their purchase of Caesengi and its buildings and paddock and the old miser's offer to lend them the mortgage himself at eleven and a half percent, Valmai saw again, in vivid detail, Tim Horen extract a blank sheet of paper from his attaché case with a numbered lock, and suggest they should both sign and date it as a further token of the total trust they had in each other. The house that was hers would become theirs. Share and share alike. So much trust had landed her in this pickle. Blank sheets of paper should be filled up with fairy tales and left unsigned until the end of time. This was what she would like Peris to understand and passionately agree with.

'What you need is a first class lawyer.' Peris said. 'And I can give you one. Bill Pryce of Pryce, Prydderch and Oates. He knows his oats! And he likes my pictures. He's got two of my watercolours and his name down for two more. When I can find the time to do them.'

It was time for her to get back to the darkroom. There were loads of things for her to develop. Why did she have to be so damn busy? Valmai stood up anxious to please, asking if there was something she could do to help.

'Well, now you mention it my dear, there is one thing. A spot of baby-sitting. Next Thursday. Unless of course you are going to Mari Emrys's party?'

'Goodness me, I'm not going!'

Valmai's smile implied that she was far too unimportant to be invited.

'It's such a bore but Mari Emrys thinks he ought to meet the man who runs the Wirral Festival. You know what she's like. Push, push, push. She thinks there's a chance this chap will commission an opera from Gareth. I only hope she's not raising his hopes all for nothing. You know how he hates parties. He doesn't want to go, but I tell him we daren't refuse or Mari will never forgive me. As if he cared. Sometimes I think he hates himself for not achieving his potential. Poor lamb. It's no joke being an artist. And even worse being an artist's wife. Would you Val my pet? I'd be ever so grateful.'

Valmai was even more grateful for the term of endearment. And the address of a good lawyer to whom she could mention Peris's name. There was enduring value and advantage in their continuing friendship. And a warm corner for her in this busy enviably creative household.

III

Little Ruthie was loaded with her soft toys and tucked up in her bed. Near the rubber plant to the left of the front door Peris was struggling with the clasp of a blue necklace she had chosen to wear. Valmai stood by, nursing her hands, ready to help.

'I'd rather be you than me,' Peris said.

She moved under the weak light that hung from the high ceiling and twisted her neck so that Valmai could deal with the clasp.

'You can't say that. You look wonderful.'

'On a night like this? Not for long. It's pouring old women and sticks. You make yourself at home in the Snug. There's a shepherd's pie in the micro. Marks and Spencers best. And if she wakes which I don't think she will, tell her one of your stories. She likes the wind blowing. Is that unusual in a little kid? I used to hate it. Where is that husband of mine? Dragging his feet as usual. I told him to start getting ready hours ago. It's all for his sake anyhow. What do I get out of it? I'll drive and he'll drink. That's about the size of it. What will you do? Watch telly?'

'I might write a bit.'

Valmai murmured the confession. Her quiet smile was an invitation to further enquiry.

'Magic from the east, innocence from the west.'

'Gracious...'

'There's more to you than meets the eye. There always was. This is for the collection, is it?'

'I thought if I could adapt a folk tale motif and give it a modern setting – something young people could relate to...'

Peris clenched her fist and winked in acknowledgement of a notable piece of cunning.

'Suitable for readers in their early teens. The competition restricted to unpublished authors. And the prize? Come on. How much?'

Valmai smiled in her most modest way.

'It's not the prize. Only three hundred pounds.'

'Quite right. It's the good name that counts. Eisteddfod

winner. Cover yourself with glory.'

Gareth Garmon arrived downstairs sketching out excuses.

'Couldn't we phone?' he said. 'Such a filthy night.'

Peris shook her head. She had dressed herself to go out and do battle fully armed on his behalf.

'Gareth you want something to think about. Valmai's got a lovely idea for a libretto.'

'Oh no. It's too childish really. It wouldn't be good enough.'

Valmai's protestations were weak and ineffective.

'People are always telling me about plots I should use.' Gareth said. 'I've got more than I can handle already.'

'"Magic from the east. Innocence from the west." Just you think about that while you're sulking over your drink in the corner at Mari Emrys's party.'

When they were gone, comfortable as she was in the room Peris called the Snug, Valmai could not settle down to write. Gareth's attitude had irked her. He didn't even enquire about the setting or the nature of her story. There was a great deal to discuss that would have been useful to him. He went on often enough about how much he wanted to write an opera. It could have been worth talking about. Transposing a medieval folk story into a modern setting. It was the kind of thing that could be done. And now she couldn't concentrate because she was wondering why men should treat her the way they so often did: with a kind of humorous contempt that made her tremble with the effort of suppressing the hurt. It wasn't fair, but then nothing in life was fair. Peris often insisted a woman had a duty to herself. Valmai accepted this as an article of faith and yet in practice she had been in the habit of letting men tread all over her. Was it because she was so uncertain of her looks, so despairing of her implacable plumpness, she felt obliged to be grateful for any attention? Tim Horen had taken to her fullness of figure and that had given her great relief and even joy until it turned out to be a complete fool's paradise.

In the music room there was a full length mirror in which she could look at herself. She was alone in a large house keyed up for inspiration, haunted with the unquantifiable ambitions of Peris and Gareth Garmon. The first step was to take a good look at herself and where better than in the workshop of the man who smouldered with misgivings that could not be all that dissimilar to her own? Were his problems all that greater than hers? Did his frustrations arise from the lack of opportunity or a sheer inability to say something new? He may have mastered the medium but did he in fact have something new and fresh to say? Perhaps he shared her sense of an invisible audience surrounding her, leaning back and making mute open-ended gestures that said, in fact, well, come on then, say something, make a sound that will startle and delight this inert assembly. She was staring intently at her whole figure in the mirror when she heard a rustle behind her. Little Ruthie stood in the open doorway dragging an outsized fluffy rabbit along the floor with one hand, and the index finger of the other weighing down the corner of her mouth.

'Ruthie! Bare feet on bare floor!'

Valmai masked her guilt with excessive exuberance. Gareth's work room was a sanctuary into which she should never venture uninvited.

'Where's my Daddy?'

Ruthie on the other hand could camp under the grand piano whenever she felt like it. If she waited long enough her father would join her on the floor and invent some new game for them to share.

'Up you come! Lets go to the Snug and I'll tell you a story. Would you like Aunty Val to tell you a story? Of course you would. I'm one of the best story tellers in the world, aren't I? Did you know I was writing a book? Well I am you know. Mind you, it's a big secret. So you won't tell anyone will you? I might win a prize you know. A big prize. We'd like that wouldn't we? Mummy would like it. And so would Daddy. And he might write a song about it. You never know do you?'

In the large armchair Ruthie was reluctant to let go of her fluffy rabbit and snuggle down against Valmai's ample bosom. Valmai reached out to pick up the exercise book in which she had been trying to write.

'Here's my story,' she said. 'Shall I read some to you?'

'Where's Daddy?'

Ruthie raised her head expecting an answer.

'He's with Mummy. At Mari Emrys's party. They'll be back soon. Do you know what my story is about? It's all about a beautiful princess from the East who marries a king in the West, and when she gets to his court the big men in the King's Council take against her because they say her skin is too dark. They say this princess is not fair enough. She's only good enough to work in the kitchen. Wasn't that terrible?'

Ruthie scanned Valmai's face to find out whether or not she was expected to agree.

'The kitchen boy was nice to her. "You're not black" he said. "You're gold" Wasn't that nice of him. People should be nice shouldn't they? We are nice, aren't we?'

Ruthie considered the proposition before she smiled and nodded. Valmai was able to give her a hug.

'Of course we are.'

There was a prospect of a channel opening and a free flow of chatter passing between them. Given time she could get to know the child better than her mother did. The more chatter the less mystery. The child was silent only because no one took the time to listen to her. She was perfectly capable of talking away. They had seen as much when she sat on the rocking horse chatting away with an older child who was a complete stranger.

The headlights of a car flashed across the window and they heard the crunch of tyres moving over the gravel.

'Goodness!' Valmai said. 'They can't be back already. Surely.'

Strange voices outside made Valmai stiffen with apprehension. She clutched little Ruthie more tightly. The door bell rang more than once. There was no choice but to answer it. There was a police car outside. The police officer under the portico had already begun to apologise for the intrusion before he recognised Valmai.

'Good God, Val!... What the hell are you doing here?'

Valmai trembled with alternating flushes of fear and indignation. This was Tim standing within two feet of her. Could he have come looking for her? He wasn't in uniform. Wet curls and a long raincoat. A hero turned enemy. She could only stand her ground, as she had every right to do and wait for the man to explain himself.

'What do you want?'

She was as cold as she could be but he pretended he could barely hear her. That's how he always was. Once he got over his surprise he was all jokes and joviality. She'd show him jokes.

'Official business.' He said. 'We're chasing asylum-seekers. You're not one of them by any chance?'

She steeled herself to make no response.

'The thing is, Val, all these outhouses. We would like permission to take a look at them.'

'It's not my house.'

Tim was amused.

'Well that's a relief anyhow. I tell you what, a cup of tea wouldn't come amiss. Parched we are. My partner and I. A cup of tea wouldn't come amiss. He could come in and chaperone. In case you're worried.'

His insinuating humour infuriated her.

'Go away.'

Val could only manage a hiss. This man was still ready to presume on the fact that she had once idolised him and the frightening possibility was that part of her still did.

'I'll call...'

'Not much use for that Val old girl. We are the police and we're here already. And who is this young lady?'

Little Ruthie had appeared behind Valmai, still dragging her fluffy bunny along the floor. Tim Horen knelt down ready to take Ruthie into his confidence.

'What's your name then?'

'Don't frighten her. She's a very nervous child.'

'Just like you then.'

Ruthie saw a man all smiles and jokes kneeling in front of her. He wanted something. Aunty Val didn't want him to come in the house. So if the man kept kneeling outside the front door everything would be all right.

'You live here don't you?'

Ruthie nodded.

'Tell me something. Have you seen any foreign looking children hanging about?'

'Of course she hasn't.'

'Is that so? Why is she nodding then? Where are the parents? If she's nodding she must know something. Mr. and Mrs. Garmon, isn't it? Where are they?'

'They've gone to a party.' Val said. 'I'm looking after Ruthie. If you want any permission you'll have to come back and ask them tomorrow.'

As though she were enacting a master stroke, Val closed the large front door. She turned to confront Ruthie.

'Did you see that, Ruthie? I shut the door in his face! Now let's get you back in bed, young lady. All warm and cuddly.'

IV

It was after school and Valmai was perfectly entitled to remain at her desk and work with fresh determination on her story. The reappearance of her ex-husband had been a fright: now it was up to her to transform it into a stimulation. Who were these asylum seekers he talked about? Strange people from the east. If she could bridle her imagination, the empty desks could become a further source of inspiration: they were there on behalf of an audience of children eager to learn what would happen next. The princess from the East was trapped in the royal kitchen and needed rescuing, and Valmai needed a silent classroom in which to concentrate on the most effective way it could be done. All solutions lay within bidding distance of the tip of her tongue until Adele Watkin-Wyn breezed in, in her usual imperious manner, and Valmai had to push her notes under a pile of exercise books and give the impression she was busy marking.

'I can't say I've ever come across this kind of thing before. Not on this scale anyway. A gallon of milk yesterday. And today a tray full of turkey-slice-dinosaurs. That's what she says anyway. I've just got to believe her. How am I supposed to know what they get up to in the kitchen? Did someone switch off the intruder alarm? Do you know anything about it?'

Adele was both forthright and ambitious, and in a head-teacher at least three years younger than herself, Valmai found this an unnerving combination. Like her sharp nose and the glint in those rimless spectacles they were designed to advertise the woman's relentless efficiency. She wanted to take Valmai into her confidence whenever it suited her. There was no sympathy there or understanding for any form of artistic aspiration. The follies and inefficiencies of school life were obstacles that Adele saw deliberately strewn across her path to higher things.

'I've had to call the police. She insisted on it. Cooks can be so touchy. And this one is as touchy as they come. She says some-body switched off the intruder alarm. And the caretaker backs her up. They want to put the blame on the teaching staff. I don't want a civil war in the place if I can possibly avoid it.'

'Of course not.'

What else could Valmai say? There were members of staff who were known to switch off the alarm because the horrid noise was liable to go off and disturb their lesson and frighten the chil-dren. Valmai considered herself unambitious professionally. She was a teacher because she identified with children and she felt herself in some way dedicated to protect the sacred age of inno-cence. The noise of that unreliable alarm bell was a crude intrusion. If this concern made her appear childish and spineless in Adele Watkin-Wyn's glittering eye, then so be it. When the great day dawned and Valmai was awarded that prestigious prize then the headteacher might be grateful to bask in whatever reflected glory became available. The fact was she could not remember whether she had turned the alarm off or not lately. Adele Watkin-Wyn would never understand that there was a part of her brain that had to be a reservoir of fantasy: the well from which she could draw the stories that would satisfy the childish thirst of her readers.

'Don't let this go any further, but I have my suspicions about cook and caretaker. It's a well know fact that he's carrying on with cook's best friend. There could be some kind of collusion going on. I dare not say it of course. But that friend of hers is in what is known as casual catering. You haven't seen any turkey dinosaurs racing around the ice cream stalls on Beulah Beach, have you?'

In her more relaxed moments Adele Watkin-Wyn liked to exercise a bizarre sense of humour. Valmai tittered obligingly. It helped to conceal her distaste for the kind of sterile gossip that lay behind the headteacher's arbitrary comments. If they were a reflection of the real world she was better off cocooned in her fictional fantasies. Adele marched to the window.

'Who's that out there standing in the middle of the school yard? It must be somebody from the police.'

Adele sighed and then straightened her back.

'I'd better go and see about it.'

What the dark princess in the kitchen needed most of all was a friend. The kitchen boy was a comfort but he did not have the power to organise her escape. And Valmai did not wish to have recourse to supernatural intervention. She had been on the verge of a notion of disguise and escape by water, all due to the dark princess's own resilience and strength of character, when Adele came, full of her self-important fuss, bursting into the sanctuary of an empty classroom. Valmai's concentration had been broken and there was nothing left but to go home to her first floor flat and hope that some revelation would present itself while she was preparing her single supper. Outside a police van had already arrived at the canteen area. A scene-of-crime team had started work. In order not to be involved she needed to keep well out of sight: to reach her Mini without being spotted by Adele Watkin-Wyn and dragged in to the petty details of the trivial investigation. She made her escape only to find Tim Horen leaning on the roof of her trusty Mini with both his large fists propping up his chin.

'You've still got it then? Your little mini-mouse?'

He was grinning away, as ever excessively pleased with himself. What could she say when she was trapped between two hostile forces? If she still had her little car it was no thanks to this maverick policeman who had the nerve to operate a law and order all his own. She couldn't even get in her own car. When other people were a danger every relationship was a risk. Any moment now he would be trying to get round her, playing on her weaknesses, trying to kindle a fresh flame out of a dead fire.

'I'd like a chance to talk,' Tim Horen said. 'Can we go somewhere for a drink? Or even a cup of tea?'

Valmai had begun to tremble so much she was having difficulty in stopping her head shaking.

'Between you and me, Val. I think my solicitor is pushing it a bit.'

Valmai found her voice.

'I've got a solicitor too.'

'Well there you are. That's the way it goes, isn't it? By the time they've both sliced off their whack we'll both be worse off, won't we? I didn't want to send the letter anyway. The trouble is, Nellie's expecting again. You know how it is. Another mouth to feed. And a policeman working hard to pay for his mistakes. It was a mistake and I admit that now. A big mistake. Still, you're better off without me. Are you still writing stories?'

He wasn't at all put off by the fact that Valmai was glowering at him.

'I can remember you reading to the kids, you know. When I looked through the classroom window. "What care I for my goose feather bed, What care I for my riches O!" Bloody good that was, singing it too. The kids were riveted. Never seen anything like it. "I'm off with the raggle-taggle gypsies O!" I'll tell you what I'll say, although he's bound to say I shouldn't. Bugger him. In the end it's you and I that should decide these things. I'll tell you this, and we can shake on it here and now if you like. A gentleman's word is his bond. I'll settle for one third of the sale price. And then we can be friends. For old times' sake.'

'You are no gentleman.'

She had found something appropriate to say and was saying

it as forcefully as she could.

'You never were. And never will be.'

'Hang on. I'm trying to be reasonable. I'm trying to be friendly.'

'You are nothing but a common cheat and a liar. Pretending to be a policeman. I'm not afraid of you. I've got good people on my side.'

'Have you now? That's very interesting. It wouldn't be the Squire of Caesengi, would it? Are you one of his spare women?'

'Get off my car. You don't know what you're talking about.'

'He's got a lady friend. I can tell you that much. A policeman gets to see a lot you know. In the course of his duties. The seamy side of life. Not fairy stories. We were looking for asylum-seekers. "You seek 'em here, you seek 'em there". And who should we find tumbling about in the hay but the great composer Gareth Garmon and the girl's choir conductor, the world famous Mari Emrys. She was conducting him alright. Fortissimo, as they say in the trade! What about it then? Do we have a deal?'

He stood back to allow her to get into her car. He tapped the window and she wound it down. She took a deep breath and found the strength to speak.

'You'll hear from my solicitor.'

VI

There could never be a good time to tell a best friend the very thing she would most prefer not to know. The longer she put it off the worse the world around her came to appear. School, once such an agreeable workplace, had become infested with ill-will and suspicion. Hostilities had broken out between teachers and kitchen staff. Locks appeared where none had existed before: even on the spare refrigerator where she had been accustomed to store her lunch-time sandwiches. Children in her class became infected with the same ill-will until they began to appear to her as grown ups in disguise, rent with petty jealousies and mean- ingless dissensions.

Her burden of knowledge cut off her escape route to Caesengi where she could at least relax and relieve her busy friend by playing with Ruthie and telling her stories. Why should she be turned out of the garden when she was not guilty? He was guilty. The great frustrated genius. How could that Gareth conduct a clandestine affair with a woman he so loudly professed to dislike? Was that part of his discordant music: or was it a universal male attribute, to conceal one deception by fabricating yet another? It was true of the duplicitous policeman she had once loved to distraction. Deception was second nature to him. He said so himself. He admitted it early in their relationship. He explained how disguises were a professional necessity and she had been quietly thrilled to be taken into his confidence. It didn't bear looking at because it could only mean that she herself had been guilty of self-deception, which could be the greatest deception of all, and where did the shadow of guilt come to an end?

She was marooned in her first floor flat as she struggled to account for Gareth Garmon's behaviour. How could a composer who spent so much time groaning and moaning that he was giving birth to a succession of mediocre mice instead of a musical mountain, find time and energy to conceal an affair, let alone conduct one? The time that they had given him to wrestle with a composition by taking Ruthie out or going on unnecessary shopping expeditions to Llandudno or Chester, he spent wrestling in the hay with that obnoxious Mari Emrys who he himself insisted had a voice like a frog and a face like an unwashed dinner plate. How could the man bring himself to say it?

Words once spoken could never be taken back. They were written in the air like musical notation waiting to be heard. So how had he brought himself to say such things? And what words could she find to inform her best friend of her husband's monstrous betrayal? Wild imaginings like weather fronts raged in her mind beyond the control of rational discourse.

Valmai abandoned all hope of completing her story. The dark princess could never escape from the kitchen because she herself was incapable of escaping from her own dilemma. Over and above this, there was always the certainty that Tim Horen would find out her address – he used to say a policeman could find out anything – and that he would turn up at her door and by his blandishments and black arts push her into a fresh seething cauldron of self-deception. The probability he would arrive on her doorstep grew into a solidifying certainty. When her door bell rang again and again with passionate urgency she took time to steel herself to answer it.

It was her wronged friend Peris who stood on the doorstep. It appeared that she had learned of her despicable husband's infidelity. She was unwashed and in a dishevelled state. Women overcome with grief were reputed to tear their hair. Peris's hair was certainly in a state.

'She's here, isn't she? Where is she?'

Her voice was harsh with accusation. She pushed Valmai aside with such force, her shoulder banged against the door. She continued to rub it as Peris dashed up the stairs.

'You're jealous of me. You always were. Don't think I've never noticed it. I've always tried to help you. Always. And this is what you do to me. Where is she?'

'Ruthie? She's not here Peris. I don't know why you think she should be here.'

'What's in this room? This door is locked. Why do you keep this door locked?'

'It's not locked. The handle doesn't work properly.'

Valmai raised the door knob and the door opened. The room was filled with furniture she had been unable to find room for when her mother died. To look at it was in itself a sadness. Behind her Peris slid slowly to the floor, her face wet with tears that kept flowing.

'You think it's all my fault,' she said. 'You think I neglect her. You'll tell everybody I neglect her. I was only out of the house for half an hour. It was urgent, the delivery. I don't know why I have to do everything myself. I thought she was in bed. Gareth likes to put her to bed when he has time and tell her a story. There was more to see to. I couldn't believe she wasn't there this morning. You know what she's like. Likes to snuggle in a corner with a heap of her toys. So self-contained.'

'Where was Gareth then?'

'Rehearsing. Where else. Always bloody rehearsing. O God in heaven what can have happened to her? You know the awful things you read about in the papers. Paedophiles. Abducting children. Oh my God! Murdering them. I don't know what to do.'

Valmai folded her arms in a resolute manner.

'Go to the police,' she said. 'I'll come with you.'

'No. Not yet. Gareth said "not yet". He's gone over to Mari Emrys's place. It's just possible, he says. She adored the rabbits. She would play there in the old stables for hours. What are you closing your eyes for? He is the father, isn't he? It's his job to go to the police.'

'Let's go back to Caesengi,' Valmai said. 'Search the whole place from top to bottom.'

'I thought you might have taken her just to teach me a lesson.'

She held out her hand so that Valmai could lift her up.

'Why should I do a thing like that, Peris? I'd never do a thing like that, would I?'

Peris was staring at her as though seeing her friend for the first time.

'I'll tell you one thing. I'll never let her out of my sight again.'

Once again she was overcome with grief and remorse. She held on to Valmai as they manouvered their way down the narrow stairs. Outside in the street Tim Horen was leaning against a police car and smiling cheerfully.

'Would I be right in thinking you ladies are looking for somebody?'

Peris began to tremble so much Valmai had to continue holding her.

'Funny little thing. Very reluctant to detach herself from her new-found friends. Especially the leader of the band. So I thought to myself I'd collect old Val and see if she could do the trick. And am I right in thinking...?'

'My daughter. My daughter?' Peris said. 'You've found her. O thank God. Where is she?'

'They're all there in the chapel vestry at Glanbranas. Under police escort you might say. Amazing piece of detection all based on a turkey slice shaped like a dinosaur. Bit of a story there for you, Val. When you come to think of it a bunch of kids all the way from Azerbaijan living off the land. Talk about a children's crusade in reverse. When I say unaccompanied they are not without a leader. The only one with a smattering of English, and where did that come from? Manna from heaven or dinosaur slices? That's the one your little girl is stuck to. Like a limpet. It's all very interesting really. Shall we go in your car or in mine? Lovely day, isn't it? Saint Somebody or other's Little Summer.'

In the back seat of the police car, Valmai struggled with her thoughts and emotions. It was a lovely day. In the gardens there were raspberry canes with fruit on them and rows of sweet peas still in bloom. The last leaves on the trees glittered with the colour of a false spring. Sitting in the front Peris released her tension by laughing at every joke the great Tim Horen chose to make. She thought all her troubles were over. Ruthie recovered and life would go on at Caesengi as it had always done. Tim was chattering about the Law broken in so many directions that you had to tip toe through it as if you were walking barefoot through broken glass. Valmai was convinced she had heard him use that one before. And saying it was a weird and wonderful world. Peris was so overwhelmed with relief that she kept laughing and even laid her head on Tim Horen's shoulder. He loved that. It was more than a hobby and a sport. It was an absolute necessity for him to play around with vulnerable women and make them even more stupid than they were already. It was something to do with power and it was just as unfair as magic in folk tales.

'You've got to know how to handle people,' he was saying.

Valmai knew from experience that the attention he was getting would propel him into a cycle of open boasting.

'Not everyone's got the knack. And then when they don't speak your language, where are you? You've got to find other means of persuasion and making yourself understood. And there are plenty of them. I had a bunch of Chinese once. Poor bloody peasants looking for fields to harvest. It only took me a couple of hours but I had them eating out of my hand. I call it my special mix of sweet and sour.'

Before they reached the village, Tim drew up at a broken gate. A pot-holed lane led down to a clutch of ruined farm buildings half hidden by straggly trees that once served as windbreaks.

'Scene of the crime,' he said. 'When I saw them I could hardly believe my eyes. They were crouching in a row in a hay bin. Like chicks in a nest all big eyes and open beaks. They were on their own. The adults had vanished. Picked up in a cattle lorry and taken to a job in Cheshire.'

'And Ruthie? My Ruthie?'

'There she was all pink and well fed. And doing her level best to look like the rest of them.'

Peris began to shake with spasms of alternating sobs and laughter. Valmai put an arm on her shoulder to comfort her.

'She is so strange,' Peris said. 'She's so lovely. So special.'

When they arrived at Glanbranas chapel a policewoman had arranged the children on benches in the vestry. The minister's wife and two members of the chapel had made sandwiches and some of the children were still eating.

'Ruthie! Ruthie, darling. Come to Mummy.'

Peris's arms were outstretched in a dramatic gesture. She became conscious that the chapel women were watching with open curiosity. Ruthie didn't move.

'That girl. That one!'

Peris drew Valmai's attention to the older girl who was holding Ruthie's hand.

'We saw her talking to Ruthie on the rocking horse. You saw her, Val! That one. She ought to be arrested. That one.'

Tim Horen nodded sagely.

'Well in a manner of speaking she is already.'

'Inciting children. Breaking into people's homes. Ruthie. Come here at once. We must go home. Daddy is getting terribly worried.'

Under pressure, the habit of obedience reasserted itself. A link was broken. Nothing was said.

The journey home was a silent gloomy affair. Tim Horen had

run out of jokes and humorous comments. He concentrated on driving and his own thoughts. Valmai made one or two attempts to talk to Ruthie. Peris seemed to discourage the effort by drawing Ruthie closer to her side. When they came in sight of Caesengi the policeman broke out into a cheerful song.

'Here we are again... happy as can be...'

Peris gave Ruthie sporadic hugs in an attempt to make her respond with a grateful smile.

Gareth Garmon was pacing up and down under the portico, clutching his hands like a footballer on the touchline waiting to be called on to the field of play. There was a flurry of excitement as Peris pulled Ruthie by the hand and delivered her into her father's arms. From the police car Tim Horen and Valmai watched the family reunion. Gareth gave them a brief wave and brief thanks before their backs were turned as they entered the house and closed the door.

'There you go,' the policeman said. 'That's as much of thanks we are likely to get. Big house isn't it? Make a very nice detention centre. Did you tell her about hubby's hanky-panky?'

Tim murmured his question close to Valmai's ear and she shifted away resenting his assumption of intimacy.

'Well, they do say, never come between husband and wife. You'll only get hurt in the collision. Off we go then.'

On their way back to the town Tim drove well within the speed limit. There were things he wanted to say but for once he was at a loss to find the words to say them.

'Funny old world we live in,' he said.

'You've said that before.'

'Yes but all the way from Azerbaijan for God's sake. Pinching school milk and dinosaur slices. Anyway they had a go. If you put that in one of your stories nobody would believe you.'

Her attitude was so discouraging he lapsed into silence. When they reached Valmai's place he determined to speak.

'I tell you what Val. You give me twenty five percent of the sale price, at your convenience, of course, and we call off the legal dogs. Then we can be friends again. After all we didn't have such a bad time together, did we? How's that for an offer?'

Valmai took her time to answer. She opened the door of the police car and stepped out.

'See my solicitor,' she said.

Glasshouses

I

Angharad Hobel turned a well dressed shoulder against the sharp breeze blowing across the channel. Fashion photographers could take exotic models and pose them against the most desolate surroundings. They were well paid to suffer the indignities and discomforts. And they were young and relentlessly vigorous. Angharad was forty and rich, and she felt the cold. She did not intend to put up with it.

'You drag me down here,' she said. 'What am I supposed to see? Visions of cloud-capped towers? Glass miracles? I can see the clouds. Where the hell are the towers?'

She clamped her hand on the smart hat she was wearing as though she were tempted to throw it away. The tide was out and on the mud flats below where they stood, a surprising variety of sea birds were feeding. She had little interest in their habits or their habitat. In the distance, abandoned derricks and cranes made a black melancholy montage against low clouds that threatened rain any minute.

'We are in this together.'

Gareth Pengry raised a clenched fist above the rusty railings he was leaning against.

'And this place in the end will give us what we both want. That's the point I'm trying to make.'

'You've got a big idea of yourself haven't you?'

'Yes I have.'

The young man smiled broadly and put up a hand to protect his oiled brushed-back fair hair from the gusting wind. His baby-faced good looks emphasised the ten year difference between them. It was more than a community of interest that held them together. They enjoyed each other's company.

'If we play our cards right, you'll get the father and I'll get the girl.'

He held his breath and pressed his lips together so that she could see how daring he felt he had been.

'You are the cheekiest little bastard. You really are.'

Whether her anger was simulated or not he behaved as though it were a squall that had to be weathered.

'As soon as I heard I knew I had to get in touch with you.'

'My God, it's going from bad to worse...'

'Please. Don't misunderstand me. It's terrible of course. A tragedy. I know she was your best friend long before she became his wife. Of course I know it.'

'You are a cold-blooded little sod. You really are.'

'I know she was a wonderful person. Nobody knows that better. She was good to me. Took me under her wing. She was sorry for me. Brought up by a bullying Baptist. She thought my old man was much too harsh with me.'

'Dear, dear.'

'We have to stand back and see things clearly. Janet was wonderful. Of course she was. She was also the chief obstacle to Dan Melor's career. All that talent going to waste. Because of her Welsh obsessions. What else can you call them? Janet kept him on a pedestal, and his hands and his brain petrified with purity.'

'And now she's out of the way, Master Pengry has a master-plan to release them.'

'We've got to set him free!'

'We?'

The sharp edge of sarcasm did nothing to deter him.

'This derelict dock site is part of the equation. He still has it in him to bring it all back into life. And we are the ones to help him. My nous for management and networking and your money. Even in the earliest stages the finest vision will get nowhere without financial backing.'

'And that's it,' she said. 'Q.E.D.'

'It's the main part of it. In the meanwhile, you should have a new house to build. All in glass and concrete. And the children's hospital badly needs a new extension which will be known as the Angharad Hobel Wing.'

'My goodness! Breathtaking! And all this because the slip of a girl turned you down. Life never ceases to amaze me.'

'This is what architecture is all about.'

In the direction of the desolate dockland Gareth waved his hand as though it held a magic wand.

'You take the ruins of the past that lie all around you and transform them into laboratories of the spirit made from the newest and the best materials. It's the life of art, Mrs. Hobel, and the art of life. The way I see it, if you want a happy ending, you've got to make it happen.'

As she picked her way carefully across the patch of waste land, her chauffeur heaved himself out of his seat ready to open the door. Gareth chased after her.

'He's living in the most awful discomfort.'

Gareth spoke with urgent sincerity.

'Woodfires, smoke and damp everywhere. Dan's terribly lonely. And Ceri is difficult. Gone off on a pilgrimage. Angharad. You're not offended with me, are you?'

He dared to hold on to her arm.

'Shall we keep in touch?'

Gently she released herself and walked towards the car.

II

The precise moment was 8.28 on a cold January morning. Who could blame the sun? It shone out of nowhere on a dull day: a sudden visitation to be welcomed. Blame the brow of the hill. Or the great lorry that also came out of nowhere. Janet was late for a school she didn't really need to attend. Yet another missionary journey to help acclimatise incomers' children; incorporate them, give them the heritage, the language, transfuse them with the colour of the community. She was dazzled, blinded, too much sun in her eyes killed her. It happened and it couldn't unhappen. The memory scarred, not the landscape. No point in returning to the spot. No one has the inalienable right to exist. Not even Janet. So wise and so beautiful. A most perfect person.

Not in cold logic. That is why cold logic belongs to the grave. This is the daily bread of thought Dan chews and cannot swallow. It lasts longer than sorrow.

Angharad needed to restrain herself from passing remarks. An old habit. Part of a soured nature. She was dressed like a rich woman on her way to horse trials, wearing suede boots, a thick jacket and a headscarf. To be alone with Dan was also an excitement to be contained. She could steady herself by contemplating the condition of the ancient cottage: picturesque perhaps, hidden in the slope of a neglected garden, and chronically uncomfortable. For him it was a necessary background that he made almost noble. She saw him like an exiled king, sitting in his high-backed patriarchal chair nursing his hands in his lap, resolutely stoic, a carved monument of suffering. He was no longer the dark taciturn young man she had been in love with before he was captivated by the delightful Janet. Now there were lines on his hollowed-out cheeks and his hair was grey and she could worship him even more: pour the solicitous oil of her silence over his motionless head. She sat opposite him in the inglenook and when she leaned back on the settle she could glimpse the sky through the chimney. From the wood above the garden came the scent of bluebells. The garden was overgrown and in summer it would become a jungle. Alone in winter had he kept warm while he searched for solace in the stars above the chimney? Even now on a reasonably warm day he soothed his frayed nerves by feeding the open fire with sticks and brushwood, found some comfort staring at the fitful flames.

'I'm rather concerned about Ceri.'

She loved his slow thoughtful way of talking, and to protect herself from excessive feeling, often pretended to be impatient with it. The facts he needed to unburden himself with seemed as heavy as the dolerite stones of which the cottage was built.

'She won't go back to college. Not interested in taking her degree. She wants to concentrate on her consciousness. Light and love she calls it.'

'What about Taizé? I thought...'

Angharad cut herself short. It hardly mattered what she thought. She was there to listen.

'Not rigorous enough for her.'

He seemed at the point of venturing a craggy smile. The inclination faded. He was too concerned about his only daughter.

'Too happy-clappy,' he said. 'She wants harsh discipline and she thinks she's found it. A guru can't go wrong, can he? All he does is wait for a disaster to happen. You've got to work out your own salvation, I told her. That's exactly what I'm doing, she said.'

'You've got to look out for yourself.'

Angharad's bracelet jangled as she expressed the depth of this conviction.

'I don't know what to think. About anything really. Amazing isn't it? From a man who thought he knew everything'

This time he did smile as though he rather enjoyed disparaging himself. For Angharad there were detectable cause and effect. The girl had lost her mother and was in search of another prop to lean on. She was childless herself and had been much concerned with a worldly career so she had no immediate measure of the depth and extent of emotional bond between mother and daughter. In whatever move she decided to make it was an important factor. At the moment, alone in these solitary surroundings with the man she had loved for so long, it was as much as she could cope with to restrain the urge to take him in her arms and comfort him.

'This chap she calls Father Ambrose. He's an ex-con.'

She had to wait while he mustered the energy to carry on. Precipitate comment could drive him into a silence she might never penetrate.

'Janet helped to set him up at Glyn Euryn because he promised to learn Welsh. Which he has after a fashion. Sent to prison for a crime he didn't commit although he was happy to admit he committed plenty of others. Hardened criminal he was. He says so himself. In prison he saw the light.'

'Good Lord.'

She could not suppress a troubled response. She knew more

than he did about criminals. They had circulated her worldly progress like sharks around a whaler. They smelt money ten miles off.

'There's no reason why he isn't quite genuine. He runs what you might call a Retreat supported by a market garden. The inmates do the work. At the moment my problem is that Ceri sees it as her destiny to look after plants and cultivate her soul. She may well be right of course. She always was a stubborn little thing. Janet used to say it was because she had red hair.'

The name was out. All they could do was gaze grimly into the smouldering wood fire and think about her. How close they had been away at school. Ministers' daughters. Exiles in a foreign land, sent away, they afterwards assured each other, to get a private education on the cheap. Janet crept into her bed because her feet were cold. Icicles on the eaves above the window. That girlish voice with the trace of a lisp eagerly in search of good causes, wonderfully unaware of her charm and good looks. Even now Angharad could feel those old familiar twinges of envy. When did it begin? When she realised it was always Janet the boys wanted to talk to. She needed a brisk cause for action, such as a pan and brush to sweep up the ash spreading over the stone hearth.

'Is it so pointless?'

He didn't expect an answer. He spoke as though she wasn't there. She squared her jaw. It was time to speak out.

'You know what I think. You need something decent to eat. I've got a picnic basket in the car. It's not such a bad day. We can go down to the beach. Cemaes cove. A picnic on the rocks. And then when you've eaten I've got some very important things I want to discuss with you.'

He stared dolefully at Angharad as though she were a visitor from another life.

'I don't go out much,' he said.

'Well it's time you did. In my chauffeur-driven Mercedes. You remember John Ifor, don't you?'

'Your bodyguard...'

It was the glimmer of an old joke and she laughed with relief.

'He'll look after us. He's getting too fat but he knows which side his bread is buttered.'

Mention of the chauffeur, who was also Angharad's second cousin, made Dan Melor reluctant to move. It suggested the complexities of an outside world he was still anxious to avoid. She was compelled to work up a fit of indignation.

'Look at you! As far as I can see all you are doing is sinking deeper into a feather bed of gloom and despondency. That's not something Janet would have approved of. Ever. She believed in action!'

'And look where it got her.'

'Dan Melor. That is a terrible thing to say. Just terrible. She was in no way responsible and you know it. And she would have hated to see the mess this place is in. I can tell you that. And she would have loathed to see you sinking into a state of paralysed self-pity. Are you coming out? Do I have to go on my knees and beg?'

His smile was sudden and spontaneous and it made her want to hug him.

'Well, now I come to think of it I am quite hungry.'

He stretched himself and took her arm to lead her through the low doorway of the country cottage. He paused for a last question.

'What will he do, John Ifor? While we are on the beach?'

'Read.'

She smiled gaily.

'He works his way through paper-back thrillers. Ideal he says for a sedentary occupation. And he still drums his fingers on the steering wheel. Don't you remember?'

III

Father Ambrose lay on a battered sofabed in what he called the office at the far end of the largest greenhouse in the nurseries at Glyn Euryn. Beyond the dirty windows two camellia bushes were shedding their red blossom as the end of the petals turned yellow. It was a site where there was always more work unfinished than tidied up. He was covered by a horse blanket and his large feet in their earth-caked boots dangled beyond the length of the bed. The work was too much for him. He had an ear infection and a fever. Ceri brought him a glass of water with which to swallow an antibiotic tablet. She urged him to be patient and rest.

'I tell you what's patient,' he said. 'A dray horse in its stall. That's me, Ceri, old girl. An old dray horse in his stall. Waiting for the knacker's yard.'

Nothing could suppress his good humour while she was around. Under his close-cropped white hair his large blue eyes stared at her with unblinking benevolence. Deafness made him raise his voice and yet what came out was a hoarse rough-edged whisper. The clerical collar dangled around his neck looked more like an off-white necklace since he wore only a kahki singlet under a crumpled alpaca jacket. The beauty of the girl among the blooms in his greenhouse made him smile. The dirt on her overall and the way her auburn hair was held back by a working headband enhanced her good looks in his eyes: the peach colour of her cheeks seemed that much more rare and delicate.

'Suspicious little bugger,' Father Ambrose said. 'That friend of yours. He's not as young as he looks either, is he? Bloody babyface. D'you know who he reminded me of? D.S. Polson. Chief Inspector if you please before he retired on his fat pension. The lying bastard. Pardon my French won't you, but it does help me to get it off my chest every now and then. Like squeezing a pimple. The old complaint. He's the one that cooked the books and sent me down for seven years. Your little chum's got that look about him. Never believes a word anybody says because he never tells the truth himself. You like him then?'

'I did once.'

He tilted his head and strained to hear her soft voice.

'Have I hurt your feelings?'

She smiled and shook her head.

'That's what we all live by isn't it, when you get down to it. Feelings. Got to govern them of course. How do we do that? That's the trick. How now brown cow?'

He swallowed the tablet with a bit of fuss and gulped down

the cold water complaining he had been born with a bloody narrow throat.

'I get a bit peevish you know when I'm tied down like this. Brings back the old days. The bad side of me comes bubbling up like scum on boiling jam. It's like when you lie in your cell and the world is shrunk to a grey wall and your eye is as dull as a dried pea. You want to be set free. Let that cell door open! You can't be free unless someone sets you free. And even in the end when it's all behind you and you're out and about you can't be free of your own nature. Do you trust him?'

'I thought I did.'

She could give nothing less than an honest answer to this old man who was never as extremely old as he looked. The things he had suffered were etched on his face and had left an aura around his awkward white head.

'I'm not so sure any more.'

'Faith means trust in my book. You find out for yourself, Ceri Melor. And don't you let me take advantage of you either because your mother was good to me. She understood things you know. Better than an old lag like me. If you give it an ear you're bound to hear her voice. I think I believe that. The answers she found are bound to be floating around in the air around us. Like music for us to play. I believe that. It's a terrible pain but it can't be all loss. I've come to believe that. The music is still there. Waiting to be played. Where are you off to?'

'I want to put fresh flowers on her grave.'

'Of course you do.'

'I won't be gone long. I know there's a lot to do.'

Father Ambrose looked at the girl with unlimited benevolence.

'This isn't a greenhouse I told him. It's an oasis. That made him look more suspicious than ever. A rest home I said for ex-cons. A clinic for the misfits of this world. Funny isn't it? Simple ideas can make clever people so suspicious. I suppose he is clever, isn't he?'

Her shy response was enough to make him realise Gareth Pengry still meant a great deal to the girl. She was vulnerable and she had to learn to protect herself.

'He wants to muscle in on your life,' he said. 'Well, that's the way it is. Nature is very purposeful. Natural selection and so on. The predatory male. You take your time, my girl. That's all I'm saying. Remember you have a duty to yourself.'

IV

Angharad Hobel was pleased with the change of mood in Dan Melor when he transferred from the untidy gloom of his cottage retreat to the luxurious interior of her Mercedes limousine. He still smelt of woodsmoke and neglect and his square chin was unshaven but he was clearly amused by the situation: the upholstery and the gadgets, 'smoke and mirrors' he called them, the broad dependable shoulders of the chauffeur, the gliding progress of vehicle. 'More like gliding than riding,' he said. She made a quiet joke about him not being disgusted by a display of wealth and his reaction was childlike and charming. It reminded him, he said of the Sunday School outings of his early childhood. 'A dream chariot to carry you along.' She was privately thrilled to see a man so stern of aspect and so obviously having undergone a period of prolonged suffering, laughing and joking with the chauffeur who also enjoyed having such a passenger so unexpectedly agreeable.

The blue sky also helped. White clouds were piling up along the mountains but the sun shone on the water. They drove through the sand dunes and the pine forest. John Ifor the chauffeur produced a privileged key and they drove to a reserved car park hidden in the trees. The sandy cove among the rocks, where they settled, gave them a view of the tranquil sea and, across the bay, of a fishing village turned tourist centre and beyond, the massive outline of a nuclear power station out of commission. John Ifor to whom Angharad still referred playfully as her bodyguard brought the leather travelling bar and the picnic basket. Dan carried folding chairs and a motoring rug. Pretending to be out of breath but laughing and whistling John Ifor returned to his much loved chariot, his paperback and his sandwiches. He said if all went well he would even take a nap.

They ate and drank well. Angharad was carefully affectionate without referring at all to old times. Dan at least looked capable of relaxing and for the time being forgetting his tribulation. They drank more wine from their stainless steel tumblers. Angharad sat, prim and regal, on one of the folding chairs. Dan stretched out on the car rug his chin tucked into the polo neck of the grubby white pullover he was wearing. He squinted at the sea and the sky as he sipped the red Burgundy. It was all so calm and immemorial, conducive to a confessional mode.

'I have to admit things were not all that marvellous between us. Not all the time.'

She stiffened in an attempt to conceal her eagerness to listen.

'She thought I was idle. She was right too. Right about most things. I am lazy.'

Although she would never believe that she restrained herself from saying so.

'But never riven with disappointment. Deeply frustrated and so on. She was wrong there.'

'Did she say that?'

This was meant as an inquiry not a protest.

'Not in so many words. She was so active. She thought I was consumed with unattainable dreams. That may have been true in my youth. But we grow out of these things. Everyone does.'

'Janet spoilt you.'

He didn't pause to ask in what way.

'She was so clear about everything,' he said. 'Those razor sharp ideals. So easy to cut yourself on them. You could call it a quiet way of living dangerously. Love me, love my causes. So she led and I followed. She dared and I scrambled to keep up. She allowed me my little hobbies. She shared them as far as she could spare the time and the effort. Painting ruins and so on. Studying the rocks and the remote past. The comforts of research. Pleasant pastimes.'

Angharad's patience gave out.

'Do you want to know what I think? She suffocated you. That's what I think.'

'Good Lord. Do you really?'

He filled his tumbler with the last of the Burgundy bottle. He wanted to consider this surprising verdict with studied impartiality. She had gone too far to turn back.

'I knew her before you did, Dan Melor. And loved her too. I know how demanding she could be. Not for her own benefit of course. Always for a cause. With a capital C. Part of her attraction I suppose. Nothing to impair her perfection.'

She sighed and became suddenly despondent. She was comparing her present self to her dead friend and finding herself wanting. Dan Melor, for his part, found this unexpected morose silence rather consoling. He raised his tumbler in Angharad's direction in a gesture of homage to an elegant presence.

'You look so well,' he said. 'And you've done so well. Getting and spending did not necessarily waste your powers eh? More fun too in the market place. Did you find that?'

There were traces of old friendship and old frankness to enjoy with the fragrance of the wine. She had looked him up and taken him out and he would show quiet appreciation.

'Fun?'

Angharad's neat nose wrinkled with distaste.

'That wasn't a word I used. Sol Hobel was a driven man and he drove me along with him.'

'Join the club!'

She ignored his unexpected frivolity. Perhaps he had drunk more than usual. Before his tongue became any looser there were things he had to know. He had to be made to understand her situation as thoroughly as she was prepared to understand his.

'Sol had two interests in life. Money and sex. And in that order.'

Her bluntness shocked him into giving her closer attention.

'Two things people could never have enough of he said. He would make them the foundation of his fortune. Make his hobby his business and his business his hobby. And so on. That was the way he talked and the way he lived. I had a lot to put up with.'

Dan gave a discreet sigh to show sympathy. He was in the company of a more exotic creature than either he or Janet had ever imagined. This is what happened in the years between: the transforming of people. He made a solemn effort to try and remember what Angharad Owen had been like when they were young. The effort was overshadowed by the overpowering memory of Janet. If she had been with them now she would have been so deeply sympathetic to her old friend and so understanding. That was one of the great things about her. In spite of all her demanding ideals she was unfailingly tolerant. And what about this Sol Hobel creature? Had he been anything more than a choice candidate for the fifth circle of Hell?

'He was clever of course. And so quick. One of the first to see the profitable link between advertising and telecommunications. A finger in every pie. It was the end of him really. Rushing around the sub-continent setting up deals. Off to Kashmir with an unknown woman for rest and relaxation. Some awful fish disease and he was gone before anybody could help him. The victim of a twin obsession with secrecy and celebrity. He never got his knighthood.'

He listened both appalled and impressed. In the wide world Janet's best friend at school had acquired such a depth and so much resilience. From the same sheltered background she had survived and triumphed in a piratical business world. Janet would have admired that surely? And what had he done? One much admired house in Aberdaron and another like it in Donegal. Taught architecture and landscape. Those who can, do. Those who can't, teach.

'Dirty mags of all shapes and sizes. Then into advertising and mobile phones. And on to global ambitions. "Always buy, never sell." "Timing is of the essence." "Knowledge is Power." I can hear him now. And too much fish finishes him off. And in the end his barren wife gets the lot. He could buy a bank but he couldn't make a baby. The Hobel name comes to an end with little me. How he would hate that.'

Her flow of reminiscence came to an abrupt end.

'We mustn't live in the past or we'll have no future. My God I've got to sound just like him. Is there any more to drink?'

Dan rummaged obediently in the leather bar and shook his head.

'Anyway I've got my millions and you've got your daughter.'

Dan Melor sat back on the sand, grasped his boots with his hands, and began to rock himself to and fro.

'Well I can tell you,' he said. 'I'm in a permanent state of being deeply puzzled by everything.'

'You were in shock. That's understandable.'

'I think it goes back further than that, to be honest. There were too many puzzles I couldn't solve. Then they became problems.'

'Well dear...' She sounded decisive. 'Start working out a puzzle by designing a house for me.'

'Is that a commission?'

'The first of many. If you'll take them. You see. I'm being very open. Very unladylike. I think we could have a future together. Nothing too binding. Nothing to inhibit you. A free collaboration.'

'Where is it? This new house. Where do you want it?'

'I thought Castiglione della Pascaia. But I have an open mind about it. We could do some preliminary research. That would be fun.'

Dan was smiling and shaking his head.

'From what you've told me we live in two different worlds,' he said.

'We don't have to. What I want more than anything is to release your potential. Oh my God I'm sounding like Sol again. I have faith in your creativity. It means more to me than I can say. There you are. I'm begging again.'

'I'm sorry,' he said. 'You are being marvellous.'

He walked from where they sat to the edge of the sea. The sand was smooth and scattered with a myriad worn shells of every size and colour, everywhere the evidence of the perpetual ebb and flow. The vast emptiness of the waters lay before him. When he turned he saw the woman still seated on her chair among the rocks. On the road next to the foreshore the large

Mercedes was parked and as far as he could detect at such a distance the chauffeur was asleep at the wheel.

Returning to Angharad he was in a more positive mood.

'There's no reason why we couldn't take a look,' he said.

V

In the light rain a solitary goldfinch perched itself on a twig of the straggling cotoneaster that grew outside the potting shed window. Her hands deep in compost, the girl stood motionless in order to absorb every detail of the young bird's bright colours and nervous ticks. How long would it stay in such close range on such a trembling perch. Ceri held her breath.

'This is where I find you.'

Gareth's voice was soft and attentive. Ceri did not move. The bird's wing twitched giving a glimpse of a gold flash.

'After searching the world...'

The bird flew off. Ceri turned raising her hands covered in compost to discourage him from coming closer.

'How can we be alone without me touching you?'

It was something he had said to her before. A first time, when he'd held her face in his hands and kissed both her eyes before kissing her lips. He used words like 'seal' and 'pledge' and they had lodged in her mind, too available, too easily recalled, however much she tried to dismiss them as hackneyed and absurd. They had a painful capacity for insisting on their own significance. At this moment they drained the blood from her cheeks.

'You never answered my letters. You are blaming me. How could I come to her funeral? I didn't hear anything. I was in Helsinki. I loved her. You know that. She meant so much to me. You know that.'

'Not as much as your career.'

He was as attractive and as confident as ever. It would have been too easy to give way to him.

'Ah, that's it! You've convinced yourself I let your father

down. It's not true you know. He knew I had to go out into the wide world to prove myself. To see how far I could go. Now I've been and I've seen. And I'm more convinced than ever of the man's wisdom. And his genius. And more convinced than ever how much I love his daughter.'

The moment she smiled he took her in his arms. She held her compost covered hands up and it seemed an odd gesture of surrender. His hands were renewing acquaintance with every contour of her body and for the moment she allowed it to happen.

'I talked to you all the time.'

He murmured fervently but it was his hands that made more evident what he wanted to say.

'In my head. All the time.'

'I didn't hear you.'

'This is what matters most,' he said. 'Being together. It's all we are in the end. What we can hold. What we can feel. Talking isn't enough. You are your body. What else? What else?'

Ceri pushed at his shoulders with her wrists. She needed to breathe and to bring the situation under her control.

'Stop. Gareth. Stop and listen to me.'

Father Ambrose appeared in the open doorway. He wore a rug over his shoulders and his nose was running. He wiped it with a large red handkerchief.

'Everything alright in here then?'

Apart from the hoarseness, his voice was as benevolent as ever. His smile as much as his large figure blocked the doorway. The rug on his shoulders added to his bulk. Gareth was angry and embarrassed.

'Is there no such thing as privacy in this place then?'

Father Ambrose lowered his head to give the question some thought.

'Good question,' he said. 'I suppose there is. For those who really need it. Never thought of it as all that much of a luxury myself. See you later then.'

He was gone but he left an atmosphere distinctly deflated behind him.

'The old fool,' Gareth said. 'The old phoney.'

The expression on her face made him attempt a change of tone.

'Well he is a bit of an old fraud, isn't he? Once a con man always a con man.'

'He was never a con man,' Ceri said. 'He was a burglar. He belonged to a gang. The Bombsite Boys. All under fourteen. That's how he started. They broke into cinemas at three o'clock on a Sunday morning. In the end he was put in prison for seven years on a false charge. And an extra three for attacking a prison officer. All in all it gave him time to think. He's a man who's seen the light.'

'Is that so?'

In spite of himself scepticism broke in.

'My mother thought so.'

It was an immediate and effective brake. He stretched an arm to touch her and let it fall again.

'Your mother thought the best of everybody,' he said.

'Including you.'

'Listen. I'm very serious. I've thought a great deal about this. I want to pay my respects. Put flowers on her grave and so on. I loved her more than anyone apart from you. And then, I don't care what it sounds like, I want to propose to you. Over her grave.'

The more solemn he sounded the more Ceri appeared to enjoy her advantage.

'Propose what, Gareth?'

'Don't try and make me look foolish. Marriage of course. What else?'

'I thought nobody got married in Denmark any more.'

'Listen. I've never been more serious. We love each other. You can feel it now. The pulse. It's an electricity at the core of our being. The rhythm of creation for God's sake. Not just sex in the head. One body's need for the other.'

'Not just me, Gareth. Surely any woman would do.'

'I'm serious,' he said. 'Sex is us. You and me together. I can't live a proper life without you. In you.'

She turned away from his grasping hands.

'Gosh. The blazing revelation to come. The ultimate orgasm.'

'I'm serious, Ceri. Just listen.'

She elbowed him away and walked over to the single cold water tap to wash her hands with clinical deliberation.

'Soft flesh and hard flesh,' she said. 'Fucking and more fucking. The epicentre of existence.'

'Well it is, for God's sake. When you get down to it. When you're dead, you're dead. And that's the end of it. So why not live to the limit while you're alive? Can't we get out of here? I want to talk. You are making me say all the wrong things. Not what I want to say at all. I love you. Don't you understand?'

'You know what my mother said to me about you? She liked you. She said you were very likeable. Very charming. Only insufficiently rooted.'

'Is that what she said? And that's why I find myself in this grotty potting shed. I'm here to be rooted.'

'There are things that we have to learn,' Ceri said. 'That's why I'm here.'

'What for instance? Tell me what.'

'You really want to know?'

'Of course I do.'

'Well for a start, God loves the dead and the decomposing as much as he loves the living.'

'You've had the most terrible loss,' Gareth said. 'I can understand that. I can feel it. You're distraught. That's what it amounts to.'

'I was. I'm not any more.'

'You're still grieving.'

'Not even that anymore.'

'I wasn't here to comfort you. I should have been here to comfort you.'

'Well you weren't, were you? You were busy elsewhere.'

A statement of fact, not a reproach. She was drying her hands on a rough towel and appeared excessively calm.

'I've learnt things here. I'm at peace now.'

'Here! Cheap labour, that's what you are. You're being conned.'

'You are angry. Because you want me. The question is, do I want you?'

'Of course you do. You know that. We are made for each other.'

'Not the way you are, Gareth. You have to learn too.'

'Learn? In this place! No, thank you.'

'Well. There we are then. You'd better get away quickly. In case you become infected.'

VI

'Well if you won't have him you won't have him. And that's all there is to it.'

The red plush library of the country house hotel had been reserved for their exclusive use. Angharad made a joke of it: a conference for two or three, she said. She was in charge. Dan Melor was liable to lapse into depths of introspection. John Ifor was elsewhere. Ready to respond to any summons she might make. Her mind was always quickly made up. Pick up Gareth Pengry and bring him back here when I give the signal. Meanwhile he could kick off his shoes, toast his stockinged feet in front of a hotel fire and immerse himself into another action-packed paperback, his Mercedes also comfortably stabled in the ample garage at the rear. The unseasonable weather restricted everything. Rain blurred the celebrated view from the library window of the gorge and the waterfall and the serried ranks of rocks and dripping pine trees.

'Sol found him useful. 'Garry boy' he used to call him. Like all the Welsh, Sol said. Pliable. Ingratiating. Eager to please and even more eager to get on. I stuck up for the boy. I never saw anyone more eager to get on than you, Sol Hobel. And talk about pliable. All your rules are made of plasticine.'

Dan gazed into the middle distance, a judge unable to sum up or decide on a final verdict. His craggy features hovered on the brink of a smile as he disentangled Angharad's humour from strictly relevant evidence.

'He did a good job on the warehouse in Cwmbran. Sol was pleased with that. And the place in Chalfont St. Giles. Not that I ever liked it. I'm a Mediterranean person myself. I can see why now if I ever doubted it. I've only got to look out of the window. John Ifor loves it too. He's got friends you know in a God-forsaken village south of Naples. Believe it or not John Ifor was a talented footballer in his youth. Travelled to Naples with a Bangor team for some cup final or other. The coach was trundling down a side street in search of their cheap hotel and it was followed in hot pursuit by an ex-prisoner-of-war on a bicycle. He'd recognised *Cae Dafydd Motors* painted on the back. The birth of a beautiful friendship. John Ifor says that that was the moment he realised for the first time he was living in a small world.'

Dan Melor smiled briefly then lapsed into judicial mode.

'I could be doing him an injustice,' he said.

His fingers twitched indecisively as he dangled his hands between his legs.

'I wouldn't call him a thief. A pupil has to imitate. And borrowing is never the same thing as stealing. And there is such a thing as legitimate ambition. I would never deny that. But he's manipulative. I think that's what got on my nerves.'

'The fact is, he has an enormous admiration for you. You could say that's what he and I had in common. He thinks you are a genius.'

Dan was too preoccupied with judgement to deny the allegation.

'Shall I order some coffee?' Angharad asked. 'This is the end of May for God's sake and I'm shivering.'

'Not with me,' Dan said. 'He couldn't manipulate me and didn't even try. But with Janet he knew exactly how to play on her sympathy. And she was wonderful to him. I must have resented the way he found of taking advantage of her good nature. And he was always on such good terms with himself. He's made for politics. All the tricks and twists and turns. I'm not. And of course he always had his eye on Ceri.'

'Well if you can't stand him you can't stand him, and that's it.'

Angharad plucked at the bell-pull.

'There are moments when I simply can't stand hotels. All I want is a home of my own. All my own. And for you to design it. Everything else can wait. That's what I feel about it.'

'I'm too old for competitions,' Dan said. 'I gave up all that sort of thing years ago.'

'I know exactly how you feel.'

She sat opposite him in an identical red plush library chair.

'It can be corrosive. Being too competitive can corrode the spirit. I saw it all with Sol Hobel. So many twists and turns. You end up with perversion. At least he did. Okay. Strictly no competitions.'

The coffee was brought in and they sat opposite each other sipping in silence. Angharad put down her cup and began to twitch with a fresh anxiety to please.

'It doesn't have to be Castiglione della Pascaia,' she said. 'I have the bit of land there because Sol thought it might bring him in neighbourly touch with a powerful Italian politician. Andreotti, I think it was. Some Christian Democrat anyway who fell from grace. So then he never bothered to build. Perhaps if we looked elsewhere... I rather fancy Aix en Provence. There's a jolly nice village outside with a smashing view of Mont Sainte-Victoire. What do you think?'

His continuing silence drove her to a minor panic.

'It doesn't have to be anywhere special,' she said. 'So long as it's you and me.'

Dan Melor had closed his eyes and was shaking his head.

'It doesn't matter about me. Or about my new house. All glass and stone and concrete. Well, it does matter. But what matters most is that you should start work again. Give your genius a chance. That's what I want more than anything else in the world.'

'I've misled you,' Dan said. 'And I'm deeply sorry. You are a wonderful person. We always thought so. Janet and I. I can't leave. I can't go with you.'

'You're worrying about Ceri. She wouldn't be pleased about me...'

'It's not that. Ceri is like her mother. Well able to stand on her own feet. It's not easy to explain. I want to be free. I've learnt this since I've been alone in the cottage. Maybe I was always a hermit inside. A hidden hermit. Is it the stream that erodes the rock or the rock that deflects the stream? I've discovered I can quite happily spend the rest of my life contemplating moss and lichen on dry stone walls. I never want to build anything bigger than a hut from now on. Self sufficient. Independent.'

Angharad paced about the room wretched with disappointment. 'Such a waste,' she kept saying. 'Such a waste.'

Melor was smiling with relief.

'I could be no good at it,' he said. 'But I have to try. Then we'll see won't we? I suspect it might take just as much energy as building the Taj Mahal.'

VII

The wind had scattered blackthorn blossom across the narrow lane and then swept it on to the green verge like white confetti. Dressed in her working overall the girl, carrying flowers in the crook of her arm, could still have been going to a wedding. This was a short cut to the church yard. The fields on either side were overpopulated with ewes and their lambs. The bleating competed with the birdsong. At the gate a pair of yew trees had grown tall enough to form an arch. Beyond there was the smell of mown grass. Only half of the circular graveyard had been skim-cut. For the rest, the fitful sunlight glittered on the succulent green grass. When Ceri reached the black gates, Gareth Pengry stepped out to greet her. He was smartly dressed in a light brown suit, silk shirt and blue bow-tie. He smiled in the hope that she would be pleased to see him. She stood still and clutched her flowers more tightly.

'Ceri,' he said. 'Ceri. Darling. I want to apologize.'

For a moment longer she was prepared to listen.

'You are right of course. You are always right. All the same there are some very suspicious characters lurking around Glyn Euryn. They are obviously on the run. Hiding from something. And why call him Father? When was he ordained? It's none of my business of course. Except that I'm concerned for you.'

Her silence was disconcerting. She was waiting for him to step aside. He spoke as he did so.

'I've been to the grave. It's a wonderful spot. It's the kind of place she would have chosen... You know what I mean. So atmospheric. Romantic would be the word. The remains of the central arcade of the old church still standing. Even the weeds are beautiful.'

As he followed her through the gravestones he was finding it difficult to stop talking. There were dead flowers to be disposed of in the compost corner of the churchyard. In the parking space in front of the lych-gate she could see a new car that had to be his. It was small but it looked as smart as its owner where he had parked it in the shade of an overhanging yew. Gareth found a place to sit on a horizontal slate tombstone. He had a concern for his dress. Ceri knelt in the grass to arrange the fresh flowers she had brought from the greenhouse at Glyn Euryn.

'I've been thinking a lot about marriage,' Gareth said. 'How it used to be when all these people were alive. Such a fateful sort of business. Every future depended on it. That's what made me say I wanted to propose to you over your mother's grave. There's a story somewhere where the fate of a nation depends on an oath taken over a grave. That sort of thing. Are you listening to me?'

'Of course I am.'

There were weeds already growing out of the mound of earth. She pushed at them with a rusty trowel left at the grave-side. The soil was something to stir. Into the metal holder inside a porcelain vase she stuck the stems of white irises.

'I think we have to get married because we are bound together in so many ways. Words are hopeless. We should be in bed together, not arguing in a graveyard. All the same this means something. We both loved her and we both love each other. I call all these tombstones to witness! We've got to work together. The future depends on it.'

He raised his arms in what was intended as a half-humorous appeal. He promptly lowered them when he saw she was not inclined to smile. He slapped his knees in a business like gesture.

'There's so much to attend to,' he said. 'We've got to do something about your father. For the sake of the country. Your mother would understand. All that style and skill and vision were never more urgently needed. Our country is at a turning point. I really believe that. And his kind of architecture has a vital part to play. That's if we are ever going to count for anything in the modern world. Do you know what I mean?'

She sat back on her heels and surveyed him calmly.

'You're looking very smart,' she said. 'All dressed up.'

'I wish you'd listen to me,' he said. 'I've got such huge plans for us. We have a duty to apply your father's principles, lessons, ideas, vision. Whatever you like to call them. We've got to reach out to each other, Ceri. You've got to tell me what you are thinking.'

He waited patiently to hear her speak. He adjusted his jacket to appear a model of rational expectation. Ceri used the trowel to point at the mound of earth.

'The first moment and the last moment are buried here. So they can't be all that much different.'

Gareth showed her he was willing to make the effort to understand.

'I have to go over every moment of her existence before the end. And the end is the beginning. That is what we have to make out. The meaning.'

He nodded sympathetically.

'I see what you mean. We have all our lives to think about that.'

Her back stiffened.

'That's where you are stupid, Gareth Pengry. Absolutely stupid. You are walking through your life with your eyes closed. You don't see anything. Oh, go away, will you. We don't have the same purpose. We don't have anything in common.'

'All right. All right. I've told you I'm willing to learn. Just listen. For your father's sake. Angharad has asked us both to lunch at Cefn Helig.'

'Mrs. Hobel, you mean? Great friend of yours is she?'

'Great friend of your mother's too. She wants to help. Help us and help your father. You can't ask for more than that can you?'

Ceri's head was shaking. Gareth blundered on.

'I can drive you back to Glyn Euryn, so that you could change.

228

Put something nice on. You know how pretty you can look.'

'Pretty!'

She filled the trowel with soil and hurled it at him. He was taken unawares. He looked down at the stains on his shirt.

'Don't distract me, you stupid boy.'

Her body shook with sobs.

'Go to your rich woman. She'll give you what you want. I can't.'

The tears were pouring down her cheeks and mingling with the dirt on her hands. He looked at her in amazement.

VIII

At Glyn Euryn, as far as she could, Ceri Melor maintained a steady routine. She divided her time equally between the kitchen, the nurseries, the fields, meditation and reading. Among the inmates she was a respected figure. She had taken to wearing a grey cloak with a hood that from a distance could be mistaken for a nun's habit. Father Ambrose admitted that he found routine difficult himself. Coming out of prison he said left him with the eternal temptation of messing about. A project here and a project there, meant nothing finished and broken prayer. The trouble with a Rehabilitation Centre was there was too much to rehabilitate. He called Ceri *The Spirit of the Place* and urged her to wander about more, not to work so hard and to keep an eye on him so that he didn't become lax and lazy. "I need you to keep an eye on me," he would say. "Be as stern as you can, my lovely."

Driven in by the weather, Ceri set to scraping the walls of what used to be the housekeeper's sitting room. It was a small compact space with a high ceiling and she was intent on converting it into what could be called a place for meditation rather than a chapel. The wallpaper had an elaborate flower pattern that would have been too distracting. It had to come off. The walls then would be painted battleship grey, as grim as a cell, Father Ambrose said. So perhaps it would be relieved by an icon if they could find one both unobtrusive and inspiring, and a lamp with a steady flame. There was one square window offering a neat view of a single oak tree in the park that could in itself become an object of contemplation.

Midmorning Father Ambrose appeared with two inmates, Nigel and Oggie, unable to work on the outhouse roofs and ready to scrape the walls or whatever else Ceri required them to do. At Glyn Euryn the men were allowed to wear what they liked provided they learned the verse for the day. Both Nigel and Oggie had tattoos, shaved heads and belts with chains. Nigel wore two belts because he was missing two vertebrae. Father Ambrose patted him on the shoulder and said, 'we won't ask how that little accident happened.'

'Now then lads,' he said. 'We're very privileged, aren't we?'

To demonstrate their agreement both men got to work with a will.

'Good lads,' Father Ambrose said. 'Good lads. Ceri, could we go down to the kitchen for a minute. I need your advice.'

The kitchen had the merit of being large, which made up for the lack of modern equipment. One great wall plug served a number of battered machines. Father Ambrose insisted that Ceri occupied the single armchair while he made the tea.

'She's been here again,' he said. 'Chauffeur-driven limousine and all. Talk about an offer you can't refuse. The biggest glasshouse north of Aberystwyth and the house adapted and equipped. Who could ask for more?'

His hoarse voice was an appeal for support.

'She's a very determined woman,' Ceri said.

'She was going on again about how close she was to your mother. Can't wait to see you, she said. Little Ceri.'

'I don't want to see her.'

The girl was adamant. Father Ambrose sighed.

'There must be a catch in it somewhere. What is it you've got against her?'

'You have to do what you want, Father.' Ceri said. 'This is your project.'

'Oh, bloody hell. What I want doesn't matter a raspberry. This place will carry on one way or another. What I want to know is what you think. Is it the dirty money? I don't mind dirty money. I'll tell you why. It goes back a long way. My mother went messing about with Yanks when my dad was away at the war. On the game you might say. For money. Fags and chocolate. I learnt to steal on the bomb sites. For money, fags and chocolates. That's what makes the world go round. Money. All we want to do is put it to better use. What's the lesson in that? Put my greedy soul to rest.'

'Where her money goes, she goes,' Ceri said. 'She'll be here every minute. She won't be able to resist it. She's that kind of woman. Looking for something she can take charge of.'

'She said, "no strings attached"'.

Ceri gave a bleak smile.

'They all say that.'

'Why not believe her? Why not?'

'If she came,' Ceri said. 'I'd have to go. This place couldn't be what I was looking for.'

'What are you looking for, for God's sake?'

'You know very well, Father. They used to call it poverty, chastity, obedience. I don't know whether I could ever make it. But if that woman took over I know I never would.'

Father Ambrose paced about the kitchen before bursting out.

'Isn't it the very devil,' he said. 'If I had any money I'd have to put it on you! That settles it. Let's have another cup of tea to celebrate.'

IX

They sat, an elegant pair, facing the concourse under the mighty glass roof of the Galleria, lifting spacious menus in front of their faces from time to time, like conspirators not wishing to be observed or overheard, although it was unlikely anyone could have been looking at them. Shoppers and tourists sauntered to and fro absorbed in their interests, happy to be at leisure. A brace of carabinieri, huge and decorative, drifted by: swordfish in the aqueous light of a giant aquarium.

'Glyn Euryn's very weird. And they are very weird,' Angharad

Hobel said, not for the first time. 'The best thing we can do is forget about them and get on with it. Get something done.'

Gareth Pengry was in complete agreement. He raised his menu again and stared intently at the dishes on offer.

'It's unhealthy,' he said. 'That old fraud is in love with her.'

'I did what I could.'

Angharad rubbed the tips of her fingers along the crisp pink cloth that covered the table in front of them.

'If somebody hates you, there's nothing you can do about it.'

'I don't think she hates you,' Gareth said. 'I wouldn't say that.'

'It's Janet,' Angharad said. 'It's all her fault really. Such an impossible idealist. Quite impossible.'

She sighed and shook her head.

'We were so close when we were young. Until she snatched Dan Melor under my very nose.'

The waiter brought them plates of risotto and a bottle of wine from the Alto Adige. Gareth was hungry. Angharad played with her food. She pointed her fork at Gareth and became brutally frank to cheer herself up.

'You've got to prove you are an architect not a butterfly, Gareth Pengry. It's all very well looking at the Villa d'Este and the Villa Olmo, popping over to Pesaro to take a look at the Villa this or the Villa that. You've got to get down to it. My dreary bit of land in Castiglione. Make the best of it. And get over being a love-sick swain.'

'It's such a waste...'

'You can't go on saying that. They weighed us up, Pengry and found us wanting. They prefer cherishing their precious souls to getting things done. What's the difference between that and massaging your own ego. Can you tell me that?'

Gareth pushed his plate aside and began to draw on a menu with a black felt pen.

'That's the spirit, my boy! Get down to it. Make a good job on my house and you've got a sleeping partner. In the commercial sense of course. A new place up in Cardiff and one on part of Sol's nefarious premises in Charlotte Street. Hobel and

Pengry. Or should it be Pengry Partners? Glasstowers in Cardiff Bay. Museums from Milford Haven to Mold. I want to get things done. What else is Progress?'

They were smiling and in harmony together.

'So we've got a bargain?'

She offered him her hand and he took it. With her other hand she played with the beads of a bulky red necklace she wore, as she said, as a charm against bad luck or evil chance.

'Bargains make the world go round,' she said. 'And what on earth is wrong with that?'

Unconditional Surrender

"It has been said that the human psyche could never recover from Hiroshima... *Unconditional Surrender* makes us appreciate this afresh."

– *Times Literary Supplement*

"A superb work of fiction." – *Kirkus Review*

"...captures the crowded uncertainty of a historical cusp." – *Publishers Weekly*

"In *Unconditional Surrender*, Emyr Humphreys gives us as satisfying and as resonating an experience as any of his earlier novels." – Gillian Clarke

The Gift of a Daughter

"a tense drama that works towards a troubling close."

– Paul Binding, *The Independent*

"A deeply rewarding novel, a book of consistently inquisitive, restless intelligence." – *New Welsh Review*

Ghosts and Strangers

"a rich, innovative, intriguing literary feast... Humphreys is often described as 'the doyen of Welsh writers' and this innovative, subtle, multi-layered volume reveals why." – *Planet*